# POISON

# POISON

## Sally Spencer

SEVERN
HOUSE

First world edition published in Great Britain and the USA in 2021
by Severn House, an imprint of Canongate Books Ltd,
14 High Street, Edinburgh EH1 1TE.

Trade paperback edition first published in Great Britain and the USA in 2022
by Severn House, an imprint of Canongate Books Ltd.

severnhouse.com

*British Library Cataloguing-in-Publication Data*
A CIP catalogue record for this title is available from the British Library.

ISBN-13: 978-0-7278-9095-5 (cased)
ISBN-13: 978-1-78029-826-9 (trade paper)
ISBN-13: 978-1-4483-0564-3 (e-book)

*All Severn House titles are printed on acid-free paper.*

Typeset by Palimpsest Boc
Falkirk, Stirlingshire, Scot
Printed and bound in Great
TJ Books, Padstow, Cornw

*This, my fiftieth book for Severn House, is – coincidentally – being published in the year of my fiftieth wedding anniversary, and I dedicate it to my wonderful, beautiful wife, who gives my life meaning and purpose.*

An angry man is full of poison.

Confucius

# JUNE 1930

# PROLOGUE

His little brother had broken his train set – had wound the key so hard that now, though there was still a whirring noise from within the tin locomotive, the wheels simply would not turn.

It had been an accident – he knew it had – but that didn't matter. A wrong had been committed, and would have to be avenged.

But how could the punishment be administered?

He thought about it for a whole week before he came up with the idea of poison.

He didn't think of it as poisoning, of course. He was far too young to even know the word.

No, as he saw it, he was simply going to do something which would give his worthless brother a very poorly tummy.

Once he had determined the form of his revenge, he set about collecting the ingredients necessary to enact it. In the garden, he found a dead bird (already covered with maggots) which, once he had plucked the feathers and cut away the bones, proved an ideal foundation for his concoction. A wriggling worm – which ceased to wriggle once bludgeoned with his trowel – was added to the mix. Other less exotic ingredients followed – a little baking flour, a little pepper and (to sweeten the taste) a large quantity of sugar.

All this his small hands pounded with a stone until it had been reduced to a mush, and then – the day before his family was due to set off on their annual holiday at the seaside – he offered the fruits of his labours to his victim.

His brother took a sniff and pushed it away.

'I'm not eating that,' he said.

'But you must,' the poisoner urged him.

'Why?'

'Cos it's got magic powers. I saved up all my pocket money and bought it off a gypsy.'

'What will it do?'

'It will make you very, very strong.'

'As strong as you?'

'Stronger. It will make you the strongest boy in the world. And the cleverest. You won't have to do what I say no more. You'll be the boss of me.'

If he had been in his brother's shoes, there were a number of questions he would have wanted to ask.

'Where was this gypsy?'

'How did she get the paste?'

And most important of all – 'Why would you buy me something that will give me power over you?'

But his brother, seduced by the promise of the magic to follow, asked none of these.

'All right, I'll take it,' he said.

'Before you do, there's something I've got to tell you,' the artful poisoner said. 'If you ever talk about this to anybody, the gypsy's curse will fall on you, and you'll die. Do you understand?'

His brother nodded – but that was not enough.

'You have to promise,' the poisoner insisted. 'Cross your heart and hope to die.'

'Cross my heart and hope to die,' his brother said dutifully, making the appropriate gesture.

He forced himself to swallow nearly half the mixture before admitting he could take no more.

The result was not immediate – but when it did come, it was most satisfactory. First he turned almost green, then he started to vomit – and he continued to retch even when his stomach was empty.

Their parents called the doctor, and after the briefest of examinations, rang up for an ambulance.

For a whole day and half, the poisoner was looked after by a neighbour (who spoiled him outrageously to compensate for the distress he must have been feeling). Then, in the afternoon of the second day, the parents returned from the hospital. Both of them looked pale and exhausted, and he was pleased about that, because although he'd only intended to punish his brother, it was good that he'd punished them, too.

'Come into the lounge, Jordan,' his father said.

'Yes, Daddy,' he replied, obediently.

But though he called this man his daddy, he knew he wasn't really, because one of the bigger boys, a bully called Eddie Brooks, had told him all about it, in the school playground.

*'Mrs Gough isn't your mummy.'*

*'Yes, she is.'*

*'No, she's not. I heard my mummy talking, and she said that Mrs Gough bought you from an orph . . . an orph . . . from a home for babies that nobody wants.'*

*'Well, if she bought me, she must have bought Arthur as well.'*

*'No, she didn't – Arthur came out of her tummy.'*

He hadn't asked his mother whether or not it was true, because he'd long ago decided that asking questions was a sign of weakness. Besides, he didn't need to ask, because he knew instinctively that what Eddie Brooks had said was true.

Now that they were in the lounge, the man who was pretending to be his father sat down and hoisted him onto his knee.

'You must have been very worried about your little brother,' the father said softly.

'I was,' said the poisoner, because though he wanted to shout proudly from the roof tops that Arthur was in hospital because *he* had put him there, he knew even then that this would not be a wise course of action.

'Well, you mustn't worry anymore,' the father said. 'He's still very weak, but the doctor says he should be fine.'

'What . . . what made him poorly?' the poisoner asked, secretly crossing his fingers.

'We don't know,' the father admitted. 'It might have been something he ate, but he says he's only eaten the same as us.'

'I feel so sorry for him,' the poisoner said.

But he didn't really – he was only saying the words to mask his sigh of relief that his brother had stuck to his word, and not spilled the beans.

'You do realize this means we can't go on holiday as we planned, don't you?' the father asked.

The poisoner shook his head in astonishment. Caught up in all the excitement, he simply hadn't thought that far ahead.

'Why can't we go?' he asked, before he could stop himself.

'Well, Arthur could be in hospital for several more days, while they do all the tests, and we can't just go off and leave him, now can we? He'll be expecting us to visit him every day, won't he? And I expect he'd like to see you, too, if the matron allows it.'

If it was me in hospital, they'd go on holiday, he thought. They'd say they were sorry to leave me – but they'd still go.

'But . . . but we can go on holiday later, can't we?' he asked, feeling his lip start to tremble.

'I'm afraid not, old chap – not this year,' the father said.

'Daddy only gets two weeks holiday a year, and these are the two weeks,' chipped in the mother.

The poisoner was crying now, because when you are only seven this sort of thing simply shouldn't happen to you.

He felt the father smoothing his hair and saying softly, 'There, there, never mind. Next year we'll have a super holiday to make up for it.'

It was heartbreaking not to be going on holiday, but he knew – deep down inside himself – that if he'd been offered a straight choice of the holiday or his revenge, he'd have gone for the revenge every time.

4TH MAY 1981

# ONE

I t seemed to George Baxter as if it had been a hundred years since he had last taken this car journey from his home to police headquarters, and now that he was finally here, he found himself fighting off a powerful urge to instruct his driver to pull off again.

And perhaps the driver sensed this internal struggle which was going on behind him, because he said, 'I could drive round to the back entrance, if you'd prefer it, Chief Constable.'

Baxter shook his head, and got out of the car. If he was going to return at all, he would return through the front door, he told himself.

He walked in through the main entrance. The sergeant behind the duty desk came to attention, and saluted.

'It's good to have you back, sir,' he said.

Baxter nodded. 'Thank you, sergeant,' he said.

He walked over to the bank of lifts and pressed a button. The door slid open immediately, as if the lift had been waiting for him – so maybe that was a good sign.

He rode to the top floor, and breathed a sigh of relief when he saw that there were no balloons or banners to herald his return. He knew there should not have been – he had issued instructions that he wanted no fuss – but he wasn't entirely sure how much weight his words still carried with the officers under his command.

As he crossed his outer office, his secretary smiled at him.

'We've missed you, sir,' she said.

Well, she'd have to say something like that, wouldn't she, he thought. But did she mean it?

His desk didn't look like *his* desk – instead, it looked like the desk of the man he had once been, but who could now be lost forever.

Feeling like an interloper, he sat down at the desk.

The telephone rang. Its harsh scream seemed more like a

protest than a welcome, and when Baxter picked it up, he noticed that his hand was trembling slightly.

'Mr Baxter, this is Jordan Gough calling,' said the voice on the other end of the line. 'I'm just ringing to welcome you back to Whitebridge.'

'How did you know I was here?'

'I run a newspaper. It's my job to know such things.' Gough paused. 'I hear you've been away studying international policing,' he continued.

Bollocks! Baxter thought.

'Oh, that's what you've heard, is it?'

Gough laughed. 'Not really – but it's what I'll be putting in my newspaper, and that will be sufficient to *make* it the truth, as far as everyone else is concerned.' Another pause. 'I have two reasons for ringing you, Mr Baxter. The first, as I said, is to welcome you back.'

'And what's the second?'

'I'd like a favour.'


Detective Chief Inspector Monika Paniatowski looked across the big desk at her ex-lover.

'You're looking well, sir,' she said.

It wasn't exactly a lie. He did look well – certainly a lot better than he had during his crisis – but with his white hair and face that just avoided being gaunt, he was nothing like the big ginger teddy bear he had been when she first knew him, back in the days when *he* was a chief inspector, working in another county.

'So I'm looking better, am I?' Baxter mused. 'And what does that mean exactly? That I don't look as if I'm suddenly about to froth at the mouth, and run screaming from the room?'

'Sir . . .' Paniatowski began, imploringly.

'I'm sorry, Monika,' Baxter said, before she could go any further. 'It's just that from the moment I entered the building this morning, I sensed people looking at me – studying me and wondering if I'm about to crack up again.'

'I wasn't doing that, sir,' Paniatowski said.

'I know you weren't,' Baxter told her, 'and I'm grateful.' He took a deep breath. 'Before we get down to police business, I want to get some personal business out of the way. All right?'

'All right,' Paniatowski agreed, sensing that she had very little choice but to agree.

'I've had a lot of therapy since I went away, and while I still blame myself for what happened, I don't blame myself as much as I used to do. But what's much more important – from your perspective – is that I no longer blame you *at all.*'

What he was talking about, of course, was the death of his wife, Jo. He had not met her until long after he and Paniatowski had broken up, and while the Baxters had lived in Yorkshire there had been no problem. It was when George Baxter had taken the job in Whitebridge that the trouble had started. Jo had been convinced that her husband still cared for Monika – and, who knew, maybe he did – which had resulted in her taking more and more solace from the bottle and eventually driving her car off the road in the middle of the moors. The coroner had ruled it an accident, but nobody believed that.

And now George Baxter was telling her that he didn't blame her at all for Jo's death.

She could have said, 'You should *never* have blamed me, because I had absolutely bugger all to do with it.'

But instead, all she said was, 'That's good, sir.'

'Now,' Baxter continued, 'down to business. I've had a phone call from Jordan Gough. I assume you know who he is.'

Oh yes, she knew who he was, all right. Jordan Gough owned betting shops, supermarkets, pubs, restaurants and houses for rent. He had never run for public office himself, but there were a number of town councillors who always seemed to vote in a way which didn't exactly damage his business interests. And whilst it was true there was no evidence that he was currently as bent as a corkscrew, Paniatowski would have been amazed if it turned out that he wasn't.

'Yes, I know who he is,' she replied, non-committally.

'He would like to talk to you. He has made himself available, at his home, between eleven o'clock and noon.'

'Can I ask you what the purpose of going to see him is, sir?' Paniatowski asked.

'You can ask, but I can't tell you,' Baxter said.

Paniatowski bristled. 'Listen, sir, if you're not even going to brief me properly . . .' she began.

'I didn't say I *won't* tell you, I said I *can't*,' Baxter interrupted her. 'All I know is that he rang me up personally and made the request, but declined to give me any details.'

'When members of the public want to talk to us, what they normally do is come to headquarters,' Paniatowski said, between clenched teeth.

'Yes, that is what they normally do,' Baxter agreed, 'but Jordan Gough isn't exactly an ordinary member of the public, is he?'

She and Baxter had made their peace, Paniatowski thought, but it wasn't set in stone. In fact, it could turn out to be no more than a truce, so the wisest thing to do would be to smile and agree with him.

Yet she simply couldn't do it!

'Every member of the public is an *ordinary* member of the public,' she heard herself say. 'How could it be any other way, when each and every one of them has exactly the same rights and obligations?'

'Jordan Gough is Whitebridge's biggest public benefactor,' Baxter said. 'He keeps half a dozen charities afloat, and since he's taken control of the *Whitebridge Evening Telegraph*, the paper has been firmly behind whatever action the police have pursued.'

'You forgot to mention that he owns Whitebridge Rovers, and keeps ticket prices for its supporters much lower than those of any other First Division club in the north-west,' Paniatowski said sourly.

'And so he does,' Baxter agreed. 'All of which means, to my way of thinking, that if he prefers to talk to us in his own home, we cut him a bit of slack.'

Actually, that didn't sound unreasonable, Paniatowski agreed silently – and but for one very important fact, she might well have been willing to cooperate.

'It shouldn't be me who goes to see him, sir,' she said – because, like it or not, the elephant wasn't only in the room, it was standing on her bloody foot.

'Why shouldn't it be you?' Baxter wondered.

'Jordan Gough and I have history.'

The chief constable looked surprised.

'Tell me more,' he invited.

'This happened back when I'd just been promoted to detective sergeant,' Paniatowski said, and she was thinking to herself that that felt as if it was some time back in the Stone Age.

'Go on,' Baxter encouraged.

'There was a gang of lorry thieves on the loose in Mid-Lancs. This gang was operating over several jurisdictions, so a number of forces were involved in the investigation, including Whitebridge. And none of these forces were getting anywhere, because the robbers left no clues behind, and never struck in the same place twice. And then some bright spark at Lancaster University constructed a mathematical model which suggested that the epicentre of the whole operation was in Whitebridge.'

'So all the other forces were happy to drop their investigations and let Whitebridge take total charge,' Baxter guessed.

'Dead right,' Paniatowski agreed. 'The investigation was a hot potato, and the quicker they could pass the responsibility for it on to somebody else, the happier they were.'

'And the team you were on at the time was given the case, was it?'

'No, there wasn't any team – it was just me.'

Baxter smiled uncertainly. 'Because even back then, everyone recognized you had the makings of a great detective?' he suggested, only half humorously.

'No,' Paniatowski replied. 'It wasn't like that at all.'


DCI Bullock has never told Paniatowski to her face that he fought tooth and nail to keep her off his team, but he doesn't need to. He speaks to her as little as possible, and even when directly addressing her, he rarely looks in her direction.

But he is looking straight at her now, across the desk in his office.

'You've heard about these stolen lorries, haven't you, DS Paniatowski?' he asks.

'Yes, sir.'

'Well, I want you to investigate them.'

'On my own?'

'That's right. It's your big chance to make a name for yourself.'

No, it isn't, she thinks, what you're offering me is my big chance to fall flat on my arse.

The simple fact is, he is not alone in wanting her gone. The whole criminal investigation department resents the presence of a female sergeant, and – even worse – fears that if she somehow makes a success of the job, more women will follow in her wake.

From their viewpoint, this is the perfect case to pass to her, because the chances are that pretty soon the robbers will decide that they've pushed their luck far enough in this particular area, and will move on to somewhere else.

She knows all this, but yet she walks willingly into the trap that has been set for her, because if she does manage – against all odds – to pull this off, she will be made.

And if she doesn't pull it off?

Well, could things be much worse than they already are?

Even before she's left the inspector's office, she is eliminating some possibilities in her mind and storing others for future examination, and by the time she reaches her own desk, a strategy is already starting to emerge.

Opening the file, the first thing she checks on is what loads the stolen lorries were carrying.

If they had been transporting cigarettes or alcohol, the cargo would have all been sold off almost before the lorry was reported missing. But none of them had. Instead, they had carried tins of pineapple chunks, mattresses, and sacks of flour – all things it would be cumbersome to shift on the black market, and really not profitable enough to justify the risk.

So where were all the tins of pineapple chunks, mattresses and flour sacks now?

The chances were they were lying at the bottom of some old, abandoned quarry, of which there were many out there on the moors.

So then, it was obvious that the lorries had not been stolen for their cargoes, but for themselves.

Then why had none of the lorries ever been recovered?

Either because they'd either been taken to some other part

of the country or because they'd been dismantled locally for their parts.

'If they'd been taken south, I was buggered right from the start,' Paniatowski told Baxter. 'If they were being dismantled, then I had to find out *where* they were being dismantled – and wherever it was, it had to be quite a large site.'

'Somewhere like an old cotton mill or an abandoned factory?' Baxter suggested.

'Yes, somewhere like that,' Paniatowski agreed.

'That shouldn't have been too difficult in a place the size of Whitebridge,' Baxter said.

'You didn't know the place in the 60s,' Paniatowski replied, stung. 'You may think it's a bit of an industrial wasteland now, but you should have seen it back then – there'd been so many mill and factory closures that half the town looked like a bomb site.'

She approaches her task methodically, dividing the town into grids and searching each grid thoroughly before moving on. She is putting in sixteen- or seventeen-hour days, and all the time has to endure the jibes from other members of the CID.

*'Solved the case yet, Sergeant Pantyhose?'*

*'When can we expect an arrest then, Miss Crash Hot Detective?'*

It's on the seventh day that she comes across the scrapyard just inside the town's boundary. It stands like an oasis of activity in a desert of abandoned and derelict buildings, and is encircled by a high wall with imposingly large gates.

The sign on the gate says 'JG Enterprises Scrapyard.'

What it *doesn't* say is that it buys and sells scrap, or when it is open for business. There isn't even a telephone number. There's no bell-push, either, but it's plain from the sound of banging and crashing from the other side of the wall that someone is in there, busily working away.

Question: When is a scrap-metal business clearly not a scrap-metal business?

Answer: When it's a front for something else.

Paniatowski parks in the shadow of one of the nearby derelict buildings – and waits.

She's been there for about an hour when the lorry appears. It is so old and battered that it looks almost as much of a wreck as the smashed-up car it is transporting on its tailboard.

The lorry sounds its horn three times, then pauses and sounds it twice more. The gates begin to swing slowly and mechanically open, and the lorry starts to edge forward. By the time it is well inside the yard and the gates are beginning to close, Paniatowski's car, which has been right on its tail, is inside too.

Her palms are sweating and her heart has gone into overdrive. She is an intruder here. She has maybe thirty seconds before she's noticed, and another half a minute before someone comes across to her. She has to use her time well.

She gets out of her car, and makes a sweeping visual search of the junkyard. There are plenty of things here that she might have expected to find – several dozen wrecked cars piled on top of each other, a crane to do the heavy lifting and a compactor to reduce selected vehicles to cubes of compressed metal. But at the far end of the yard is a large building which is producing all the noise she heard from the other side of the wall.

'This is private property,' says a harsh voice to her right. 'What the bloody hell do you think you're doing here?'

She turns to see a square-built mean-looking man in a boiler suit.

'There's . . . there's nothing on the gate to say I can't come in,' she tells him. She is acting intimidated – although, in all honesty, most of it is not an act at all.

'There's nothing on the gate to say you *can* come in,' the man rasps. 'You're lucky the dogs are fastened up at the moment,' he points across the yard at two big dogs straining against their chains, 'because if they weren't, they'd have you by the throat.'

A new man arrives on the scene. He is in his middle thirties, and wearing a smart suit which seems quite out of place in these surroundings.

'What seems to be the problem, Len?' he asks.

'It's like this, Mr Gough,' the other man begins, 'this woman . . .'

'This *lady*!' Gough interrupts him, with a hard edge to his voice.

'I'm sorry, Mr Gough, I meant this lady,' the man in the

boiler suit says, and Paniatowski notes that while he might, indeed, be tough, Gough still frightens him. 'She . . . this lady . . . sneaked in right behind the wagon.'

Gough looks at Paniatowski questioningly. 'Is this true?' he asks.

'Certainly not!' Paniatowski says, indignantly.

'No?'

'No! I did not *sneak* in at all. I couldn't see any way into the yard, so I waited until a lorry came, and then I followed it.'

'And why did you want to do that?'

'Somebody said you could get used cars from here cheaper than you could from a regular dealer, and I have a friend who needs one.' Paniatowski smiles. 'But it's obvious, just looking around, that I've been misinformed, so I'll just apologize for the intrusion and go.'

Gough returns the smile. 'No problem at all – and if you promise to buy me a drink the next time we run into one another, we'll say no more about it.'

'Good God, did it ever occur to you that you could have poisoned your whole case – not to mention torpedoed your career – by doing that?' Baxter said.

'Of course it occurred to me,' Paniatowski said. 'That's why I was very careful how I handled it. I didn't go anywhere I was specifically prohibited from going, and I carried out no search apart from a visual one of things that were clearly on display.'

'You didn't announce you were a police officer.'

'No, but I didn't deny I was one, either.'

'I suppose you were, strictly speaking, within the letter of the law,' Baxter conceded grudgingly. 'So you decided this was the place the stolen lorries were being taken, did you?'

'No,' Paniatowski said, 'I didn't have enough to go on to be so definite, but I certainly had enough to make it too likely a prospect to ignore.'

The following day, she is taken off the case.

'No point in wasting any more of the taxpayers' money when you're clearly getting nowhere,' DCI Bullock tells her.

What he doesn't tell her is that it will go down on her record as her first failure as a detective, but they both already know that it will.

She could tell him of her suspicions at this point, but she knows that though she trusts her own instincts, the chief inspector would quickly dismiss them. So she says nothing, and meekly accepts the new duties assigned to her.

It is late afternoon. She has come off duty and is back at the derelict building opposite the scrapyard, only this time she is armed with a camera fitted with a telephoto lens (which she has had to empty her bank account to purchase).

She does not know how long she will have to be here, but she will stay forever if needs be.

As it turns out, it is not forever at all – though it certainly feels as if it has been at least that long when, on the fourth day of her observation, she sees the lorry.

There are three things which distinguish it from all the other wagons she has seen entering the yard.

The first is that it is much newer, and in better condition.

The second that is there is no mangled corpse of a car – or any other pieces of junk – strapped down to its flatbed.

But it is the third thing which gets Paniatowski really excited. There is a piece of sacking hanging down from the flatbed and covering the middle section of the back of the lorry. It could be seen as accidental – the sack might easily have been lying on the flatbed, and got picked up by the wind, yet prevented from blowing away entirely by the fact that the one edge was snagged onto something.

Yes, that was what the casual observer was meant to think, but Paniatowski is not fooled. The sacking is there for no other purpose than to cover the back number plate.

As the wagon navigates its way through the slowly opening gates, a sudden breeze blows up, temporarily lifting the sack clear and exposing the number plate. The opportunity only lasts for a few seconds, but Paniatowski has her camera at the ready, and the moment is captured on film.

\*      \*      \*

Paniatowski presents the photograph to Bullock. 'This lorry was stolen on the M6, late yesterday afternoon,' she says. 'The picture was taken at Jordan Gough's scrapyard, about two hours later.'

'*About* two hours later! Are you saying you don't know exactly when the photograph was taken?' Bullock asks, disapprovingly.

Paniatowski shakes her head. 'No, I'm saying I don't know exactly when the lorry was stolen. It could have been anytime in the half-hour or so the driver was working his way through his plate of egg and chips.'

The chief inspector looks at the photograph with the air of a man who feels obliged to look at a snap of someone else's children.

'You were supposed to be working on the burglaries on the Wilton estate yesterday,' he says.

'I was working on them,' Paniatowski protests. 'I was off duty when I took this photo.'

'An officer who is working on an active case is never off duty,' the chief inspector replies.

You bastard! Paniatowski thinks. You bloody sanctimonious bastard.

'Maybe you should tell the rest of the team they're never off duty, then, since they were down at the pub while I was carrying out my surveillance,' she says aloud.

'Sir,' Bullock says.

'What?'

'Maybe you should tell the rest of the team, *sir*.'

Paniatowski suppresses a sigh.

'Maybe you should tell the rest of the team, sir,' she repeats, dully.

The chief inspector gives the photograph another cursory glance. 'All right, you can leave this with me,' he says.

'What are you going to do next, sir?' Paniatowski wonders.

'That's really not your concern, now is it?' the chief inspector replies airily. 'Thank you, sergeant, you can go now.'

Paniatowski doesn't move.

'You're going to raid the scrapyard, aren't you, sir?' she asks.

Bullock scowls. 'As I said, it's really not your concern.'

'I want to be in on the raid,' Paniatowski says stubbornly.

'I'm sure you do,' Bullock concedes. And a small smile creases the edges of his mouth, as if he's starting to get some malicious pleasure from this. 'But you see, sergeant, it's what I want that matters. And what *I* want, if I do carry out a raid, is to have it conducted by experienced officers.'

'I've done all the groundwork,' Paniatowski tells him. 'I've earned the right to be there.'

'Every investigation is a team operation, in which we all play a part – and you've already done your part,' the chief inspector says.

She should leave it at that – she *knows* she should leave it at that – but there is a rage bubbling and gurgling in her gut, and if she walks away now, she'll never forgive herself.

'If the newspapers got hold of it, they might think it was a bit strange that I wasn't included,' she says.

'Are you threatening me, DS Paniatowski?' the chief inspector snarls.

'No, sir,' Paniatowski replies, as innocently as she can manage at this particular moment. 'I'm part of the team, so I would never leak the story – but one of my friends in the station who'd heard about it just might.'

'You have no friends in this station,' Bullock sneers. 'Don't you know that, Detective Sergeant?'

It is meant to crush her, but she just shrugs her shoulders philosophically and says, 'Well, if that's true, I suppose there's nothing for it but to give in gracefully. Thank you, sir.'

She is almost at the door when Bullock says, 'Wait a minute.'

She turns around. 'Yes, sir?'

'If I do decide to raid the place, I'll probably include you in the team,' Bullock says.

'What made Chief Inspector Bullock change his mind?' Baxter asked.

'He never said, and I never asked,' Paniatowski told him.

'Perhaps at the bottom of his dark woman-hating soul there was one tiny corner of light which recognized the justice of your request,' Baxter suggested. 'Or perhaps he was worried that whatever you'd said, you would go to the newspapers.'

'What's more likely is that he decided he needed a scapegoat in tow, in case something went wrong,' Paniatowski said.

'And did anything go wrong?'

'No – or at least, it didn't go wrong *during* the raid.'

It has taken a full twelve hours to obtain the search warrant, but they are finally ready to go.

There are four vehicles involved in the raid – three cars and a Land Rover. DCI Bullock is in the Land Rover, as befits a general leading his troops into battle. Paniatowski, virtually relegated to the role of camp follower, is in the back of the third car.

But before they can pull off the dramatic made-for-television raid, it is necessary to go through the boring procedure of reasonableness, and this part of the operation is entrusted to a detective constable, who is even lower down the pecking order than Paniatowski is.

The constable walks up to the double gates. He comes to a halt and examines the gate in an attempt to find a bell. He's been told there *is* no bell, but is aware that if he doesn't look, then in court the defendants' barrister will demand to know *why* he didn't look.

Having ascertained that no bell has been installed since Paniatowski last saw the gate, he raises his right fist and hammers on it. As expected, there is no response, so he lifts the megaphone – which he is holding in his left hand – up to his mouth, and says, 'This is the police. We have a warrant to search this yard. Please open the gate immediately.'

There is no response, and he signals this to the waiting convoy, before making sure he himself is standing well clear.

The Land Rover, which has a battering ram welded to its front, leads the assault. When it hits the gates, they groan and splinter, but do not give way. The Land Rover backs, and rams the gates a second time. This time, they open wide enough to see a crack of light on the other side. The Land Rover snorts and pushes, pushes and snorts, and finally the gates reluctantly give way.

The Land Rover enters, and pulls off to the side. The three cars sweep past it, and fan out.

Half a dozen boiler-suited workmen stand at various points around the site. They make no move as the police officers are rapidly disgorged from the cars. They look as if they are in shock, and maybe that is just what they are.

Paniatowski is not looking at them. Instead, her gaze is directed towards the workshop at the end of the yard, where a man in a smart suit is looking directly back at her. He doesn't move, either, but his stance suggests it is not shock which is affecting him, but rage.

'Do you see now why I shouldn't be the one who goes to see him, sir?' Paniatowski asked.

'Was it your testimony in court that got him sent down?' Baxter asked.

'No,' Paniatowski said. 'It never got to court.'

'So he has no criminal record that can be directly attributable to your actions?'

'He has no criminal record of any kind.'

'Then, for God's sake, Monika, what are you bothered about? It was a long time ago, and he's probably forgotten all about it by now.'

'He hasn't forgotten,' Paniatowski countered. 'And if you'd been there back then, and seen the look in his eyes for yourself, you'd know he won't have forgotten. It doesn't matter to him whether it happened five minutes ago or a hundred years ago – he wants his revenge, and he'll not be at peace until he's had it.'

Baxter laughed as if he found the idea quaint or amusing – but it was so obviously a forced laugh.

'You're both different people now,' he said. 'You're a detective chief inspector, which puts you in a much stronger position than you were in when you were a young detective sergeant. And Gough will have changed too. He's a rich man now, and he'll have long since put his criminal activities behind him. In fact, he might have taken being arrested as a wake-up call, and been completely legitimate since then. Rather than hating you, he may actually be grateful to you.'

'Jordan Gough will never change,' Paniatowski said firmly. 'Send somebody else.'

Baxter sighed. 'I obviously haven't made myself completely clear,' he said. 'When I told you that Gough wants to talk to you, I was speaking in specific terms. He doesn't want to talk to any old police officer. He doesn't even want to talk to any old detective chief inspector. He wants to talk to DCI Paniatowski. In fact, he says he won't talk to anyone else.'

'Then I guess that means he won't be talking to anyone at all,' Paniatowski said.

Baxter shook his head angrily. 'Wrong!' he said. 'Because he is such a huge benefactor to this town – and because we as a force rather like having the backing his newspaper gives us – we will provide him with what he wants. And what he wants is you, Monika. Is that clear now?'

His sudden anger had taken her by surprise, and she found herself wondering if, when he had said he no longer blamed her for his wife's death, he was being strictly truthful. Was he perhaps always searching – consciously or subconsciously – for some reason to be angry with her? It was looking more than likely.

'If you order me to go . . .' she began.

'I am ordering you to go,' he interrupted her.

'. . . then I will do as I've been instructed. But it will only end in tears, you know, George.'

His anger was gone, and was replaced by a deep pity, though she could not say whether the pity was for her, for himself, or for his dead wife.

'Perhaps it will end in tears,' he conceded. 'But you should have learned by now that in this life, *everything* ends in tears, sooner or later.'

# TWO

Whitebridge could be located on maps dating as far back as Tudor times. It had been a market town then, and looking along the narrow twisting streets at its centre, it was easy to picture reluctant pigs being herded by bad-tempered drovers, rickety wasp-infested wooden stalls selling seasonal fruits and vegetables, and wily Flemish traders holding up woven cloth for the inspection and admiration of the unsophisticated local yokels.

Once beyond the old town, however, any evidence of the Middle Ages had been obliterated by the utilitarian brutalism of the Industrial Revolution, and the skyline was dominated by the cotton mills which had once played a big part in making Britain the workshop of the world.

But times had changed, as times always do. It was over a decade since the last cotton loom had been in use. Now, some of the mills had been converted into warehouses or direct factory outlets, but there were still a fair number which stood skeletal and lonely, a mocking reminder to those old people who had confidently believed that cotton would be king forever, that they couldn't have been more wrong.

On the other side of the canal from the mills lay the rows upon rows of terraced houses which had once been home to the tacklers and weavers who had worked in the mills.

Beyond this were the greener pastures of the semi-detached and detached homes of senior clerks and assistant shop managers. Here, some wit proclaimed, even the sparrows coughed more genteelly, and it was through this suburban utopia that Paniatowski and Crane were driving when Crane said, 'There's a lot of things that puzzle a southern boy like me about the north, boss.'

Paniatowski grinned. Crane was not your average bobby, because there really weren't many bobbies who were poets and had a first-class degree in English from Oxford University. Yet though this might have encouraged many young men to feel superior, Crane gave no indication that it had this effect on him. He was, in fact, a hard-working officer who never tried to exploit either his background or his undoubted good looks – and Paniatowski liked him a lot for that.

'Is there something in particular that's troubling you at the moment, Jack?' she asked.

'Yes, there is,' Crane admitted. 'In most towns around here, the south side of town is the posh side. That's right, isn't it?'

'Spot on,' Paniatowski agreed.

'But in Whitebridge, it's the north side that's posh. Why is that?'

'It's all a matter of the prevailing winds,' Paniatowski told him.

'That's a bit enigmatic, boss,' Crane said.

'Yes, isn't it, just?'

They drove on a little further, then Crane said, 'Oh, I get it!'

'Then explain it to me.'

'In the old days, when there were something like thirty cotton mills in this town, the factory chimneys would be spewing out all kinds of crap into the air.'

'It was like Dante's Inferno,' Paniatowski said. She smiled again. 'Dante was an Italian poet, you know.'

Now that was just the sort of thing that her old boss, Charlie Woodend, might have said, she thought, and wondered if she, too, would eventually end up wearing hairy sports jackets and smoking Capstan Full Strength.

Crane was grinning too. 'Italian, you say,' he mused. 'Anyway, if there was no wind, the smoke would just hover there – rather like the black cap on a hanging judge . . .'

'Nice image,' Paniatowski said.

'. . . but if there was a wind, it would blow away and gas the people who lived downwind of the mills. And since most of the wind comes from across the moors to the north, it was always best to catch that wind *before* it mingled with the smoke.'

Paniatowski tried not to look at him too fondly. 'I'll make a detective out of you yet,' she said.

'Can I ask you about Mr Gough?' asked Crane, whose restless mind had already moved on.

'Of course.'

'Why couldn't you prosecute Gough once you'd raided the scrapyard? Didn't you find any evidence?'

'We didn't find the lorry. It had taken so long to get the search warrant that by the time we hit the place, Gough's gang had finished its work. But we did find other evidence.'

'Like what?'

'We found a garage workshop which was clearly set up for no other purpose than to dismantle heavy vehicles. We found a number of tyres of the size and brand of those on the stolen lorry. We found some steel bars and brackets which could well have formed a part of the chassis, and a drive shaft for that particular model of lorry. We also found engine parts which had had their serial numbers filed down or burned off with acid. Oh, and we found a couple of seats.'

'What about the cab?'

'That was probably one of the cubes of compressed metal sitting out in the yard.'

'So did the chief constable think you had enough of a case to prosecute?'

'Yes. It would have helped if one of Gough's crew had been willing to confess, but they were represented by Spider Markham – the best bent solicitor money could buy – and they weren't saying a word. But even without them, we had a good case. The only way Gough could explain the tyres and engine parts was to say that some feller came into the yard and sold them to him – which is a pretty weak story by anybody's standards. Then there was the fact that the garage was clearly a chop shop, and couldn't be anything else. Each piece of evidence was circumstantial, but what tied it all together was the photograph I'd taken of the lorry being driven into the yard.'

'Something happened to that photograph, didn't it?' Crane guessed.

'Back then, we were based in the old police building on Whitworth Street, but that was due to be demolished, and we were moving to our current headquarters. That being the case, there didn't seem to be much point in spending money on maintenance. So it wasn't entirely surprising when a water pipe in the evidence room burst overnight, and destroyed both the photograph and the negative.'

'Was that deliberate?' Crane asked.

Paniatowski shrugged. 'It could have been. It wouldn't surprise me if Gough had found a way to bribe some bobby who'd got himself up to his neck in debt with hire-purchase payments. But it could also have been an accident, because, as I said, the old building was in a terrible state. Whatever the cause, the chief constable and prosecuting barrister decided between them that without the photograph there simply wasn't enough evidence to go forward.'

'Gough must have been jumping for joy,' Crane said.

'I don't think Jordan Gough believes in joy,' Paniatowski said. 'I'm not even sure he believes in happiness – at least, if he does, he showed no signs of it that day.'

Gough is standing opposite the police station, and the moment Paniatowski appears in the doorway, he crosses the road to join her.

'Have you been waiting for me?' she asks.

'Yes.'

'For how long?'

Gough shrugs, as if it doesn't matter. 'Maybe an hour,' he suggests. 'Or it could be an hour and a half. I haven't been keeping track.'

'That's quite a while.'

'I'm a patient man. I can wait as long as it takes.'

She believes him, because there is not even the slightest hint of impatience in his voice. There is no hint of anger, either. In fact, she can't pin down a trace of any emotion in his flat voice and immobile features.

'So what do you want, Mr Gough?' she asks.

'I want to talk to you.'

'Well, here I am, so talk away.'

'Would you like to walk with me a little, Detective Sergeant Paniatowski?' Gough asks.

She can think of no reason why she should, but she says, 'Why not?'

Because to refuse his request might lead him to think she is frightened of him, and though it shouldn't matter one way or the other to her what he thinks of her, it does – it bloody *does* – and she isn't about to give him the satisfaction of thinking he's scared her.

They walk in silence until they reach the corporation park, and once they are inside the gates, next to the ornamental fountain, Gough looks around and says, 'There isn't much chance we'll be overheard here – unless you're wearing a wire.' His ice-cold blue eyes gaze straight in to hers. '*Are* you wearing a wire, DS Paniatowski?'

'No,' she says.

'Would you mind if I checked?'

'Yes. I would mind very bloody much.'

Gough thinks for a moment, and then laughs – though the laugh is totally devoid of humour.

'No, you're not wired,' he decides. 'You had no idea I'd be popping up like that, so why would you have been prepared? And you wouldn't lie to me anyway.'

'Wouldn't I? And what makes you think that?'

'You wouldn't lie to me because you'd take no pleasure in nailing me through deception.'

'Are you sure of that?'

'Yes.'

'So suddenly, you're an expert on me.'

'I'm learning to be,' Gough says. 'Anyway, to get back to the point, it's because of you I was arrested – because of you I was *handcuffed* – and I'll never forgive you for that.'

'I really don't give a damn about your forgiveness, Mr Gough,' Paniatowski tells him.

'Oh, but you should, because I'll find a way to pay you back – a way to humiliate you as you've humiliated me. It may take years, but I don't mind, because, as I told you earlier, I'm a very patient man.'

'Why has Gough specifically asked to see the only bobby who ever nicked him?' Jack Crane asked.

'I don't know, Jack,' Paniatowski admitted, 'and that's just what's bothering me.'

'Maybe the Chief Con is right, and now Gough's had time to think about it, he's grateful to you for setting him back on the straight and narrow. That's possible, isn't it?'

'Anything's possible,' Paniatowski agreed. 'It's possible that Inspector Beresford will take a vow of celibacy – but I'm not holding my breath waiting for it to happen.'

Crane chuckled. Colin Beresford – the boss's number two, and oldest friend after ex-DCI Charlie Woodend – had what was euphemistically called 'a roving eye' and so was known to everyone else on the force as 'Shagger' Beresford – a nickname which did not entirely displease him.

'Anyway, I'm far from convinced Gough *is* on the straight

and narrow,' Paniatowski continued. 'True, nothing has ever been pinned on him since that one time, but nobody gets as rich as he is, as quickly as he has, by strictly legitimate means.'

'It could be an interesting meeting,' Crane said.

Yes, Paniatowski agreed, it most certainly could.

They had left the respectable suburb behind them, and were in what Crane had called the 'posh' part of town. Here, some of the houses were large enough to be called mansions, and had gardens which almost earned the title of grounds.

The Gough house was surrounded by a six-foot-high wall, into which had been set a pair of ornamental gates which fell just short of looking genuinely antique. When Paniatowski pressed the button on the gatepost, the gates slowly swung open, and they got a clear view of the mock-Georgian house which lay at the end of the driveway.

'And they say crime doesn't pay,' Crane commented wryly.

The house sat on what was probably three-quarters of an acre of land, and the garden was landscaped, with rolling lawns which were only broken up by the occasional flower bed.

'All that's missing is a few peacocks,' Crane said sarcastically, when they were parking in front of the house, and as if waiting for its cue, a peacock – with its tail spread out in all its glory – appeared from around the side of the building.

Paniatowski rang the doorbell and her ring was answered by an olive-skinned man who had a hard, muscular body, and could have been anything from forty to fifty years old. The man was dressed in a grey suit which was – as near as damn it – a uniform.

'Mr Gough is waiting for you in his study,' he said in a most superior manner, before either of the officers had time to speak. 'Follow me.'

He turned.

Paniatowski stayed where she was.

The man hesitated for a second, then repeated, 'Follow me,' as if he thought that she had misheard him the first time.

'Get your notebook out, DC Crane,' Paniatowski told Jack. 'What's your name?' she asked the man in the grey suit.

'I am José Cardoza,' the man said reluctantly.

'Are you Spanish or Portuguese?'

'I am Portuguese.'

The sight of the notebook had rattled José. It often had that effect, Paniatowski thought – especially on people brought up in dictatorships, as he must have been.

'Mr Cardoza says he's Portuguese. Make a note of that, DC Crane,' she said.

Crane obligingly made a scribbled comment in his notepad.

'Do you have a work permit, José?' Paniatowski asked.

'Yes, I . . . of course I do.'

'Good,' Paniatowski said. 'We'd like to see it once we've talked to your boss.' She paused, and José hovered uncertainly. 'Well, don't just stand there – take me to your leader,' she told him.

José Cardoza led them into a hallway which was about the size of Crane's flat, and then along a corridor panelled in polished walnut and floored in oak. The further they went into the house, the more the servant appeared to be regaining the confidence he had lost when the notebook was produced, so that by the time they finally came to a halt in front of double teak doors, he seemed to be almost back to his earlier supercilious self.

'You are to knock and enter,' Cardoza said, before turning and heading down the corridor.

'Your boss seems to be inordinately fond of wood,' Crane called at his retreating back.

'Mr Gough is fond of anything that costs a great deal of money,' Cardoza replied, over his shoulder.

They waited until the servant had disappeared, then Paniatowski said, 'You take the lead, Jack.'

'Me, boss,' Crane replied. 'Why not you?'

'It'll be good practice for you,' Paniatowski told him.

Besides, she added mentally, it leaves me free to observe the way that Gough reacts.

Crane knocked, and they entered the room. Their instant impression of the study was of bookcases weighed down by large, leather-bound volumes. It seemed less a place where work was done, and more like a film set – a faithful copy of what Hollywood designers thought an English aristocrat's study should look like.

Gough was sitting behind a large imposing rosewood desk. He was wearing what was obviously an expensive tweed jacket, and a silk cravat. He was probably intending to look like a prosperous country squire, Paniatowski thought, and she had to admit that he was making a pretty fair stab at it.

The last time she had seen him had been a year earlier, when she'd caught sight of him across the room at some official event or other, but he seemed to have aged at least a decade since then. He had always had a tendency to be slightly plump, but now his face looked positively haggard.

'Good afternoon, Mr Gough,' Jack said, from just inside the door. 'I'm DC Crane, and this – as you probably know – is Detective Chief Inspector . . .'

'You can stop right there, lad,' Gough said, holding up his hand. 'I wanted to have a talk to the organ grinder, not her monkey, so why don't you be a good boy and just piss off?'

'How dare you talk to one of my officers like that, Mr Gough?' Paniatowski said, furious.

Gough gave her a mirthless grin. 'You'd be surprised what I dare to do.' He paused. 'Although, thinking about it, maybe you wouldn't be surprised at all.'

Paniatowski turned smartly on her heel. 'We're leaving, Jack,' she said to Crane.

'Just a minute,' Gough said. 'If you leave now, all that will happen is that I'll ring your chief constable again, and he'll order you to come back. And that would be rather humiliating, wouldn't it?'

'If he did that, I'd refuse to come,' Paniatowski said.

'And I'd insist that you did. And because your boss is a little unsure of himself, having only recently been released from the nut house – and because he's afraid of what I may say in my newspaper – he's going to take any refusal from you very badly indeed.'

He was right, Paniatowski thought. Baxter would find that very stressful. At best he'd make her life a bloody misery. At worst, it would tip him over the edge – and the last thing she wanted was to be responsible for that.

'If you want my advice, your best move would be to bite the

bullet and get the meeting over with now – because you'll hate yourself even more if you have to do it later,' Gough said.

He was right again, she thought. If she had to do it, it was best to do it now.

'Wait outside, Jack,' she said.

Crane looked at her questioningly – and perhaps a little disappointedly – then did as he'd been ordered.

'I suppose I should offer you a seat,' Gough said, gesturing to the chair on the other side of the desk.

'I'd prefer to stand,' Paniatowski told him.

Gough shrugged. 'Please yourself.'

He pressed a button on his desk, and José immediately appeared through a side door, as if he'd been standing there waiting.

There really was something rather theatrical about the whole thing, Paniatowski thought.

'Go over to the drinks cabinet and mix a vodka and tonic, José,' Gough said.

'I don't drink on duty,' Paniatowski said frostily.

'Maybe that's just as well – because I'm not offering you a drink,' Gough told her. 'It's for me.'

He'd set a trap to make her look gauche, she realized, and she'd walked right into it.

With a smirk on his face, José went over to the drinks cabinet at the back of the room, and mixed the drink.

Gough waited until the Portuguese had left the room again, then took a sip of his vodka and tonic, smacked his lips with satisfaction, and said, 'Somebody is trying to kill me.'

Paniatowski blinked. 'I beg your pardon?'

'Somebody is trying to kill me,' Gough repeated.

'Who?'

'If I knew that, I wouldn't have needed to call in the Filth to help out, would I?'

'You enjoy being rude to me, don't you, Mr Gough?' Paniatowski asked.

'I enjoy being rude to most policemen,' Gough replied, 'but when it's you, Detective Chief Inspector Monika Paniatowski, I have to say that I really bloody revel in it.'

'And all because I arrested you, so many long years ago?'

'That's part of it, of course – I never forget a slight – but it isn't the whole picture,' Gough said. 'I also dislike you for pretty much the same reason I dislike the *Mona Lisa.*'

'Oh, I'm really getting to enjoy this little parlour game of ours,' Paniatowski said. 'What shall we play next? Pin the tail on the donkey?'

Gough scowled, as if annoyed that she was refusing to follow the script he had mapped out for her. 'The reason I don't like the *Mona Lisa* is because I want to own it and I can't,' he said.

'Are you saying that there are some police officers who you *do* own?' Paniatowski wondered.

'If I did own a few bobbies, I wouldn't be stupid enough to admit it to a squeaky clean cop like you, now would I?' Gough asked.

Paniatowski sighed. 'If you called me here just to take the piss out of me, it's such a thin joke that you're the one who ends up looking like a complete fool,' she said.

Gough suddenly shuddered. 'It's no joke,' he said. 'Somebody is trying to kill me. I don't know who it is, but God knows, there's enough folk in Whitebridge who'd be glad to see me dead.'

'So how's the killer going about his work?' Paniatowski asked, almost whimsically. 'Is he tinkering with the brakes of your car? Have you felt a sudden gust of wind as a bullet rushes past your head? Or is some knife thrower using your chest for target practice?'

'You're not taking this seriously,' Gough complained.

'Then say something to *make me* take it seriously,' Paniatowski suggested.

'I think that maybe somebody's trying to poison me.'

'And what leads you to that conclusion?'

'Five days ago, I started getting this pain in my gut. At first I thought it would just go away, but it got worse and worse until, in the end, I thought I was dying. That's when I threw up – and kept on throwing up until I was vomiting blood.'

'Well, you seem to have recovered – or you wouldn't be enjoying your vodka and tonic quite so much,' Paniatowski said, unsympathetically.

'For hours after I stopped being sick, I felt as weak as a baby.'

'And what did your doctor say about it?'

'I didn't go to the doctor.'

'Why not?'

'I'd already puked out whatever had got into my system.'

'So you had a bad gut and built it up in your mind into a murder attempt,' Paniatowski said. 'That's paranoid.' She grinned. 'Still, it must be hard *not* to be paranoid when everybody's against you.'

'You're still not taking me seriously,' Gough barked.

'Well spotted,' Paniatowski agreed. 'All right, let's play it your way. You've been poisoned. Have you done anything to prevent it happening again?'

'I'm not a complete bloody idiot, so of course I've taken precautions. The only food I eat has been prepared by Mrs Adams, my housekeeper.'

'And you trust her, do you?'

'With my life.'

'If she's your poisoner, that's exactly what you are doing.'

'Mrs Adams wouldn't poison me,' Gough said.

'And how can you be so sure of that? Is it because she's very loyal? Or perhaps it's because you're such a lovely person that she could never think of hurting you?'

'The reason she'd never poison me is because she'd be far worse off with me dead than she is with me alive.'

'Would you like to explain that?' Paniatowski asked.

'No,' Gough said, 'I don't think I would.'

'So you trust your housekeeper,' Paniatowski conceded. 'What about when you're eating and drinking outside the house?'

'I've stopped eating in restaurants, and if I go to a reception, I stay well away from the canapés.'

'What about drinks?'

'José watches the bar. I only ever have drinks that have come from a bottle that someone else has already been served from.'

'The barman might slip something into the drink.'

'Not with José watching. He's an ex-policeman who has also worked as a bodyguard. He was trained to spot things like that.'

'Well there you are, then, you seem to have everything pretty well covered,' Paniatowski said.

'And what if he doesn't try to poison me next time? What if he picks me off with a sniper rifle, or puts a bomb under my car. Do you see what I mean?'

'Of course I see what you mean,' Paniatowski said. 'After all, that sort of thing happens every other day in Whitebridge.' She sighed. 'I'm afraid you've a made a mountain out of a molehill, and I'm not prepared to waste any more of my valuable time on it,' she continued, before turning and walked towards the door.

'Wait!' Gough said, and she thought she detected not just urgency, but also fear in his tone. 'There were the anonymous letters.'

Paniatowski stopped, and turned around again. 'What anonymous letters?'

'There were three of them. They were made up of words cut out of glossy magazines. The first two just said he was going to kill me, but the third one, just before I got ill, said – "You've Been Poisoning The Life Of This Town For Years And Now I'm Going To Poison You".'

'Let me have a look at them,' Paniatowski said.

'I haven't got them anymore. I burned them.'

'Now why would you do that?' Paniatowski wondered.

'I got angry that anyone would dare to threaten me – *me!* So I got rid of them.'

Paniatowski laughed. 'How very convenient for you.'

'I don't expect this sort of attitude from a public servant,' Gough said, and now his desperation had given way to anger. 'There's not another officer in the Mid-Lancs Police who would have treated me with such contempt.'

'You've clearly not met my sergeant,' Paniatowski said. 'But if you wanted an arse-crawler, why didn't you ask for someone else?'

'Because I want the best – and that's you,' Gough told her. 'Look, I'm sorry about the way I treated you earlier, but I'm so scared that it's affecting my judgement. Couldn't you help me?'

It was a nice pull-back, this confession of vulnerability and show of humility, and it almost worked.

Almost – but not quite.

'Even if you're not playing a game – and I'm almost certain you are – you've given me nothing to work with,' Paniatowski said. 'If the age of miracles ever comes about, and you can give me some kind of evidence, then I'll look into it. Otherwise, I'm done with you.'

She turned to the door again, and this time she had reached the corridor before Gough spoke again.

'Don't you dare abandon me in my hour of need!' he shouted. 'Come back here right now.'

Well, she certainly seemed to have got under his skin, Paniatowski thought, so the morning hadn't been entirely wasted.

Crane was angry – not angry enough to want to plant his fist in the centre of Gough's face (which would have been Inspector Beresford's instinctive reaction in a similar situation), nor yet angry enough to devise some fiendish psychological way of making him suffer (which was more Sergeant Meadows' style), but still sufficiently angry to realize that a stroll round the garden, breathing deeply as he went, might be a wise move.

It was when he reached the back of the house that he saw the gardener, bent over and weeding one of the flower beds.

The gardener noticed him, and straightened up. 'Who are you?' he asked, in a voice that was heavily accented.

'Detective Constable Crane,' Jack replied. 'And who are you?'

'My name is Alonso.' The gardener grinned. 'Mr Gough going to be very disappointed.'

'About what?'

'That they only send a detective constable to arrest him. He think nothing but the big chief is good enough to put the chains on him.'

'Why should I arrest him?' Crane wondered.

'Because he is the rotten piece of fruit that need to be removed before he turn the rest of the barrel bad.'

'I take it you don't like him,' Crane said.

The gardener shrugged. 'I am not alone. Most peoples don't like him but some are afraid of him, and some are in his debt.'

'And are you afraid?'

The gardener puffed out his chest. 'No, I am not afraid.

I fought for my country in Angola and Mozambique. I have medals for my bravery.'

'So you're in debt to him?'

'To him, and to my bastard cousin José. I owe them for getting my work permit and for paying for me to travel from Portugal – and I am paying so much in interest that I will never be free of them.'

Looking at the man closely, Crane could see the resemblance to grey-suited José Cardoza.

'I thought that Portuguese families stuck together and helped each other,' Crane said.

'Mostly they do,' Alonso agreed. 'But my cousin is a swine. When the dictator Salazar was in power, José was a member of the secret police. Have you heard of the Taraffal Camp?'

'No,' Crane said. 'I don't think I have.'

'It is a prison on the Cape Verde Islands. It is where that bastard Salazar sent his political opponents to be tortured – and José was one of his top torturers.'

'From what you've just told me, he sounds like a very nasty piece of work,' Crane said.

'He is worse than that. He is a very evil man – and that is why Mr Gough likes him so much.'

Crane was not in evidence when Paniatowski left Gough's study. She had never expected him to be, because he was a spirited young man, not some naughty schoolboy who would wait meekly in the corridor after his banishment.

It was a pity he had been banished, though, because she would have welcomed his perspective on the strange conversation she had just had with Jordan Gough.

The fact was, she still didn't really know what the conversation had been about.

Was he simply playing games with her – summoning her like an underling, because he knew that he could?

Or did he really think his life was in danger, as – at some points in the conversation – he had seemed to?

Whatever the case, she was almost certain that he would try to make things as difficult as possible for her back at police headquarters.

Well, she had no regrets about how she had handled the meeting – she couldn't see how she could have done it any other way – and if a storm did break, she would just have to ride it out.

As she stepped out into the sunlight, she saw Crane sitting in the car, talking into the police radio, but by the time she reached the vehicle he had hung up, and he was looking at her with excited expectation.

'Has something happened, Jack?' she asked.

'Something certainly has,' Crane replied. 'We need to get over to the James Hargreaves Building on Clegg Lane as soon as possible, because there's been a rather messy murder.'

# THREE

Many of the cotton mills in Whitebridge had been built next to the Leeds and Liverpool Canal. There were two good reasons for this. The first was that the mills needed a constant supply of water for their steam engines, and the canal was a convenient source. The second was a question of logistics: before the coming of the railway, transportation by water was the quickest, cheapest and most efficient way to move goods, and the narrow boats on the canal journeyed back and forth to the port of Liverpool, bringing raw cotton from India and America on their outward trip, and taking back finished cloth on their return.

The Madras Mill had been one of these. It had fronted onto Clegg Street, which had been a cobbled street, like most of the streets in Whitebridge (until just after the War, when the council, in the name of modernity, had asphalted it). There had been an iron foundry across the road from it. The back of the mill had opened onto the canal, and looked out at another mill on the other side of the water – though 'looked out' was perhaps the wrong term, since all the windows in the mill were high above eye level, so that while they could admit the necessary light and some air, the workers would not be distracted by the view.

It was no longer called the Madras Mill. Now that it had been developed as a residential unit, it was known as the James Hargreaves Building.

'I wonder who James Hargreaves was,' Paniatowski said, as they approached Clegg Street.

'Oh, he was a mill owner who lived just down the road from here, in Oswaldtwistle,' Crane said. 'He invented the spinning jenny, which was a multi-spindle spinning frame, in the middle of the eighteenth century. It revolutionized the weaving industry.'

'It's really coming to something when outsiders know more of our history than we do ourselves,' Paniatowski said, almost under her breath. 'Smart-arsed southerner.'

'That's me,' Crane agreed happily.

Clegg Street – or Olde Clegg Lane as it was now known – was a wide street, since it had been designed to allow enough room for two large horse-drawn wagons to pass each other, and the developers who had renamed it had also reinstated the cobbles, in tribute to a past they would have hated if they'd actually had to live in it.

A police presence was already well established on what Paniatowski still thought of as Clegg Street. There were two uniformed constables posted thirty feet to the left of the Hargreaves Building, and another two the same distance to the right. For the moment, their only job was to prevent pedestrians and vehicles going down the street, but as news of the murder spread – and it was remarkable how quickly that could happen – they would be fully occupied holding back the small crowd of thrill-seekers.

Two more constables had been posted at the door of the building, and one of them quickly stepped forward to open the chief inspector's door for her.

'Thank you, constable,' Paniatowski said frostily, 'but I'm blessed with a good pair of hands, and I could probably have opened that door myself.'

'Sorry, ma'am,' the young bobby replied, confused.

A feeling of guilt gushed through her. The lad was only trying to be helpful, and she was just feeling prickly, she told herself, but after a meeting with Gough, who wouldn't be?

'No, *I'm* the one who should be apologizing, constable,' she said awkwardly. 'It was a kind thought.' She paused for a second. 'Has Dr Shastri arrived yet?'

She'd known the constable would say, 'No, ma'am,' before she'd even asked the question, because there was no sign of Shastri's legendary – and apparently indestructible – Land Rover on the street, but by asking it, she had at least guided the conversation back on to a formal business-like level.

Paniatowski and Crane entered the foyer of the Hargreaves Building. It was a large space – arguably larger than a small block of flats justified – and whoever had designed it seemed to be in love with black glass and marble. A porter's desk stood in one corner. The only other furnishings were two leather sofas, several pot plants, and a couple of abstract sculptures. It might have looked fine and dandy in Manhattan, but in Whitebridge it merely seemed pretentious.

Paniatowski grimaced. 'Listen, Jack,' she said, 'if I unexpectedly come into money, and decide to blow it on a flat in this place, I want you to shoot me.'

Crane nodded. 'Under the circumstances, it would be the only kind thing to do, boss,' he said.

They took the lift up to the third floor – the penthouse floor – which was where the victim had been discovered. Two more uniformed constables were on duty outside the apartment, and a couple more loitered in the hall, waiting to be given something to do.

The living room, which led off the hallway, had picture windows offering a view with the corporation park in the foreground and the edge of the moors beyond, a view which must, Paniatowski thought, have added a few thousand pounds to the selling price.

The victim himself was lying where he had fallen, in the centre of the living-room floor. Until he had been examined by Dr Shastri, it could not be officially stated that he'd died from a blow to the head, but the fact that the back of his skull was missing, and a considerable portion of his brains lay spread over the oriental carpet, strongly suggested this was the case.

Standing a few feet from the body was Detective Sergeant Kate Meadows. Meadows was a part-time sadomasochist, and – in spite of her pixie haircut and elfin figure – a full-time scary person. She was also easily the best bagman Paniatowski had ever worked with.

Paniatowski bent down and gently prodded the corpse. It was in full rigor, which meant that the victim had been dead for at least ten to twelve hours.

'Who found him, Kate?' she asked.

'His cleaning lady,' Meadows replied. 'She asked me if it would be all right if she cleaned up the mess.'

'And what did you say?'

'I thanked her for her diligence, but pointed out that she was probably in shock. I got one of the uniforms to drive her to the infirmary for a check-up.'

Paniatowski nodded. 'So what can you tell me about our victim?'

'His name was Tom Crawley,' Meadows said. 'He was twenty-eight years old and a chartered surveyor. I haven't talked to the neighbours yet, because they're all young professionals, which means they're out busy impressing other people with just how clever they are. But I have got a list of their names from the concierge.'

'Concierge!' Paniatowski repeated, raising an eyebrow.

Not a caretaker – or even a porter – but a *concierge*. If that didn't make this a high-class murder, she didn't know what did.

'And what can this concierge tell us about our Mr Crawley?' she asked.

'Not a great deal,' Meadows admitted. 'He's only here from eight to five, so he sees very little of the tenants, but the fact that there were periods when he didn't see the victim at all leads him to suspect that Crawley may have been travelling.'

'Hmm, and have you reached any conclusions of your own?' Paniatowski said.

'Only that he either had a rich daddy or a source of income other than his work,' Meadows replied.

'I thought chartered surveyors were quite well paid,' Paniatowski said.

'They are,' Meadows agreed, 'but there's stuff in this apartment that even a successful young surveyor shouldn't have been able to afford.'

'Like what?'

'Like the carpet he chose to expire on.'

Paniatowski examined it. 'They sell carpets like that in Hadley's Furnishing for around fifty quid,' she said. 'Not exactly cheap, I'll grant you, but if he could afford this place at all, he could easily cough up that much for a carpet.'

Meadows laughed. 'You wouldn't find anything like this in Hadley's, boss. This is a genuine Persian silk carpet. He'll not have seen much change out of a thousand pounds.'

Paniatowski whistled softly. 'Are you sure about that?'

'Certain,' Meadows replied. She knelt down, and turned back one corner of the carpet. 'It's hand stitched. Look at the knots. They're all slightly different to one another, aren't they?'

'Yes, I suppose they are,' Paniatowski agreed.

'If this carpet had been factory-made, they'd all have been identical. Then there's the fringe – on the carpets you can buy at Hadley's, the fringe has been sewn on at the end of the process, but here it's an integral part of the carpet. And finally, there's the design – you can see it distinctly on the back of this carpet, because the pattern is made up of different coloured silks, but on a cheaper carpet, the pattern is nothing more than dyed on, so the back of it is very fuzzy.'

'Sometimes I'm astounded by the depth of my own ignorance,' Paniatowski said.

Meadows grinned. 'Don't blame yourself, boss – it's not your fault you weren't cursed with a privileged upbringing.'

The lounge door opened, and Dr Shastri entered the room. Yet *entered* did not quite catch the essence of what the doctor did, Paniatowski thought. Perhaps *glided* might have been a more accurate description for the movement of this small brown – strikingly beautiful – woman, wrapped in a dreamlike cloud of colourful sari.

The doctor looked down at the body.

'Humpty Dumpty sat on a wall, Humpty Dumpty had a great fall. All the king's horses and all the king's men, couldn't put Humpty together again.' She sighed. 'But perhaps where the combined armed forces of Toyland have failed, a simple Indian doctor might just be able to pull it off.' She smiled. 'I'm sorry. Where are my manners? Good morning, Monika. Good morning, Kate.'

'Good morning, Doc,' they chorused obediently.

Shastri did have a first name, but the only person who seemed to know it was Paniatowski's daughter, Louisa. And even if they had known it, it would somehow have seemed wrong to use it.

'Listen, Doc . . .' Paniatowski began.

'I know,' Shastri interrupted her, 'you want the results as soon as possible.' She shook her head. 'I once rescued a poor donkey from an Indian brick factory because I could see he was being worked to death. I took it home to my mother. She was not pleased – I had gone to school with a satchel and crayons, and come back with a great hairy animal – but she became reconciled to it, and he soon became one of the family.'

There were any number of questions she *could* ask, Paniatowski thought, but she restricted herself to saying, 'And the point of this story is . . .?'

'I am like that poor donkey, but there is no one to rescue me.'

Paniatowski grinned. 'Don't try to make me feel sorry for you, Doc,' she said. 'You absolutely adore being worked to death.'

Shastri nodded. 'Sadly, you are correct,' she agreed. 'And now, as you can see, my little helpers have arrived,' she continued, pointing to the ambulance men who were standing in the doorway, 'and so I would appreciate it if you could clear the area while we conduct our grisly business.'

Paniatowski looked out of the window. A gentle rain had begun to fall, and already the cobbles were glistening. Some of the small crowd which had gathered had umbrellas, and those who didn't held newspapers or shopping bags over their heads. Unless the weather got appreciably worse, they were clearly determined to stay where they were, even though they must have known that if any of the gory details were visible to the naked eye, they were being held too far back to get anything like a clear view of them.

Paniatowski was ambivalent about such gatherings. Sometimes she thought of these people, who seemed content to wait patiently for hours, as nothing but ghouls – thrill-seeking emotional vultures. At other times, however, she would accept that it was a natural human instinct to wish to confront death, if only at second hand. On these occasions she found herself wondering whether she would have been there with them herself, if she hadn't been in her particular line of business. On the whole, she thought not. She had seen enough death as a child refugee in war-torn Europe for it to have lost any novelty value for her. Instead, it was the *reason* for a death which fascinated her – which could sometimes dominate her whole being.

Perhaps she was looking for a way to come to terms with the horrors of her childhood.

Or perhaps not.

But whatever the reason, she knew this obsession of hers was what made her such a good bobby.

The ambulance men re-appeared down below, carrying the stretcher between them. The eager crowd did not move an inch further than what was allowed by the police barrier, yet somehow managed to give the impression of surging forward. The ambulance men loaded the body into the back of the ambulance, and once they were inside it themselves, it drove off. The crowd stayed where it was for a full thirty seconds before beginning to break up and drift listlessly away.

A uniformed sergeant appeared in the doorway. He waited until Paniatowski had noticed him, then said, 'I've just had a message over the radio in my unit, ma'am. The chief constable wants to see you right away.'

'Are those the exact words his secretary used – he wants to see me "right away"?' Paniatowski asked, with a dangerous edge – which both Crane and Meadows caught – creeping into her voice.

'It wasn't his secretary I spoke to, ma'am,' the sergeant said awkwardly.

'Then who was it?'

'It was Mr Baxter himself. And yes, ma'am, those *were* the exact words he used.'

'Does he know I'm currently investigating a murder?'

'Yes, ma'am,' the sergeant said, looking increasingly uncomfortable. 'He said you should leave Inspector Beresford in charge.' There was a heavy pause while he considered the wisdom of saying any more, then he stiffened his spine and continued, 'And then, just before he signed off, Mr Baxter repeated that you had to return to headquarters immediately.'

'Thank you, sergeant, both for delivering the message, and for not trying to sugar the pill,' Paniatowski said, forcing a smile to her face. 'You can go now.'

She waited until he had left the room, then turned to Meadows and Crane. 'When Inspector Beresford deigns to show his face, tell him I want the whole street canvassed for any visitors who looked out of place, or anything unusual that's happened – both of those things in the last twenty-hours, although once we've got Dr Shastri's report, we may well have to go back even further. Have you got that?'

'Got it,' Meadows said.

'I want you, Kate, to go to his office and find out . . .' she paused. 'Well, you know the sort of things I want you to find out.'

'Yes,' Meadows agreed.

'I also need to know the second that any of the other tenants return to the building. Jack, you're to be Sergeant Meadows' running boy until I tell you I need you for something else. Got it?'

'Got it,' Crane agreed. For a second, he wondered if it was wise to say anything more, and then he heard the words, 'You're very angry, aren't you, boss?' coming out of his mouth.

'Let's put it this way,' Paniatowski said. 'At this particular moment in time, nothing would give me greater pleasure than to tear off the chief constable's bloody head, and stick it up his bloody arse.'

# FOUR

Paniatowski swept through the chief constable's outer office, brushing aside the protests of his secretary, and entered the inner sanctum without bothering to knock. Baxter was sitting behind his desk, and half rose to his feet in surprise, then seeing exactly who the intruder was, he sank back down into his chair again.

'There are certain procedures and protocols that should be observed when you enter the chief constable's office, Detective Chief Inspector Paniatowski,' he said hotly.

'Yes, there are certain procedures and protocols covering all kinds of situations – and one of them is that, if you have an instruction for one of your senior team, you don't get a lower-ranking officer to convey it,' Paniatowski countered.

Baxter suddenly looked shame-faced. 'Yes, that was wrong of me,' he admitted. 'But I was angry.' He took a deep breath, and any signs of regret melted away. 'And I'm still angry,' he continued.

'And why might that be?' Paniatowski asked.

'I'm angry because when I tell one of my officers I want something done, I expect it to be done.'

'I've no idea what you're talking about,' Paniatowski said, though they both knew that she did.

'I told you to go and see Jordan Gough . . .'

'Which is what I did.'

'. . . to find out what it was that was worrying him.'

'Which I also did.'

'And then you dismissed his worries as if they didn't matter.'

'Yes, I did dismiss them,' Paniatowski agreed. 'And the reason I dismissed them is because I suspect that they're pure fantasy. If he thinks he's being poisoned, why doesn't he go to the doctor to make sure? If he's received anonymous letters, why didn't he keep them to show to me?'

'There could be any number of . . .'

'I'll tell you why. It's because he doesn't really believe anyone's trying to kill him at all. He's playing some kind of elaborate game, and we're no more than pieces on his chess board, which he moves around at whim.'

'Why should he be playing a game?' Baxter wondered.

'I don't know,' Paniatowski admitted.

'Then maybe you should find out,' the chief constable said.

'I wonder if you'd be so concerned about this if Gough was a petrol-pump attendant instead of a local bigwig,' Paniatowski said.

'Your attitude is bordering on insubordination,' Baxter warned her.

'Only *bordering* on it?' Paniatowski countered. 'Then I have let myself down badly.'

'I could put you on a charge,' Baxter threatened.

'Do that,' Paniatowski dared him. 'I'd just love the opportunity to tell a board of inquiry about how it is now your policy to let a rich crook determine how this police force is run.'

Baxter took a deep breath and closed his eyes. His lips began to move, though he made no sound.

Paniatowski felt as if a bucket of ice water had been thrown over her, because what she was witnessing, she realized, was one of the calming techniques Baxter had been taught during his treatment. She also realized that, because of their history together, she was probably one of the few people who had the power to push him over the edge again, and she didn't want that, because some of her old affection for him was still there, however much she might choose to deny it.

Baxter opened his eyes.

'Let's start again,' he suggested.

'All right,' Paniatowski agreed.

'Maybe you're right, and Jordan Gough is a crook,' Baxter said, 'but let me ask you this – do you have any proof of that?'

'No,' Paniatowski said.

'In that case, I'd be very careful indeed what I say about him in front of other people, because some of them will not be as discreet as I am. So you'll need to watch what you say and where you say it. Are we agreed on that?'

'Yes,' Paniatowski agreed reluctantly.

'And maybe you're right about Gough being a bit of a hypochondriac who interprets an upset stomach as an attempt on his life. But that's not really the point.'

'Then what *is* the point?'

'We have to deal with life as it is, not life as we'd like it to be, and as a front-line police officer, you should appreciate that reality more than most people would. But you don't, do you? Pragmatism doesn't work with you, because you're too much of an idealist. Or to put it another way – there's far too much of Charlie Woodend in you.'

Charlie Woodend – the man who had guided her and protected her right from when she was a green detective sergeant up until the moment when he retired and she took over his job.

'Charlie was the best bobby I ever met,' she said – defensive, as always, when she thought her dear friend might be under attack.

'You're probably right,' Baxter agreed. 'He was probably the best bobby I've ever met, too – but you have to admit, he was so bloody uncompromising it's a miracle that he managed to hang on to his job until he reached retirement.'

Paniatowski smiled, despite herself. Good old Charlie! Yes, because of his refusal to bend with the wind, his career was always teetering on the edge of disaster. But though you could criticize him for that – and a lot of folk did – he always got the job done.

'The point is that Gough is a powerful force in Whitebridge, and if he really put his mind to it, he could destroy you,' Baxter continued. 'And I want to protect you from that.'

'And protect yourself,' Paniatowski said, before she could stop herself.

'Yes, and I want to protect myself, too,' Baxter agreed. And suddenly this big teddy bear of a man looked very small and very frightened. 'I know you love your job, Monika,' he continued, 'but if you lose it, you still have your family. If I lose my job, I have nothing.'

Paniatowski had to fight the urge to lean across the desk and stroke him soothingly.

She sighed. 'All right, so what do you want me to do?'

'I want you to investigate Jordan Gough's claim that someone is trying to kill him,' Baxter said.

'Couldn't somebody else do it – somebody who's not already dealing with a real case with a real dead body?'

Baxter shook his head. 'Gough has made it quite clear that he won't deal with anyone but you.'

'And what about my other case – Tom Crawley's murder? Do I just drop that?'

'No, of course not,' Baxter assured her. 'You're forever saying you've got a very good team . . .'

'I have an excellent team.'

'. . . so there's no reason why, with their help, you can't handle both cases.'

It didn't work like that, or – more specifically – *she* didn't work like that. And he knew it. Once Paniatowski was on a case, it consumed all her energy. Even her kids got very little attention – which made her feel as guilty as hell, but there was nothing she could do about it.

'I want to help – really I do,' Paniatowski said. 'But handling two investigations at once simply wouldn't work.'

'In that case, I'll give the Crawley case to somebody else,' Baxter said. 'I have no choice in the matter.'

He couldn't take the investigation off her! Not after she'd seen the body. Not after questions about the murder had already started to form in her mind.

'I suppose I could put on a show of investigating Gough's allegations, and devote most of my attention to my real case,' she conceded.

Baxter shook his head again. 'That isn't good enough. Gough's not stupid. He'd never be happy with anything but the real thing. Besides, even if you could fool him, say there really is something behind his claim and he ends up dead. There'd be questions asked about why you didn't do something to prevent it, and however much I might want to, I couldn't protect you.'

'Do you actually think it's likely that there is something behind his allegations?' Paniatowski asked, incredulously.

'It may be pretty much of a long shot,' Baxter conceded, 'but it would still be a gamble to ignore it. I prefer to play it safe. I have done since the day Jo drove her car off the moors.'

It always came back to Jo, his wife, Paniatowski thought. However much he might protest that he'd come to accept that what had happened had been Jo's responsibility, rather than his or Paniatowski's, the guilt – and the blame – just wouldn't go away.

'Do you think we'll ever be comfortable in each other's company again, George?' she asked.

Baxter looked directly at her, his eyes drowning in sorrow. 'Do you?' he asked.

# FIVE

Some of Whitebridge's chartered surveyors still occupied houses in a Victorian terraced row in the old centre of town, where they rubbed shoulders with old-fashioned solicitors who could have stepped straight out of the pages of a Charles Dickens novel, and accountants who regretted the day the decision was made to abandon the quill and ledger. Go to see one of these surveyors, and you would pass through the reception on the ground floor, and then find yourself on a journey through a warren of corridors, which would often also involve climbing at least one flight of narrow stairs, before finally reaching the poky and ill-lit office of the man you had come to see.

Not so with the firm of Wilton and Brough (Chartered Surveyors Ltd.). Its offices were located in a shiny glass and concrete block in the new business park. And instead of the reception desk being occupied by a kindly but vague blue-haired lady (usually on the verge of retirement) as was common in these traditional firms, there was a bright and alert, smartly dressed young woman.

'We'd like to see Mr Wilton, please,' Meadows said to the receptionist, flashing her warrant card.

'And what exactly is the nature of your business?' the other woman asked briskly.

Meadows peered at her warrant card, as if she had suddenly begun to doubt who she actually was.

'Going by what it says on here, it would appear to be police business,' she said, reassured.

The young woman laughed lightly. 'I'm sorry, but you're going to have to be much more specific than that.'

'I'm afraid we can't reveal the nature of our inquiries at this time,' said Jack Crane – and though the receptionist did not realize it, he was making a valiant effort to shield her from Meadows.

'It doesn't really matter *what* the nature of your inquiries is,' the young woman said. 'We have certain procedures here, and one of them is that you can't see Mr Wilton without an appointment. Now if you'd like to *make* an appointment, I'm more than willing to book it for you.'

'Oh, that won't be necessary,' Meadows said, with an easy, yielding tone which was already starting to make Crane nervous. 'If Mr Wilton isn't free, I'll see Mr Brough, instead.'

The receptionist laughed again, patronizingly this time – which Crane thought was a big, big mistake.

'Mr Brough is dead,' she said. 'So is old Mr Wilton. Young Mr Wilton is in sole charge now.'

'And he won't see anyone without an appointment?'

'Exactly.'

'What's your name?' Meadows asked, in a deceptively friendly and somewhat disconcerting voice.

'It's right there in front of me,' the woman said, pointing to the sign on her desk, which read 'Miss Rathbone Office Manager'.

Meadows laughed. 'But that only gives your surname,' she said. 'I don't want that – silly – I want the name your friends call you. My friends call me Kate, so unless all your mates call you Miss Rathbone . . .'

'I'm Sarah,' the receptionist said, with some reluctance.

'A very nice name,' Meadows said approvingly. She leant on the desk, so that her eyes were at the same level as the receptionist's. 'Have you ever been in trouble with the police, Sarah?'

'Of course not,' Sarah Rathbone said.

'I could soon change that, you know,' Meadows said, almost lazily.

'I beg your pardon!' Sarah Rathbone exclaimed.

'I said, I could soon change that. Everyone breaks the law. We forget to pay our television licence or our car insurance. We drive the wrong way up a one-way street. We find a wallet in the street, and instead of handing it in at the nearest police station, we keep it for ourselves. Have you ever done any of those things?'

'No, certainly not,' Sarah Rathbone replied, outraged.

'Doesn't matter, because you're bound to have done

something else illegal,' Meadows said. 'The thing is, we all get away with these little things because the police can't be bothered to chase us up about them. But say the police were constantly watching you. I know if I was watching me, it wouldn't be more than five minutes before I was forced to arrest myself. But say *I* was constantly watching you – how long would it take you to get into trouble?'

'Can you hear her threatening me?' Sarah Rathbone appealed to Crane.

Well, he'd given her the chance to avoid this, and she hadn't taken it, so now she'd just have to muddle through on her own, he thought.

'Threaten you?' he said. 'No, I can't say I did hear that. What I *did* hear was Sergeant Meadows promising to do the job that she's sworn to do.'

'All right, Sarah, the joke is over,' Meadows said, unexpectedly.

'What do you mean?'

'I was teasing you. But a bright girl like you already knew that, didn't you?'

'Well, I . . .'

'Come on – admit it. You saw right through me, didn't you?'

'Yes, I suppose I did,' Sarah Rathbone said, dubiously.

'And I saw right through you, too.'

'What do you mean?'

'When you said I couldn't see Mr Wilton without an appointment, I knew you were only teasing me,' Meadows said. 'But now it's time we got serious again, Sarah, so I'd really appreciate it if you'd pick up that phone and tell Mr Wilton that we're on our way to see him. Will you do that for me?'

Sarah Rathbone nodded, and picked up the phone.

Simon Wilton was one of those men who took himself very seriously, and expected others to do the same. Thus it came as something of a shock to be told by Sarah – who knew the rules as well as he did himself – that a police sergeant was on her way to see him, and by the time he heard the knock on his door, he had already composed the lecture which he intended to deliver to her ever-increasing chagrin.

That plan was abandoned the moment Meadows entered his office. It wasn't the fact that she was fanciable that put him off – though, in a rather unconventional way, she undoubtedly was – but rather that there was something about her demeanour which suggested that rebuking her was really not a very good idea.

He invited the sergeant and her young constable to sit down, then said, 'So what can I do for you, Sergeant . . . Err . . .?'

'I'm afraid I have some bad news for you,' Meadows replied. 'One of your staff has been murdered.'

'One of my staff, Sergeant Err . . .?'

'Meadows,' Kate said.

'I beg your pardon?'

'My name is Sergeant Meadows.'

'Ah! Are you sure you've got your facts right, Sergeant Meadows? If one of my staff hadn't turned up for work this morning, Sarah would assuredly have informed me.'

'His name was Tom Crawley,' Meadows said. 'And unless his ghost decided to take his place this morning, Sarah's definitely let you down.'

'Oh, but Tom hasn't worked here for months,' Wilton said.

'It said on his business cards that he worked for you,' Crane said.

Wilton frowned. 'He still had some of them, did he?'

'Yes.'

'He should have handed them all over to Sarah, when I fired him.' He shook his head. 'Oh my God – it's only just sunk in. Poor Tom!'

'Why did you fire him?' Meadows asked. 'Had he been dipping into the petty cash?'

'Oh no, nothing like that.'

'Well, then?'

'I must ask for your discretion, because what I'm about to reveal could involve a third party.'

There was no telling how Meadows would react when faced with pomposity, Crane thought, and he was relieved to hear the sergeant say, 'But of course, sir. Discretion is my middle name.'

'A few months back, one of our biggest clients decided his company would buy a luxury apartment for the use of important visitors. He had already found one, and agreed a purchase price with the vendor. All he wanted us to do was assess whether or not it was a fair price. I needed someone reliable to carry out the assessment, and so I gave the job to Tom.'

'This apartment wouldn't be in the James Hargreaves Building, by any chance, would it?' Crane asked.

'It would. Tom offered the vendor more than our client had, and since the client had nothing in writing, he lost it. The client was furious, and insisted I fire Tom. I would have done that anyway even without his encouragement. I simply can't have that sort of thing going on.'

'Why did you think he did it?'

'At first, I thought he had bought it on behalf of someone else. You could have knocked me over with a feather when I heard he'd moved in himself.'

'Why is that?'

'Well, I didn't see how he could possibly have afforded it. I pay a very fair salary here, but even if he'd been prudent with it, he'd have been pushed to keep up the mortgage payments. In fact, that's what I said to a chap I know who works for the company organizing the finance for the block.'

'And why would you do that?' Meadows wondered.

'Just to make him aware of the potential pitfalls in going ahead with the transaction, of course.'

'Of course!' Meadows agreed. 'Only a cynic would think you'd done it to spite Tom Crawley.'

'Well, exactly,' Wilton said. 'Anyway, when I warned him about the possibility of Tom defaulting, the chap said there was no danger of that, because he had paid in cash.'

'You said he couldn't have afforded it "even if he'd been prudent",' Crane pointed out.

'Well, yes, I did say that.'

'The implication being that "prudent" is not a word you would ever think of applying to him. Have I got that right?'

'Well, yes,' Wilton said awkwardly. 'I . . . err . . . don't want to speak ill of the dead, but chartered surveyors are well known for being responsible with their money, and Tom simply wasn't.'

'Could you be more specific?' Meadows asked.

'He was a good surveyor – maybe even a very good one – but although I know virtually nothing about what he did outside the office, I did get the distinct impression that he seemed to care rather too much for the high life.'

'But that's all it was – an impression?'

'Yes, but two or three times he's had to come to me and ask for an advance on his salary, and that would suggest that he was living above his means.'

'So how did he take it when you fired him?' Meadows asked.

'Much to my surprise, it didn't really seem to bother him. To tell you the truth, I got the distinct feeling that if I hadn't given him the sack, he would have resigned anyway.'

# SIX

I t was only just after five o'clock, but already it felt as if this had been a long, hard day, Paniatowski thought. And what made matters worse was that she was doing something that she really didn't want to do – something it was taking every ounce of self-discipline to *keep* doing.

As she drove through the gates of the Gough mansion, she saw the grey-suited figure of José Cardoza standing by the front door. She wondered what would make a man like him – a man who had known some power and some authority – accept a job in which he was little more than a servant.

Money, probably!

A lot of it!

But the really interesting question was what, in Jordan Gough's eyes, made José Cardoza *worth* a lot of money?

She parked, and before she even had time to get out of the car, Cardoza walked over to her.

'Mr Gough is waiting for you in the garden,' he said. 'You must go around the side of the house.'

'Will you be coming with me?' Paniatowski asked.

'No.'

'Then who will protect me from the peacocks?'

Cardoza looked puzzled. 'The peacocks are not dangerous,' he said.

If there was one thing worse than a psychopath, Paniatowski thought, as she was walking around the outside of the mansion, it was a psychopath without a sense of humour.

Gough was sitting at a table on the terrace, looking out at the garden. He had his shirt sleeves rolled up, and Paniatowski noticed how thin his arms were. It was almost as if the man was wasting away.

He looked up when he heard her approaching.

'You could have saved yourself all the embarrassment of coming back with your tail between your legs if you'd simply agreed to do what I wanted in the first place,' he said.

'Is that what this whole pantomime was about – embarrassing me?' Paniatowski snarled. 'Well, you're quite right, I am embarrassed. So now you've had the pathetic revenge that you seem to need so desperately, are you happy?'

The comment seemed to really amuse Gough.

'This isn't my revenge, chief inspector,' he said. 'It's no more than a whiff of what's to come – a soupçon to whet the appetite, if you like. Real revenge involves a long and complicated journey, and we haven't even left the station yet.'

'So what more do you think you can do to me, exactly?' Paniatowski wondered.

'It would spoil the surprise if I revealed any more now,' Gough said. 'But, if I may, I'd like to tell you the story of someone else who crossed me.'

'Go ahead,' Paniatowski said,

'When I was at school, there was this woodwork teacher, only a young feller but as cocky as a blood-stained South American tyrant.'

'Or as the owner of the *Whitebridge Evening Telegraph*,' Paniatowski interjected.

Gough glared at her. 'The woodwork teacher's name was Mr Cousins,' he continued. 'The other kids called him Chippie behind his back, but . . .' he lowered his voice dramatically, '. . . I had quite another name for him.'

He paused.

Paniatowski looked around the garden. In one of the trees, a bird – it may have been a nightingale – had begun to sing its farewell to the day.

'I said, I had quite another name for him,' Gough said.

'Oh, I see – you want me to ask you what that name was. And when I do, you'll say a name so foul that you think it's guaranteed to shock me. Well, I'm not that easily shocked, so just go ahead.'

'Enjoy your little victories while you can,' Gough said, 'because they're nothing but skirmishes, and when the final defeat comes, it will crush you.'

'So are you going to tell me the name or not?'

'No,' Gough said, 'you've spoiled that moment, so we'll stick to calling him Chippie.'

'Entirely up to you,' Paniatowski agreed.

'Now what gave Chippie Cousins a lot of pleasure was humiliating kids who weren't much good at woodwork,' Gough said.

'And I take it that you were one of those who turned out to be completely bloody useless,' Paniatowski goaded.

Gough looked stung. 'I never said that,' he told her.

'You didn't have to. Your tone of voice and your whole body language said it for you. And isn't the whole point of this story that you compensated for your own inadequacies by hitting out at someone else?'

'I could have been bloody brilliant at woodwork if I'd made the effort,' Gough said unconvincingly, 'but I just couldn't be bothered. So what he'd do, you see, was he'd make me stand in front of the rest of the lads, and show them whatever it was I'd been working on. "Look at this," he'd say. "Gough calls it a mortise and tenon joint. Is that what any of the rest of you call it?"'

'I imagine that was a big mistake on his part, considering how popular you must have been with your classmates.'

'Watch your step!' Gough growled.

'Or what?' Paniatowski wondered.

'He'd ask them what they thought of my mortise and tenon joint and they'd laugh,' Gough continued, ignoring the question. 'The cowardly little arse-crawling bastards would laugh, and shake their heads, as if to say that only an idiot would call the thing I'd done a mortise and tenon joint. "If you have as much trouble getting your dick into a hole as you have getting this tenon in a mortise, then you'll be a virgin till the day you die," Chippie would say. And oh, everybody had such a good time pissing themselves laughing at my expense.'

He didn't look like a man who could tell a story well, Paniatowski thought, but he was certainly delivering this particular tale convincingly enough, because as he spoke she could see the woodwork room in her mind's eye, could smell the sawdust and shellac – and could feel his sticky, painful humiliation.

'He set an example for all the playground bullies to follow, didn't he?' Gough asked. 'He might as well have painted a target on my back. And I was small for my age then. It wasn't until I got to fifteen and started weight-training that I really shot up.'

'You're talking as if you were the only one Cousins picked on,' Paniatowski said. 'Were you?'

'Not at first, no. There were a couple more kids got the same treatment for the first week or so,' Gough said, 'but their parents complained to the school, and Cousins got a right good bollocking from the headmaster.'

'But your parents didn't complain?'

'My loving dad didn't give a shit about anything but chasing other women, and my loving mum was always too bloody drunk to care about what happened to me. So after that, it was just me – and Cousins was worse than ever, because I was the only one left to make him feel good about himself, and the more I suffered, the better he felt.'

'An emotional trait he seems to have passed on to you,' Paniatowski said.

'When I got to sixteen, and knew I was strong enough to tackle a weed of a woodwork teacher, I thought about beating the shit out of him. But then I decided that wasn't good enough.'

'What do you mean?'

'Beating him up would hurt for a while, but then it would be all over. I wanted something that would go deeper than that – something that would keep on hurting him until the day he died.'

'Get to the point,' Paniatowski said. 'What was your final revenge?'

'I waited until the time was right,' Gough replied, ignoring her question again. 'It was a long wait, but I never grew impatient, because a good artist always wants to get things exactly right.'

'That's how you see yourself, is it? As an artist?'

'Yes, I . . .'

Gough stopped speaking. For a moment, he gazed with blank intensity over Paniatowski's shoulder, but when she quickly glanced backwards, she could see nothing there.

'And *then* what did you do?' Paniatowski asked.

Gough said nothing. He seemed not to hear her, she thought. He seemed, in fact, to be somewhere else entirely.

'Mr Gough?' she said.

Gough blinked several times, then shook his head vigorously, like a dog does when its ears are wet.

'I was going to give you a list,' he said, a little shakily.

'You never finished your story,' Paniatowski reminded him.

'What story?' Gough asked blankly. He reached into his pocket, and took out a piece of paper. 'The last time that you were here, you asked me for the names of the people who might want to see me dead. I think you'll find that most of them are on this list.'

He handed the piece of paper to Paniatowski. It contained a pretty long list, and she recognized the names of several of the people who had qualified for inclusion.

'There are a few town councillors here,' she said.

Gough nodded. After his moment of strangeness, he seemed to have returned to normal.

'Yes, I've often had clashes with our elected representatives,' he agreed. 'But you'll notice there are enough councillors *not* on the list to ensure that any jumped-up representative of the people who *does* oppose me is like a voice crying out in the wilderness.'

Paniatowski scanned the list further.

'Who is Arthur Gough?' she asked.

'He's my brother.'

'So why is he on the list?'

'You asked for a list of the people who hate me, he hates me, so he's on the list.'

'Does he live in Whitebridge?'

'Yes.'

'And where does he work?'

'In the main office of Gough Enterprises.'

'He works for *you*?' Paniatowski asked, incredulously.

'Indeed he does.'

'If he hates you so much, why should he work for you?'

'Because I offered him a job, and he didn't dare turn it down.'

'Why didn't he *dare* to turn it down?'

'You'll find out – eventually.'

'And is it well paid, this job he daren't turn down?' Paniatowski wondered.

Gough shrugged. 'He's never going to be able to travel first class, but it covers his basic needs.'

'I still don't see why you'd even want him to work for you,' Paniatowski admitted.

Gough smiled. 'People claim a number of things are motivating them. Some say it is a love of an individual or of humanity in general. Others claim they are driven purely by principle. There are even a few who will state quite openly that money is their one and only aim. They are all lying, even the callous ones. Or, to be more charitable – and I do hate being charitable when there's nothing in it for me – they're simply deluding themselves.'

He was playing with her again, Paniatowski realized, and her best move would be to say nothing.

'So what does motivate people?' she heard herself ask.

A lesser game-player would have smiled triumphantly, but as Gough had said earlier, this was only an initial skirmish, and his mind was focused on the whole campaign.

'There is no greater pleasure to be had in this life than watching your enemies suffer,' he said seriously. 'And before you dismiss that out of hand, think back to your own career, and ask yourself whether it was from solving a case or from watching an enemy fall that you gained the most satisfaction.'

Paniatowski made a quick mental journey through her years

in the force, and came to a halt – almost inevitably – at the night Chief Constable Henry Marlowe had resigned.

She and Charlie Woodend had been sitting in the public bar of the Drum and Monkey when Marlowe had unexpectedly appeared on the local television news to announce that he was stepping down from the position of chief constable. He had set himself against Woodend and his team from the start, at least partly because Charlie found it almost impossible to hide his contempt for men who were lazy or incompetent – and Marlowe had been both.

So how had she felt at that moment? She had been surprised, certainly. She had been relieved that she would now be able to walk into police headquarters and not have to worry about what stunt the chief constable would try that day.

But had she experienced the sort of pleasure Gough had described? She had felt pleasure, yes, but surely not as great as the pleasure she felt when taking a dangerous man off the streets, or bringing justice to a family in mourning.

Except it was not as simple as that, because the latter pleasure was satisfaction in a job well done, whereas the former was closely related to the all-too-human instinct for self-preservation.

Gough chuckled. 'I've got you thinking, haven't I?' he asked.

Yes, damn it, he had!

'Are all the other people on this list marked down for your future revenge?' Paniatowski asked, hurriedly changing the subject.

'No, not at all,' Gough replied. 'It's true they've all got in my way at one time or another, and, as a result, I had to stamp on them, but it was purely business as far as I was concerned – nothing personal in it at all.'

'But you suspect they don't see it quite like that?'

'I'm bloody sure they don't see it quite like that.'

'Tell me about José Cardoza,' Paniatowski suggested.

'What would you like to know?'

'Do you trust him?'

'Yes.'

'With your life?'

'Yes.'

'Now that is surprising,' Paniatowski said, 'because I got the distinct impression that with your jaundiced view of humanity, you don't really trust anybody. Yet now you're telling me that you trust him with the most precious thing you have.'

'I trust him because I control him,' Gough said. 'As long as I'm alive, he has a pretty good life himself. If I die from unnatural causes, he's in big trouble because I've made arrangements.'

'What kind of arrangements?'

'That's not important. What matters is that I've made them – and he *knows* I've made them.'

'It's like the sword of Damocles hanging over him, isn't it?' Paniatowski suggested.

'You're spot on there. It is *exactly* like the sword of Damocles,' Gough agreed. 'There's a sword hanging over José's head which is held in place by a single hair.'

'And since you're the one who hung it there, that makes you King Dionysius, the tyrant who rose to power through ruthlessness and cruelty, and who lived in perpetual fear of his enemies exacting their revenge.'

Gough chuckled. 'You don't expect a copper to know things like that,' he said. 'I wonder where you read it. Or perhaps you didn't read it at all – perhaps your clever daughter told you the story.'

Paniatowski felt a chill run through her. 'What do you know about my daughter?'

'I know a great deal,' Gough said. 'I know that you adopted her when her father was killed in a car crash, and that she's now a police cadet. I know you have two sons, and that they're twins, but for once my sources have let me down, and I can't find out who their father is.'

Nobody knew that – with the exception of Dr Shastri and Kate Meadows. Nor could they *ever* know – because no child should grow up with the knowledge that but for a rape, he would never have been born.

'Would you like me to tell you more about your family?' asked Gough, in a tone which could have been described as mischievous, had the words been uttered by someone less sinister. 'Shall I describe your relationship with the chief constable, and how that drove his wife to suicide?'

'You're trying to scare me now,' Paniatowski said.

'Trying?' Gough repeated. 'I would say that I'm succeeding – admirably.'

There was only one way to deal with a man like Gough, and that was to counter-attack, Paniatowski decided – and fortunately, Jack Crane had given her the ammunition to do just that.

'Damocles was a courtier, and like most courtiers, his one talent was in being able to flatter,' Paniatowski said.

'What are you talking about?' Gough wondered.

'It must have been easy to intimidate him, because, like I said, he was a soft courtier. But it won't be quite such a doddle to handle a man who has served at the Taraffal Prison, as José has.'

'How in God's name do you know about that?' Gough said, clearly shaken.

'Like you, I have my sources,' Paniatowski told him. 'And if I were you, I really would watch my back with him – because he doesn't seem to me like the kind of man who would enjoy being threatened.'

She had had as big an impact on him as she could ever hope to, so now was the time to leave. She turned around and headed for the side of the house.

'I shall expect a report from you very soon,' Gough said.

'I wouldn't hold my breath while I was waiting,' Paniatowski called, over her shoulder. 'I don't work for you, and any report I make will go to the chief constable. What he does with it is his business.'

She didn't really think anyone was trying to kill Gough, she decided, as she drove away, but if someone was, it would be very tempting to ask him if there was anything she could do to help. She sighed, because what she might like to do was irrelevant – she was a police officer, and it was her duty to protect everyone, even people who clearly didn't deserve it.

# SEVEN

I t was as Paniatowski was leaving the Gough mansion behind her that the message came over the police radio.

'Doc Shastri says the body is ready for Tom Crawley's nearest and dearest to identify, boss,' Kate Meadows said.

'And who exactly are his nearest and dearest? His parents?'

'No, his mother's been dead for a few years, and no one knows where his father is, which means that the lucky winners in the identification sweepstakes are an aunt and uncle, Mr and Mrs Harrison, who live at 17 Burnley Avenue. Do you want me to tell them the news?'

Do I? Paniatowski wondered.

Why not? She certainly had no concerns about her sergeant handling it well, because though, if she chose to, Meadows could intimidate a grizzly bear with a sore paw, when dealing with a grieving relative she could become almost unbelievably gentle and loving.

On the other hand, she was not far from Burnley Avenue herself at that moment, and as unpleasant as announcing a death could sometimes be, it might at least wash away the foul taste her encounter with Jordan Gough had left in her mouth.

'I'll take it,' she said. 'You're sure they haven't already been informed about the death?'

'Yes, boss.'

'It hasn't been in the papers, or on the television news?'

'The papers did want to run with it, but Inspector Beresford told them we weren't even sure ourselves that it was Tom Crawley, and if they used his name – and it turned out to be someone else entirely – they could find themselves paying out a small fortune in damages.'

Paniatowski grinned to herself as she pictured blunt, straightforward Colin Beresford saying just that. There really was no one else who could play the part like he could.

'So what did they say?' she asked.

'They said that a man had been found dead in the James Hargreaves Building, and that the police suspected foul play.'

'Good,' Paniatowski said. She checked her watch. 'I'll be in the Drum at eight. I'll expect everybody to be there.'

'They will be,' Meadows promised.

Burnley Avenue was a tree-lined street of pleasant semi-detached houses, and no. 17, with its nicely painted windows and neat front garden, blended in perfectly with its neighbours.

The doorbell was answered by a man in his early forties. He was wearing a cardigan which was obviously home-knitted, and a pair of well-worn carpet slippers. He had a pipe in his mouth, and removed it to say, 'Can I help you?'

'Mr Harrison?' Paniatowski asked.

'Yes?'

'And is Mrs Harrison at home?'

'She is,' Harrison said, 'but could I ask who . . .?'

'DCI Paniatowski,' Monika said, showing him her warrant card. 'Do you think I could come in?'

Harrison looked bewildered. 'Would you mind telling me what this is all about?'

'I'd prefer not to say anything until I've got you and your wife together,' Paniatowski said. 'Do you mind?'

'No, I suppose not,' Harrison said. 'You'd better come this way.'

He led her down the carpeted hallway into a tidy living room. A woman with greying hair was sitting on the floral sofa, knitting. When she saw the new arrival, she made a move to rise to her feet.

'Please, don't get up,' Paniatowski said. 'And would you sit down next to your wife, please, Mr Harrison?'

Mr Harrison sat. 'She's a police woman,' he said to his wife. 'Detective Chief Inspector Paniatowski.'

'Detective Chief Inspector Paniatowski,' his wife repeated, bleakly.

'I've afraid I've got some bad news,' Paniatowski said.

The woman gasped, although she must already have guessed that something was wrong.

'It's . . . it's not Jane, is it?' she asked.

'Of course it's not Jane,' her husband said, trying not to sound exasperated. 'How could it be? She's upstairs, isn't she?'

'Yes, yes, of course she is,' Mrs Harrison mumbled. 'Then is it . . . could it be . . .?'

'It's your nephew, Tom Crawley. I'm afraid he's dead.'

'What happened?' Mrs Harrison moaned. 'Was it an accident? Was he run over by a bus?'

'She's a chief inspector, Doris,' Harrison said gently. 'They don't send a chief inspector round when it was an accident.'

'Your husband's right,' Paniatowski said. 'He was murdered.'

'How . . . who . . .?'

'A blow to the head,' Paniatowski said. 'We don't know who did it.'

'Where are my manners?' Mrs Harrison said, starting to get up. 'You'll be wanting a cup of tea, and I think there are some ginger nut biscuits left.'

Her husband put a restraining hand on her shoulders, and forced her down again.

'The chief inspector doesn't want any tea or ginger nut biscuits, do you, Chief Inspector?' he asked.

'No, I don't,' Paniatowski said.

'What you will be wanting is for us to identify the body, isn't it?' Harrison asked.

'If you feel you're up to it.'

'I'm up to it,' Mr Harrison said calmly. 'You won't need Doris as well, will you?' he added, with a hint of concern.

'No,' Paniatowski agreed, 'one member of the family is usually enough on these occasions.'

Harrison stood up. 'I'll go and get my daughter. Look after Doris for a moment, will you, Chief Inspector?'

'Of course,' Paniatowski agreed.

Harrison left the room, and Paniatowski could hear the sound of him running up the stairs.

'I promised his mother I'd look after him, you see,' Doris Harrison said. 'As she lay there dying, I took her hand and promised I'd look after him. And now I've let him down.'

'It wasn't your fault,' Paniatowski said soothingly. 'He was a grown-up, and I'm sure your sister wouldn't want you to still be protecting him.' She paused, and assessed how far she could push things. 'Did you get on well with your nephew?' she asked.

'Oh yes.'

But it was an automatic answer – the kind of thing she would be expected to say.

'So you never had any arguments?'

Mrs Harrison hesitated. 'Tom was a bit headstrong,' she said, 'but it wasn't his fault. His father deserted our Judith when Tom was only eight. Well, that's enough to make any boy go off the rails now and again, isn't it?'

'Is that what he did? Go off the rails.'

Mrs Harrison looked down. 'He was a good boy at heart,' she said in a voice which suggested that was all she was prepared to say on the matter.

Mr Harrison came downstairs again, and when he re-entered the living room he had a pale girl of about sixteen with him.

'This is Jane,' Harrison told Paniatowski. 'I've explained what happened to Tom, and she'll be looking after her mother while I'm away.'

Paniatowski made a quick assessment of the girl. She looked calm enough – certainly not devastated by the fact that she had just learned her cousin was dead – and should be up to the task of caring for her mother.

'Shall I go in my own car?' Harrison asked.

'No,' Paniatowski said. 'I'll drive you to the mortuary, and I'll see to it that one of my officers drives you back.'

And that way, we can have a little talk without anyone else getting in the way, she thought.

As she pulled away from the kerb, Paniatowski said, 'Your wife seemed very upset when I told her about Tom.'

'Yes, she did,' Harrison agreed, non-committally.

'But you didn't,' Paniatowski pressed. 'And, it has to be said, neither did your daughter.'

'Perhaps we just hide it better.'

'Stiff upper lip, and all that sort of thing?'

'Yes.'

'I take it you do want your nephew's killer caught, don't you?' Paniatowski asked.

'What kind of question is that?' Harrison asked, with a hint of anger. 'Of course I want him caught.'

'Then if that is what you really want, tell me why you were surprised – maybe even shocked – at the news, but not too upset,' Paniatowski suggested.

There was quite a pause before Harrison said, 'To tell you the truth, I'm not sure I was even surprised.'

'Oh?' said Paniatowski, who could play the non-committal card as well as the next man.

'When Tom was eight, his dad stepped out of the house to buy a packet of cigarettes, and never came back,' Harrison said. 'I did hear he was living in Australia, though I can't vouch for that being true. What I do know is that he never contacted Judith – that was his wife, Doris's sister – again. So she was left to bring up their Tom on her own, and to compensate for him having no dad, she spoiled him rotten.'

'It happens,' Paniatowski said.

'Maybe it does, but when it does, it's usually other people who have to bear the consequences of it.'

'What has he done to you?' Paniatowski asked.

'Where would you like me to start?' Harrison wondered. 'Whenever we looked after him when he was a kid, he was a real pain. He acted as if he was entitled to do or say anything he wanted. It upset my wife a great deal, but I didn't do anything about it because I knew her relationship with her sister was very important to her, and I didn't want to see it damaged. So I told myself he would grow out of it.'

'But he didn't?'

'His mother died when he was twenty. She hadn't had much of a restraining influence on him, but without her there was no restraint at all. Take one example. A few years ago, my wife decided she really wanted to take Jane to Disneyland. It was a big thing for us, was that, normally well out of our reach. We'd never even flown in an aeroplane, let alone gone all the way to America, but it was something that Jane wanted, and Doris decided to make it happen.' He paused. 'I don't really think you want to know all this.'

'Believe me, I do,' Paniatowski said.

'Well, we had to make some sacrifices to save the money. I cut down my tobacco to half an ounce a week, and Doris gave up going to the hairdressers. We'd eat scrag end instead of best steak, and of course there were no trips to the pub. And the money started to mount up. Doris kept everything we'd saved in an old dried-milk tin in the kitchen. Then one day Tom came round, and the next time Doris looked in the old milk tin, the money was gone.'

'So what did you do?'

'Nothing. What could I do? Tom swore he hadn't taken it – and I couldn't prove he had. But nobody else could have done it.'

'And that was it as far as you were concerned? You washed your hands of him?'

'Emotionally, yes. I wanted nothing more to do with him. But I still tolerated him, because Doris begged me to.'

'But there did come a point when he went too far?' Paniatowski guessed.

'Doris was in hospital with "woman's problems" and I'd just been to visit her. When I got home, I heard a scream from Jane's bedroom. I rushed upstairs and found Tom in there with her. He'd dropped in unexpectedly, and finding that Jane was the only one at home, he'd decided to take advantage of the fact. I don't know if he'd have actually raped her, but he certainly tried to kiss her and put his hand down her blouse. He was in his mid-twenties then – and she was fourteen.'

'What did you do?'

'I grabbed him by the scruff of the neck, and threw him down the stairs. And when he was lying there at the bottom, groaning, I told him never to enter my house again. But it wasn't what I *wanted* to do.'

'What you wanted to do was beat the shit out of him,' Paniatowski suggested.

'What I wanted to do was kill him.'

'Did he ever come to your house again?'

'No. I suspect Doris saw him outside. She may even have slipped him money now and again, because however much he had, he was never averse to taking more off his foolish auntie.

But he never came back because he was afraid of me – even though he was younger and taller and stronger than I am. The man was a coward. The man was below contempt.'

'And that's why you're not surprised he was murdered?'

'If he behaved towards the rest of the world as he behaved towards us – and I've no reason to think he didn't – then the only surprise is how long it took someone to get around to killing him.'

It was a noise the girl dreaded – the thump, thump, thump, reverberating through the floorboards, which told her that the music had started below.

She squiggled down in her bed, closed her eyes, and tried to imagine she was somewhere else, very far away.

It started to work. She could almost hear the sound of birds which sang a very different song to that of the squawking sparrows and starlings she had become accustomed to now. She could almost feel the gentle caress of a benevolent sun on her bare arms. And she could almost smell the cool air of the snowy high plains and the warm sticky air of the sweating jungles.

But the feelings did not last long, because the heavy beat of the music could smother any daydream, however powerful it might be.

The door suddenly burst open, and the man was standing there.

'Why are you still in bed?' he demanded angrily. 'Why aren't you already up and wearing your make-up?'

'I don' feel well,' she protested.

'Don't feel well!' the man repeated.

He stripped back the bedclothes, grabbed her arm and pulled her roughly out of the bed. She was a pretty girl, and she was naked, but he showed no interest in that, because as far as he was concerned, she was merchandise.

He released her arm, and she slumped back onto the bed.

'I sick,' she moaned.

'Get dressed and put on your make-up like you were taught to,' the man said. 'And before you do either of those things, take a shower – because you stink.' He looked around the room. 'And another thing,' he continued, 'change the sheets. The punters pay good money, and they want the sheets smelling of springtime freshness – just like it says in the advertisements – not stiff with some other bastard's spunk.'

'Please,' she said, 'not tonight. Tomorrow I will feel better.'

'Maybe you need somebody to explain to you in your own language why you need to work,' the man said. 'Shall I ask Joey to pay you a visit?'

When he said Joey, he was talking about José.

The girl shuddered.

'Not him,' she said. 'Please, not him.'

'So will you be ready to work on time?'

She bowed her head. 'Yes,' she said, defeated.

'Good,' the man said. 'That's a much better attitude. I'll be back in half an hour to check up on you.'

Once he had left, she got off the bed and went over to her small dressing table. She looked into the mirror, and studied the face staring back at her.

Only a year earlier, she had been considered beautiful by some people.

And pure!

Oh yes!

'Beatriz looks almost like a nun,' said some of her parents' friends who were old-fashioned enough to consider that a compliment.

But what did she look like now?

Even without the paint which she was forced to wear, the face in the mirror was the face of a whore.

She would not be in this place forever, she was sure of that. She had known some of the other girls, and had exchanged a few words with them once in a while – but always cautiously, because making friends with the other workers was not allowed, and would be punished. And then, one day, they were gone.

'What has happen to the girl with the yellow hair?' she had dared to ask the man.

And because she had caught him in a good mood, he had said, 'The punters were getting bored with her, so we've moved her on.'

'Moved her on? I don' understand what that mean.'

'Sent her to another club,' the man had replied, his patience already wearing thin. 'Somewhere she isn't known yet.'

And that would happen to her, too, she accepted. One day the punters would grow bored of her, and she would be moved on.

It wouldn't make any difference. This club was in a place called Whitebridge, but for all she saw of the world outside, it might as well have been on the moon. And so they would move her to Blackbridge or Greenbridge, or whatever other crazy name they gave to their towns, and it would be just like it was here.

They had promised her that once she had worked off the debt she owed to them, they would give her money to send back to her family. She had believed it for a while, but not anymore.

Nothing in her future would ever change for the better. Instead, the living nightmare she knew now would be repeated day after day, again and again . . . and again.

She would experience the same swirling horror many times over, until . . .

Until what?

She wondered if God would forgive her if she killed herself.

She wondered if these people would do anything if she eventually got sick, or whether they would just stand back and watch her die.

She wondered if one of the punters might go crazy one night and murder her – and if anyone would care if he did.

The sound of footsteps in the corridor brought her back to the present with a crash. She needed to get showered and dressed and made-up before the man came back. Because if she hadn't done that, as he'd instructed her to, he would get his friend Joey to pay her a visit. And even as this thought passed through her mind, she felt the sticky wetness of urine run down her leg, and realized just how frightened she really was.

# EIGHT

The corner table in the public bar of the Drum and Monkey was, unlike the tables which surrounded it, old and battered. All the other tables had, in fact, arrived at the pub only a few months earlier, courtesy of the brewery, which had decided it was high time the Drum smartened up its image. The landlord had paid the local Boy Scout troop to take away most of the old tables as part of their Bob-a-Job fund-raising week, but had left the corner table unchanged.

It had been a wise decision. It would have seemed strange to both the landlord himself and to his regular customers if that space had been filled by any other table, because this was the one at which Charlie Woodend used to brainstorm with his team, when Monika Paniatowski was a mere sergeant, Colin Beresford was no more than a constable, and Jack Crane was crawling round the garden in his nappies, looking for bugs to swallow. Woodend had retired many murders ago, and it had felt odd at first to see Monika Paniatowski fill his place, but now it was as if she, like the Sphinx, had always been there.

There was no brass plaque to indicate that so many cases had been cracked at this very table, but the regulars knew all about it, and felt – with not a little pride – that they had been part of the process themselves. So when the table was not occupied by the team, it was not occupied at all, and anyone new to the pub who made a move to sit at it was told, politely but firmly, that it was already in use.

When Paniatowski arrived at the Drum that early evening, the rest of the team had already assembled.

She looked at them fondly, from across the room.

There was Jack Crane, who could have made a fortune as a pop star, even if he couldn't sing a note, because the teeny-boppers who would Blu-tack posters of this cute, handsome young man to their bedroom walls would regard musical ability as a mere irrelevance.

There was Kate Meadows, slim, pixie-like, the object of fantasy of many men, who would never belong to anyone but herself.

And there was Colin Beresford – Paniatowski's best friend. His mother had suffered from Alzheimer's disease, and taking care of her had absorbed virtually all of his free time in his twenties, so that when he finally gave into the inevitable and put her in a care home, he was a thirty-year-old virgin. But – by God – he had more than made up for those lost years since then, and had truly earned the nickname of 'Shagger' Beresford. Colin would never be as clever a detective as Jack Crane, nor anything like as imaginative a detective as Kate Meadows, but he was a solid dependable bobby, who she loved dearly.

God, I'm thinking like a bloody mother hen, she realized, with some horror.

She walked over to the table, sat down, and immediately took a swig of the Polish vodka that was sitting there waiting for her. That was better, she thought. Now she felt less like a broody chicken and more like a chief inspector in charge of a murder case.

'What have you got for me, Inspector Beresford?' she asked crisply.

'The lads out on the street haven't come up with anything at all, which is hardly surprising because most of the buildings on Clegg Street are no more than work in progress,' Beresford said.

That was true enough, Paniatowski agreed. The gentrification process was in its early stages, and while the rest of the street would eventually resemble the James Hargreaves Building, for the moment it consisted mainly of gutted shells of the former industrial buildings.

'What about the other tenants?' she asked.

'We got something there, but I'm not sure how useful it will turn out to be,' Beresford said.

'So let's hear it,' Paniatowski suggested.

'There are twelve flats – or apartments, if you'd prefer.'

'We're only simple folk here, so let's stick to flats,' Paniatowski said.

'All right. There are twelve flats. Two are occupied by young couples – one of them with a baby. Two are company flats, and have nobody in them at the moment. The rest are let out to – or owned by – single young men. As you might have guessed, all these people are fairly well heeled, either because they've got good jobs or because their daddies have plenty of brass.'

'Which makes Tom Crawley an exception, because he doesn't fit into either of those categories,' Meadows interjected.

'I thought he had a job,' Paniatowski said.

'Maybe he did, but he didn't have the job we thought he had,' Meadows replied, enigmatically.

'We'll come back to that later,' Paniatowski decided. 'You were telling us about the other occupants, inspector.'

'They're all out for most of the day, and a lot of them give the impression they're out for most of the night, as well, which is pretty much what you'd expect of well-off young men.'

'And detective inspectors worried about the onset of middle age,' Meadows said softly.

'What was that, sergeant?' Beresford asked sharply.

'Nothing, sir,' Meadows said sweetly.

Paniatowski suppressed a grin. What she had just witnessed was Meadows indulging in her favourite sport of Beresford-baiting. She could have put a stop to it, she supposed, but as long as it was kept under control – and Meadows was controlled in everything she did – it was quite funny, and served to keep Colin on his toes. Besides, she strongly suspected that while it could annoy Beresford, he was also quite flattered that someone like Meadows would consider him worthy of being prodded with the proverbial sharp stick.

'However, we didn't draw quite as much of a blank as we did in the street inquiries,' Beresford continued. 'None of the other occupants really knew Crawley – no surprises there, they didn't know each other, either – but one of them,' he took out his notebook, 'a Giles Hatton, got the distinct impression that Crawley was often away for several days at a time.'

An impression! That was pretty much what the concierge had said, Paniatowski thought.

'And what was this impression based on?' she asked.

Beresford shrugged. 'Oh, you know, the little things. He'd often nod to Crawley as they passed each other in the lobby, but for days at a time he wouldn't see him at all. Crawley's letter box would start filling up with mail, too, so you could see it sticking out of the top. There was nothing conclusive in itself, but enough for him to make a supposition.'

'Fair enough,' Paniatowski said. 'Anything else?'

'Hatton's flat is next to Crawley's. The units are all well insulated, so unless the noise is very loud, you can't hear what's going on next door. What you can hear, however, is doors to the corridor being opened, and Hatton says that shortly after each of Crawley's presumed trips, he seemed to have a lot of visitors.'

'What does the concierge – bugger it, what does the *porter* – say about all this?'

'The porter only works until six, and all these visits took place in the evening.'

'So, to recap,' Paniatowski said. 'Several times, Crawley goes away for a period of time, and shortly after he comes back, he has some sort of party. Is that right?'

'That's about it,' Beresford agreed.

Paniatowski turned to Meadows. 'So what's this about him not having the job we thought he had?'

'He was fired several months ago,' Meadows said. 'Actually, it was buying this flat – which was supposed to have gone to a client – that cost him his job.'

'He bought it!' Paniatowski exclaimed.

'That's right – and he paid cash.'

Paniatowski whistled softly. 'So how could he afford it?' she asked. 'Did he get another surveyor's job?'

'His old boss doesn't think so. The chartered surveying world is quite a small one, and he says that if somebody else had taken Crawley on, he would have heard about it.'

'So it has to have been some other kind of job, or else he has no job at all,' Paniatowski said.

'That's right,' Meadows agreed.

Paniatowski frowned. 'Are we agreed that he must have borrowed the money he used to pay for the flat from *somewhere*?' she asked.

'Yes, unless some long-lost relative suddenly died and left him a fortune,' Meadows said.

'If that had happened his uncle would have told me about it,' Paniatowski said. 'So, we have to assume that he was quite heavily in debt, and that the person he owed would be expecting at least a partial repayment.'

'It's a logical assumption.'

'So if he *did* get a new job, it had to be a very well-paid one, in order for him to be able to meet his commitments – and if he *didn't*, where was all the money coming from?'

'There were no bank statements in the flat, but there was a letter from the bank advising him that his new bank card was ready,' Meadows said. 'I spoke to the manager over the phone, and he said he couldn't possibly reveal the details of a client's bank account, even if that client was dead.'

'I'll apply for a search warrant,' Paniatowski said.

'No need for that, boss,' Meadows said. 'I'll go and see him in the morning, and get him to change his mind.'

'If you *can* make him change his mind,' Beresford said.

'I will,' Meadows said.

Of course she would make him change his mind, Paniatowski thought. She was DS Kate Meadows, and she always got what she wanted, though if her superiors had any sense (and Paniatowski did) they wouldn't inquire too closely into *how* she did it.

'Right,' Paniatowski said heavily. 'I suppose it's time to tell you about my day.'

She outlined her conversation with Crawley's uncle on the way to the mortuary.

'From what Harrison says, Tom Crawley seems to have been a particularly nasty piece of work,' Beresford said.

'Careful, Colin,' Paniatowski warned him. 'Relatives don't always give the best character references, especially relatives by marriage, and for all we know, Harrison may merely have been jealous about the amount of affection his wife lavished on her nephew.'

'But you don't really think that's the case here, do you, boss?' Meadows asked.

'No,' Paniatowski admitted. 'Harrison struck me as an honest, thoroughly decent sort of feller, but I've been taken in by con men in the past, and before we reach any firm conclusions, I want it checking from all angles. That's one of the things that I'll be wanting you to do tomorrow morning.'

The other members of the team exchanged glances which said they had all noticed that Paniatowski had said 'wanting *you* to do', and quickly reached the kind of unspoken understanding that only people who have worked together under great pressure – and know each other better than they know their own families – can possibly reach. And this understanding was that while they didn't like the way things were heading at all, they would say nothing for the moment.

Paniatowski noticed the exchange, because she, too, was part of that team – part of what had almost become a single driven entity. But like them, she decided the time was not right to comment on it.

'Inspector Beresford, I want your lads back on the streets again. I suggest you expand the area of your search. Book a spot on the local morning television news, and make a general appeal for information. Someone, somewhere, must have seen something.'

'You don't want to do the broadcast yourself?' Beresford asked.

'No,' Paniatowski replied. 'The viewers have seen my face so often that they must be heartily sick of it. Besides, it's about time you started to raise your profile, Colin, because I won't be here forever. When I've gone somebody has to be ready to step into my shoes – and I'd much prefer it if it was someone I knew would do a good job.'

The general feeling of unease around the table deepened, but Paniatowski pretended not to notice it.

'Sergeant Meadows,' she continued, 'I want you to interview all the other occupants of the James Hargreaves Building again, and when you've done that, I want a deep search into Tom Crawley's background. Who were his friends? Did he have lovers of either sex? And most importantly of all, did he seem to have any source of income? DC Crane will assist you, and if you need any more bodies to do the spade work, ask Inspector Beresford for them. Is that clear?'

Somebody needed to ask the question, and it was pretty obvious that it was going to be Meadows.

'Where will you be while all this is going on, boss?' she asked.

'I'll be looking into Jordan Gough's claim that someone is trying to kill him,' Paniatowski said.

'You'll be doing *what*!' Beresford exploded.

'You heard her,' Meadows said, in soft, quiet voice which nevertheless suggested that the discussion should end right there.

But Beresford, having slipped into his bull-in-a-china-shop mode, was not to be silenced.

'Is that because the chief constable insists that you investigate the Gough business?' he demanded.

'Well, of course it is,' Paniatowski replied, exasperated. 'You don't seriously think I'd be doing it otherwise, do you?'

'You never used to let yourself be pushed around by the armchair bobbies from the top floor,' Beresford said.

And then a look of horror came to his face as he realized, as Meadows had been trying to warn him, that what he was implying was that since she came out of her coma, Paniatowski was not the woman she had once been.

'Listen . . .' he began, remorsefully.

'It doesn't matter what I might have done in the past,' Paniatowski interrupted crisply, 'because these are not normal times. The chief constable is feeling very insecure at the moment . . .'

'Then maybe he should have thought twice before coming back off sick leave,' Beresford said.

'He's not always been the best boss in the world. We all know that,' Paniatowski said.

And the others were thinking, 'No, he hasn't, because between the time his wife died and the moment he had his nervous breakdown, he was doing his level best to shaft you, boss.'

'Nevertheless, there have also been times when he's been pretty bloody good,' Paniatowski said. 'There've been times, in fact, when he's put his neck on the line for us. Is there anybody here who disagrees with that?'

Heads shook around the table, and Beresford said, slightly shamefacedly, 'It's true, he has.'

'So I think we owe him something,' Paniatowski said.

'Besides, what happens if he goes? You do remember when Marlowe was chief constable, don't you, Colin?'

'It's not something I'm likely to forget,' Beresford said, with an involuntary shudder.

'And whoever replaces Baxter could be as bad as Marlowe – or worse. So if making a show of taking Gough's worries seriously will help the chief constable, I don't see why I shouldn't do it. And it's not as if I'll be stepping back and leaving idiots in charge. You're the best team around.' Paniatowski smiled. 'And so you bloody well should be – because I trained you.'

The rest of the team smiled back at her. They were very far from happy, she thought, but they were prepared to accept the situation – at least, for the moment.


Reyes, Paniatowski's housekeeper/nanny, appeared in the hallway the moment she heard Monika's key turn in the front door.

'Your supper is in the oven, boss,' she said. 'It will be dried up by now, but if you are later than you tell me . . .' she gave a shrug, '. . . then there is nothing I can do about that.'

Calling her boss hadn't come out of nowhere, Paniatowski thought. Someone had convinced her it was the correct form of address to use, and since whoever had done it obviously had both a slightly off-beat sense of humour and an ironic attitude to authority, she suspected – though she could not prove – that that somebody was Kate Meadows.

The rest of Reyes' English had a very different source. She was from a small village in Alicante province, and was a distant relation of Louisa's. She had learned some basic English in school, but that had been heavily supplemented by lessons from ex-DCI Charlie Woodend, who lived nearby.

Charlie, as he would be the first to admit himself, was not a natural language teacher, because in his work he had always placed more faith in imaginative leaps than he had in structure, but he was a nice man, and he had done his best. The results had been mixed. On the negative side, Reyes had arrived in Whitebridge with large gaps in her vocabulary, and a syntax which refused to be tied down by rules. On the positive side, however, whatever English she did know, she was able to deliver convincingly in a broad Lancashire accent.

'Is Louisa home?' Paniatowski asked.

Reyes shook her head. 'There is a football match tonight. She is on duty at the Rovers' *estadio*.'

Paniatowski felt a cold chill run down her back. There could sometimes be trouble at football matches, and she really didn't want her daughter anywhere there was a possibility she might get hurt.

She was being stupid, she told herself angrily. Louisa was all grown up. She was a police cadet, and capable of handling herself in most situations. And you couldn't keep your children wrapped up in cotton wool forever, however much you might want to.

'What about the boys?' she said. 'Are they asleep?'

Reyes put her hands on her hips, in imitation of the older women in her family when they were demonstrating their exasperation.

'Are they sleep?' she asked. '*Claro que sí*, they are sleep.' She gestured with her thumb at the clock on the wall. 'Just look at the time.'

Paniatowski grinned. She allowed Reyes – little more than a child – to bully her, because she recognized that she needed to be bullied sometimes, and because the girl was marvellous with Philip and Thomas.

'I think I'll just slip upstairs and see them,' Paniatowski said.

'Don' you wake them!' Reyes said threateningly.

'I'll be careful,' Paniatowski promised.

The boys were lying in single beds, next to each other. They did not look like twins, and there was a strong possibility that they were not, because though they had emerged from the same womb, only minutes apart, there was a better than even chance that they did not have the same father.

Paniatowski had been raped by three bikers. Meadows had informed her, almost casually, that the bikers had been tracked down by her 'associates' and castrated. If anyone else had told her that, she would not have believed them, but coming from Kate, she had to accept it as true.

Not that it really mattered whether it was true or not. Alive
or dead – or merely maimed – the bikers were irrelevant. They
were part of an unpleasant incident in the past, and had nothing
to do with these two little boys.

Except that they did have!

However much she might deny it, they did have.

Thomas was fair, and was a calm, happy child. Philip had
dark hair, and a dark side to his nature. While Thomas always
wanted to cuddle every cat he saw, Phillip took pleasure in
frightening them and running after them, screaming at the top
of his voice.

Had the two boys inherited this difference from their
respective fathers, or was it just something that happened? She
didn't know.

She had told Philip he must be nice to animals, and he seemed
to understand, so maybe, when he grew older, a gentler side of
his nature would emerge. But what if it didn't? What if he grew
up to be mean and vicious? She would still love him, she
thought. She didn't have any choice in the matter. Yet the idea
that he might turn into a Jordan Gough or even a Tom Crawley
filled her with fear.

Many solicitors who came into contact with the general public
– and especially the criminal part of it – had nicknames. Some
were flattering – the Spin Master or the Wizard. Some, like Piss
Poor Percy or Clueless Claude, were less so. But, as far as
Horace Markham was aware, he was the only solicitor who had
ever been known as Spider.

He did not know the origin of the nickname, but liked to
think that was because he wove a complex and tangled web in
which to catch the unwary. He was deluding himself. The name
came from his habit of resting his fingertips of both hands on
the desk in front of him, while arching the backs of his hands,
so that each hand came to resemble a headless, five-legged
spider.

Markham was one of those solicitors who did for the reputation of lawyers what Dr Crippen had done for the reputation
of the medical profession and Sweeny Todd had done for
barbers. His clients were almost all rich, and all guilty of some

serious crime. He charged them excessively for his services, and did not inquire too closely where the money they handed over to him – usually in plain brown envelopes – came from. A serious businessman and transparent philanthropist like Jordan Gough would never have dreamed of using the services of such a disreputable figure, but there was another, hidden Jordan Gough – the one who started out as a criminal and had never been able to kick the habit – and he kept Spider on permanent retainer.

Aside from Spider, there were two other people sitting around the table. One was Gough himself, and the other was José Cardoza, Gough's fixer.

'The reason I've called you here tonight is to remind you of the situation you're both in,' Gough said.

'Is this really necessary,' Spider Markham protested. 'We've been through it dozens of times before.'

'Did I say you could speak?' Gough demanded.

'No, but . . .'

'Then keep your gob shut tight, Spider.'

'Sorry,' Markham mumbled, because Gough was frightening enough on his own, and when Cardoza was also there, only a fool would not see the need for self-effacement.

'As I was saying, you both have detailed instructions, and I expect them to be carried out to the letter,' Gough continued.

'You can trust me,' Markham said, even though he knew he should have kept silent.

Gough glared at him. 'If you follow the instructions, you will be well compensated,' he said. 'But what happens if you don't?'

Neither of the other two men said anything.

'You can speak,' Gough told Markham. 'In fact, I insist you speak.'

'If I don't follow instructions, Cardoza has been told how to deal with me,' he said, with a shudder. 'If he doesn't follow instructions, I've been told how to deal with him.'

'Exactly,' Gough agreed. 'It's what's called mutually assured destruction. But it goes further than that. José might decide to forestall matters by killing you.' He turned to the Portuguese. 'That's a possibility, isn't it, José?'

'I don't know,' Cardoza replied.

'I can't help thinking that Spider here might have felt a little happier if you'd immediately answered no to that question,' Gough said.

He's enjoying this, Markham thought. The bastard's taking real pleasure from scaring me. But he's always been like that. Sometimes there's a purpose behind it – to make me do something I don't want to do. But there are other times when there's no profit in it for him at all – and he's just done it because he can.

'You're thinking too much, Spider,' Gough said. 'I don't like people thinking too much when I'm around.'

'I was just . . .'

'If José does decide to knock you off, there's a mechanism in play to punish him that he doesn't even know about,' Gough said. 'You believe that, José, don't you?'

'Yes, I believe it,' Cardoza said, looking down at the table.

'And if Spider tries to get you, José . . .'

He stopped, mid-sentence. His cunning eyes had gone quite blank. It was almost as if he were in another world – or as if he wasn't anywhere at all.

They'd seen this before, Markham thought, but it was happening more and more frequently now.

Two minutes passed in silence, then Gough asked, 'What was I saying?'

'You say that if Spider try to get me . . .' José replied.

'Ah yes, if Spider tries to get you, there is another mechanism in place which will ruin him. So it's a case of you hang together, or you hang apart – and in José's case, I mean that quite literally.'

'Are you all right now?' Markham asked, and the moment the words were out he realized he'd made a mistake, because what he'd intended to sound like concern could quite easily be interpreted as mocking a vulnerability.

'Of course I'm all right,' Gough said. 'Why wouldn't I be all right?' He ran his hand across his forehead, as if to check that it hadn't suddenly developed a gaping hole. 'I'm tired now,' he continued. 'I'm tired, and I'm sick of the sight of the pair of you, so get out!'

5TH MAY 1981

# NINE

I t was just after eight o'clock in the morning, and the canteen at Whitebridge police headquarters was experiencing the lull that always came between the day shift just going on duty and the night shift getting ready to sign out. In fact, the canteen had only two customers, a young man with heroic good looks and a slightly older woman with a pixie haircut.

Crane was drinking from a large tea mug. Those people who had known him in his Oxford days would have marvelled at the sight. Back then, he was known for his discernment. Back then, people would study him in the tea shop, as he delicately sipped from a china cup, and speculate as to what tea he had chosen to delight his palate that morning – had he shown favour to the Earl Grey, or gone for the slightly more exotic Russian Caravan?

All that was gone. He had cast it aside when he moved north, much as he had cast aside his mortar board and under-graduate gown. Now the tea he drank was industrial strength – almost strong enough to stand a spoon up in. It showed the taste buds no mercy, and after the initial shock of the first few mugs, Crane had quite grown to like it.

Meadows was not drinking tea, because she didn't believe in stimulants. She didn't drink alcohol or smoke cigarettes either, and steered well clear of the heart-attack-on-a-plate which the canteen served as a fried breakfast. It was strange then that she should treat her body so well in the daytime and yet hand it over to Zelda, her alter ego of the night, to be subjected to all kinds of damagingly nasty sado-masochistic games, Crane thought.

'So the closest thing we have to a witness is this Giles Hatton chap,' Meadows said. 'Which one of us should talk to him?'

Crane shrugged. 'Probably it should be you, since you're in charge. Or do you think it might be more effective if we questioned him together?'

'You said you knew him from your university days, didn't you?' Meadows asked quizzically.

'I certainly knew someone of that name, but I don't know if it's the same man,' Crane replied.

'Giles is not a common name round here – nor is Hatton, for that matter – so there's a good possibility it *is* the same man. In which case, I think you should see him by yourself. You can pull the old pals act. Remind him of the jolly times the two of you had down by the jolly old river.'

'But we're not old pals,' Crane countered. 'I never actually felt the urge to hit him during the time I knew him, but I certainly didn't like him.'

'And he probably didn't like you, either,' Meadows had said. 'But that was then, and this is now. People have a tendency to rewrite their own personal history, especially when they're a long way from home, and they see a familiar face.'

When Meadows was cynical, she was usually right, Crane thought – which probably explained why she was nearly always cynical.

'Still, if you think it's an important interview . . .' he began.

'I do,' Meadows confirmed.

'. . . then maybe it's better that you do it.'

'I've got a lot of things on my plate this morning,' Meadows told him. 'You'll be fine.'

Crane got a sudden glimmering of exactly what was going on. He grinned. 'This is just like a Hollywood musical, isn't it?'

'Isn't what?'

'The star can see how much the understudy wants to prove herself – or, in this case, himself – and because she's got a heart of gold, she fakes having a twisted ankle to give the understudy her – or, in this case, his – big chance.'

'You really can talk a load of crap sometimes,' Meadows said, ever so slightly defensively.

'Do I?' Crane asked.

Meadows smiled. 'All right, maybe there is the tiniest sliver of truth in what you say,' she admitted, 'but if you tell anyone else about it, Jack, I'll cut your balls off.'

And he believed she would.

It was a glorious late spring morning, and the air outside Paniatowski's house had had an almost intoxicating flavour to it. The same could not be said about the air in the narrow streets in the old centre of Whitebridge, she thought. By the time the breeze reached them, it was tainted by the poisonous fumes from a thousand car-exhausts, and even a heavy smoker would think twice before inhaling a lungful of that.

The headquarters of Gough Enterprises was on one of these streets. It was no more than a shop front, and was sandwiched, rather uncomfortably, between a tobacconist's and a business which repaired shoes and cut keys. Most of its frontage was taken up by a large plate-glass window, which displayed several of Gough's businesses, including Economy Supermarkets, the King's Head Hotel, the Excelsior Club and Casino, and Gough Turf Accountants – but all the pictures were faded and curling up at the edges.

It would be tempting to see the window display as simply a result of neglect and lethargy, Paniatowski told herself, and if this had been any other business, she might have thought just that. But she was getting to know Gough, and was sure that if the window looked this way, it was because he *wanted* it to look this way, though she still had not worked out what his motive could possibly be.

She moved a little way down the street, and waited. After around five minutes, a man stopped in front of the building, took out a set of keys, and entered. She gave him a short time to settle in, then knocked on the door.

On the street, the man had been wearing a jacket, but now he was safely inside, he had shed that, and was draped in a rather shabby cardigan.

'Yes?' he said, as if surprised anyone would call – and for all she knew, he might have been.

'Are you Mr Gough?' she asked. 'Mr Arthur Gough?'

'Yes,' the man said.

She produced her warrant card. 'May I come in?'

Gough looked alarmed. 'What's this about?' he asked. 'If it's anything to do with my brother's businesses, then I'm afraid I can't help you.'

'But this is the headquarters of Gough Enterprises, isn't it?' Paniatowski asked, faking surprise.

Arthur Gough shrugged awkwardly.

'Well, you know . . .'

'As a matter of fact, I'm not here about his businesses at all,' Paniatowski said. 'I'm here because someone has threatened to kill him. So do you think I could come in now?'

'Yes, of course, why not,' Arthur Gough said, in a voice that seemed more exhausted than defeated.

He led her into the office. There were two desks – both of which would have fitted snugly into the category of 'battered'. One of the desks had an ancient typewriter on it, and presumably belonged to the secretary. The other was a little larger, and had a telephone in one corner. In front of this desk were two visitors' chairs which had seen better days. There was a bookcase running along the back wall, but it seemed mainly to contain catalogues, and there were two filing cabinets that had an almost pristine newness about them.

'Take a seat,' Arthur Gough said, indicating the chairs in front of his desk. 'I've got a kettle in the back, so I'll make you a cup of coffee if you'd like one. You'll probably have to drink it black, though, because I'm almost certain the milk has gone off.'

'Actually, I've just had a coffee,' Paniatowski lied, 'and as I assume you've got a busy day ahead of you,' another lie, since it should have been obvious to anyone that he hadn't, 'why don't we get started?'

'All right,' Arthur Gough agreed, sitting down opposite her.

She knew that Arthur was a couple of years younger than his brother, but if she hadn't been told that, she might easily have taken Arthur Gough as the elder of the two.

He didn't look much like his older brother at all. Jordan was thickset and had a dark complexion. His arms were hairy and his eyes were mean. Arthur was much slimmer – almost weedy – and had hair the colour of straw that has been left out in the sun too long. His eyes were pale blue – almost watery – and suggested that even if he did know how to stand up for himself, he would never find the energy.

Oh, my God, it's just like my boys, she thought. Is this what I've got to look forward to in the future?

'Are you all right, Chief Inspector?' Arthur Gough asked.

'Yes, I . . . I'm fine,' Paniatowski said.

'Only you've gone quite pale.'

'It's nothing,' she said, forcing her mind back onto the task in hand. 'Could I ask you a question about your window display?'

'If you must.'

'It's not very impressive, is it?'

'No, it certainly isn't.'

'So I was wondering why you didn't spruce it up a little.'

'I did once – in the days when I knew no better. I changed the whole thing around, with new photographs and everything. It looked much better.'

'So what happened?'

'Jordan flew into a rage, and demanded I put it back exactly the way it had been.'

The more she got to understand the way that Jordan Gough's mind worked, the more this sort of thing was making sense, Paniatowski thought.

It wasn't enough for him to make Arthur take a job which was really no job at all, it had to be made perfectly obvious that this was the case – and not only to Arthur, but to everyone else as well. That was why the window display was so seedy. That was why the office looked as if it had been furnished from a Salvation Army jumble sale. It was just one more way of Jordan rubbing his brother Arthur's nose in it.

'Yesterday, Jordan gave me a list of people who might want to kill him – and you are on it,' she said.

She didn't know what reaction to expect, but she certainly hadn't anticipated that he would simply nod.

'So I'm on his list,' Arthur Gough said. 'I can't say I'm surprised.'

'Why? Is it because you actually *do* want to kill him?'

'No, it's because I know the way he thinks. If he was in my situation, and I was in his, *he* would want to kill *me*.'

'And what situation are you in?'

'I'm working for a man I despise.'

'You don't have to work for him, you know,' Paniatowski said.

Arthur smiled weakly. 'Don't I?'

'No, you could have said, "Stick your job up your arse," and gone to work for someone else.'

Arthur shook his head. 'I have a nice home, and my children go to a good private school,' he said. 'I also have a large mort-gage, and if I default on my payments, I lose the house, and I'll have to withdraw my kids from the school.'

Arthur Gough was talking as if he had no choice, Paniatowski thought, with growing annoyance. He was excusing himself from taking action by pretending there was no action he *could* take.

'You still haven't told me what's stopping you getting a job elsewhere?' she asked.

'What's stopping me?' Arthur repeated. 'Jordan is.'

'Oh, come on now!' Paniatowski said, exasperatedly.

'You just don't understand how he operates, do you?' Arthur asked, mildly. 'I'm a pretty good book-keeper – not a great one, but easily one of the best in Whitebridge – so it should be easy enough for me to get a job somewhere else. Or, at least, that's what I thought until I tried.'

'What do you mean?'

'The first company that interviewed me said that I was the perfect candidate for the job that they'd advertised, and they were looking forward to me joining the team. That was on the Tuesday afternoon. And then on the Wednesday morning, they rang me and said they'd had a re-think and decided I wasn't suitable at all, so they were withdrawing the offer.'

'And you think the reason for that was because they'd been pressurized by your brother?'

'Well, of course it was. What else could have happened to make them change their minds in such a short time?'

'It is possible they really did reassess the job,' Paniatowski said, though she didn't really think that was very likely.

'That's what I tried to tell myself,' Arthur replied. 'So I applied for half a dozen other jobs, all of which I was well qualified to do – and I never even got to the stage of being called to interview.'

'And why exactly did Jordan do this?'

'Because he's like a cat, playing with a mouse. He could destroy me anytime he wanted to, but where's the fun in that?

Far better to keep me around, and stick his claw in me from time to time.'

It sort of made sense, given what she'd learned of Gough's character, Paniatowski thought, but it really was stretching credulity to think that even he would go *that* far.

'Did he ever tell you about Mr Cousins, the woodwork teacher?' Arthur asked, reading the doubt on her face.

'Yes, he did,' Paniatowski said.

'I thought he might have. It's one of his favourite stories.'

'But he never got to the end of it.'

'So what did he miss out?'

'He told me he'd had his revenge on the teacher, but he didn't explain how he'd done it.'

'Well, Mr Cousins put in an application for the post of deputy head . . .' Arthur began.

'Hang about, I thought he was still a young teacher when he taught Jordan,' Paniatowski interrupted.

'So he was. But this is fifteen or sixteen years later I'm talking about,' Arthur explained.

'Good God!' Paniatowski said, and she was thinking that when he'd said he'd waited a long time for his revenge, it had been no exaggeration.

'Shall I continue?' Arthur asked.

'Yes, I'm sorry for the interruption,' Paniatowski said contritely. 'Do carry on.'

'Life was working out very well for him. He had a nice home, a very attractive wife, and was strongly tipped to get the job of deputy head. That was when Jordan decided things were going a little *too* well, and made up his mind to step in.'

'What did he do?'

'Cousins' wife liked having a bit of fun. I'm not saying she was a good-time girl, but she liked to let herself go once in a while, if you understand what I mean.'

'I understand.'

'Cousins was away for the week on a school trip to France, and she decided to go out to the pub.' Arthur paused. 'I can't prove any of what I'm about to tell you, but I'd stake my family's lives on it being true.'

'All right,' Paniatowski said.

'What she didn't know when she set off for the pub that evening was that Jordan had hired a private investigator to follow her. This private eye managed to produce pictures of Cousins' wife in the woods with two men. Her knickers were round her ankles, and she was holding one of the men's things in her hand.'

'You've actually seen these photographs?' Paniatowski asked.

'Not as photographs, no.'

'Then how could you . . .?'

'I'm coming to that later. When it all came out, I'm told that Mrs Cousins admitted to her next-door neighbour that she'd been drinking, but claimed she remembered nothing about being in the woods with the two men. She said they must have spiked her drink – which they probably had.'

'Are you saying these men worked for your brother?'

'What do you think?'

'So what did Jordan do with the incriminating photographs? Did he send them to Cousins?'

'No, that would just have hurt *him*. What Jordan wanted was the kind of public humiliation that he felt Cousins had subjected him to, back in the woodwork room.'

'So he showed the photographs to other people?'

'You're underestimating his viciousness again. What he actually did was wait until the day of the interviews for the deputy head's job. I remember it was a beautiful mild early summer day, and the weather put a spring in most people's steps. I imagine it certainly put a spring in Cousins' step. He was wearing a new suit, and carrying a new briefcase, and I'd guess he was looking forward to leaving workbenches behind him forever, and sitting in his very own office. He always walked to work, because it was less than half a mile from his home, and as he got close to the school, what do you think he saw?'

'Somebody had pasted the photographs of his wife all over the wall,' Paniatowski said, in a dull, dead voice.

Arthur shook his head. 'You're underestimating Jordan, again. What somebody had actually done – and by that I mean somebody who was working for Jordan – was blow up the photographs to full poster size, and *then* paste them on the wall.

Cousins tore them down, of course, and stuffed them in a bin. By the time he got to school, he looked a mess. There was paste all over his nice new suit, and two of his fingernails were torn. He pulled himself together as best he could for the interview, but it was nowhere near good enough, and he didn't get the job. When he got home, his wife was gone. I think Jordan – or somebody working for Jordan – had warned her about what to expect from him, and given her a wodge of cash to make herself scarce. The last I heard of her, she was running a whelk stall in Blackpool.'

'Is that it?' Paniatowski asked.

'No, it's nothing like it,' Arthur told her. 'Cousins had taken down the posters, right enough, but not before half the kids had seen them on their way to school. So he ended up with no wife, the same shitty job he'd always had, and all the kids – and a lot of the staff – laughing at him. He hanged himself three months later. I'm surprised it took him so long.'

'If your father had only intervened when Cousins first started bullying him, none of it might ever have happened,' Paniatowski said.

'What did he tell you about my father?' Arthur, asked, and for the first time, Paniatowski could detect a hint of both strength and anger in his voice.

'He said that your father cared about nothing except chasing women.'

'And did he say anything about my mother?'

'He said she was an alcoholic.'

'None of that's true, of course,' Arthur said.

'So what is the truth?'

'Both my parents treated him well. They bought him many more things than they bought me – many more than any other child in our class had. They never mistreated him. They never even raised their voices to him.'

'But . . .?' Paniatowski said – because there simply had to be a 'but'.

'While they tried as hard as they could to be loving parents, their hearts simply weren't it, and as Jordan got older he began to notice it. That's when he started to build up stories about them. If they didn't love him, somebody had to be to blame. It couldn't be him, so it simply had to be them. So father was a randy old goat and mother was a lush, and that's why they were like they were. The only problem was, they should, by his logic, have been treating me as they treated him, and they weren't. And so he began to hate me.'

'So your parents were loving to you?'

'They were wonderful to me.'

'Why you and not him?'

'I think they could see a certain darkness in his soul which made it hard to love him. Then again, it might be much simpler than that. Maybe they loved me more because I was their natural son.'

'Wasn't he?' gasped Paniatowski, who had certainly not been expecting anything like that.

'No,' Arthur said, as if he were surprised she didn't already know. 'They were told they couldn't have children of their own, so they adopted Jordan. I was unexpected.'

And not only were you unexpected, Arthur Gough, Paniatowski thought, but you really upset the applecart.


It was a quarter to nine in the morning when Crane rang Giles Hatton's number on the James Hargreaves Building automatic porter.

'Who is it?' asked a tinny voice from the top floor.

'Jack Crane,' Crane said.

There was a pause, then Hatton said, '*The* Jack Crane? Jack Crane from Jesus College, Oxford?'

'That one,' Crane agreed.

'Well, then, you'd better come up,' Hatton said.

Crane reached the top floor and rang the bell. When Hatton answered it, he was wearing a silk dressing gown, and had a frying pan in his left hand, containing what looked like an omelette.

'Well, well, Jack Crane,' he said, holding out his right hand. 'Do come inside. You'll have to talk to me in the kitchen, because I'm halfway through cooking my breakfast.'

'That's fine,' Crane said.

The kitchen was all shining chrome and gleaming granite. Crane looked on as Hatton spooned some mushrooms and tomatoes from a second frying pan onto the omelette, and then expertly flicked one half of the omelette over, so that it covered them.

'Jack Crane!' Hatton said, turning the mixture over. 'What the devil are you doing here in Whitebridge?'

'I'm a detective,' Crane said. 'I've been assigned to the Crawley murder case, and I've come to interview you.'

Hatton chuckled. 'Well, well, well, whoever would have imagined that the new colossus of English literary criticism – the modern-day Lord Byron – would ever end up as a flat-foot?' he asked. 'Still, it's good to see you. And it was nice of you to take the time to talk to me yourself, when you could just as easily have sent one of your underlings.'

Crane smiled. 'I have no underlings,' he said. 'If you can imagine a pecking order with the chief constable at the top, then I'm right there at the bottom.'

Hatton's face fell. 'You don't mean that you're . . . what I suppose I'm saying is . . .'

'I'm a detective constable,' Crane said.

'Yes, well, I suppose we all have to start somewhere,' Hatton said. He tipped the omelette onto a waiting plate, and took it over to the breakfast bar. Picking up his knife and fork, he cut a piece of it off, and ate it with relish.

'Delicious,' he pronounced. 'This is my speciality.' He cut off another piece. 'There's the percolator on the counter. Pour yourself a cup of coffee if you want one. It's Jamaican Blue Mountain. Costs the earth, but if you can't spoil yourself, who can you spoil?'

'I'm fine,' Crane said.

'So, you're a policeman now,' Hatton mused. 'Well, I don't want to appear boastful, but I'm an assistant deputy department head at Brocklehurst Brothers, which, as you are no doubt aware, is one of this country's premier merchant banks.'

'An assistant deputy department head! I am impressed,' Crane lied. 'So what is an assistant deputy department head like you doing in Whitebridge?'

'Well, for all its grimness, there is still money to be made in the north,' Hatton said, 'and all the young high-flyers are expected to serve for a time somewhere in the back of beyond.

It's a sort of initiation rite before you become a fully-fledged member of the club.'

'I'm sure a man with your obvious ability won't be out in the cold for long,' Crane said.

The comment seemed to knock Hatton slightly off-balance. 'Why, thank you, Jack,' he said. 'You know, back in Oxford you always seemed a little superior and supercilious, but I obviously had you all wrong.'

Hatton shovelled the remains of the omelette into his mouth. The man ate like a pig, Crane thought.

'You said in the statement you made last night that Tom Crawley had a number of gatherings in his apartment, and that they were usually held when he'd been away for a short time,' Crane said.

'That's right,' Hatton agreed.

'I was wondering if you could possibly give me a few more details,' Crane said.

'What kind of details?'

Crane shrugged. 'Whatever details happen to occur to you. The number of people present at these affairs, for example. Whether there were more men than women. If the parties ever got out of hand.'

'As I said in my statement, the walls are sound-proofed, so I've no real idea how many people there were,' Hatton said. Then a thought suddenly occurred to him. 'I don't know if you'd call it getting out of hand, but I did see a girl dragged back into the apartment once.'

'You saw *what*?' Crane exclaimed.

'I was heading for the lift when the door to Crawley's apartment opened, and this girl came out. She was rather a pretty girl actually – a little too dark to be accepted by the circles I move in, but certainly very tasty. I saw that her clothes were somewhat *déshabillé*, but before I'd had time to take full advantage of the view, somebody grabbed her from behind and pulled her back in.'

'And you didn't do anything about it?' Crane asked.

Hatton looked confused. 'What should I have done?' he asked. 'I mean, it's not as if she was being raped or anything.'

'How do you know she wasn't being raped?'

'Well, she didn't scream, did she? And she had the look of a girl who knows what's what.'

*'Never show a witness how you feel, Jack,'* Paniatowski had told him, early on in their relationship. *'You may think he's filthy pond scum, but if he once senses that, you'll get no more out of him.'*

'Is there anything else you can think of, Giles?' he asked.

'No, nothing else occurs to me at this point in time.'

'Then thank you for your help, and I'll get back to you if I have any follow-up questions.'

'How's your love life?' Hatton asked.

'Pretty much non-existent,' Crane admitted.

'Jesus! Why is that?'

Because the combination of his work and his poetry meant he didn't have the emotional energy for anything else. And because the last girl he had allowed himself to fall in love with had turned out to be a murderer.

But he wasn't going to tell any of that to a creep like Hatton.

'I just never seem to get round to it,' he said.

'I'm engaged to be married to the Honourable Cassandra Featherstone Green,' Hatton said proudly.

'Do I know her?' Crane asked, because it was obvious from Hatton's tone that he was expected to.

'I should say you *do* know her,' Hatton said. 'We were all up at Oxford together. She was captain of the St Catherine's hockey team.'

Oh yes, he had her now, Crane thought. Cassie 'Jolly Hockey Sticks' Green – a rather sturdy girl with an outdoors complexion and who, if she'd gone to prison for having a sense of humour, would have been falsely convicted.

'She's rather well connected, you know,' Hatton said. 'In fact, her uncle is chairman of the very bank I work for.'

'Now there's a surprise,' Crane said.

'Mind you, the fact that I'm engaged to Cassandra doesn't stop me having a bit of fun now and again,' Hatton said. 'In fact, if you're free one night, we might go hunting together.'

'Aren't you worried that your amorous exploits might get back to your fiancée?' Crane asked.

'Of course not,' Hatton said, 'because I'm smart, you see.'

'In what way are you smart?' Crane wondered.

'Well, there are two kinds of girls, as you know yourself.'

'Do I know that? I never realized it.'

'Well of course you do, when you stop to think about it. There's the decent girls, like Cassandra, and the good-time girls who are quite prepared to let you have your bit of fun as long as you buy them a few drinks.'

'And that's what the girl you saw in the doorway of Tom Crawley's flat was – a good-time girl?'

'Yes.'

'And it didn't occur to you, even for a minute, that she might be a decent girl who was in trouble? You didn't think it was worth the bother to check if she needed any help?'

'No, it was obvious what she was.' Hatton paused. 'Hold on – are you getting at me?'

*'Never show a witness how you feel, Jack. You may think he's complete pond scum, but if he once senses that, you'll get no more out of him.'*

'No, I'm not getting at you,' Crane assured him. 'How could I be? I wasn't even there, was I?'

'Well, it certainly seemed to me as if you were having a go at me,' Hatton said sulkily.

# TEN

At the start of any new murder inquiry, Detective Inspector Colin Beresford would assemble the team of detective constables who had been seconded from other divisions, in the basement of police headquarters. He would look down at them from the podium – some familiar faces, some new ones – and tell them just how important they were to the investigation, since only they could provide those individual pieces of information which, when fitted together, would make the case. He would pause a second, to let this sink in, then remind them that discipline – both team discipline and individual discipline – was vital to the success of the investigation, and add that any number of murderers had escaped detection because someone on the team had thought he could cut corners.

It was always a good speech, which never failed to inspire the newly promoted officers who hadn't heard it before, and even the veterans, who had sat through several such talks, came away feeling more positive and determined because of it.

Beresford's leadership skills didn't stop there. He had a real talent for recognizing a good lead when it presented itself, and for rapidly moving the team's focus in that direction. But he also had a nose for sniffing out lines of investigation which were likely to lead nowhere at all and abandoning them, when others in his situation might still be giving them serious consideration. He was feared and admired by the constables who worked under him, and strongly approved of by his boss, Monika Paniatowski. Even DS Meadows, who took the greatest pleasure in baiting him whenever the opportunity arose, had sincerely congratulated him on more than one occasion.

Yes, he really liked his job, and he was very good at it.

And yet . . .

And yet, there were times when he longed for the good old days, when he had been a sergeant, not the least bit responsible for anyone else's behaviour and free to follow his own hunches. So whenever an opportunity came his way to temporarily abandon the commanding heights of the investigation and get down and dirty in the trenches, he grasped it with both hands.

And such an opportunity had presented itself to him that morning – had rather, in fact, forced itself onto him.

He had thought that Tom Crawley looked vaguely familiar when he was examining the corpse, but later on, as evening melted into night, he had an increasingly nagging – almost worrying – feeling that part of his brain was holding back some vital piece of knowledge from the rest of it. He had gone to bed troubled (and alone) but had woken up just before dawn knowing *exactly* where he had seen the man before.

And – *voilà* – he had all the excuse he needed to do a little investigating on his own.

Whitebridge was a city, with the largest indoor market for miles around, and its own cathedral. But it was also a series of communities or circles, and these could not be considered solely in geographical terms. Thus, the Free Masons, who made up one of these circles, had their solemn lodge meetings and sociable ladies' nights without ever intersecting with the members of the Transport and General Workers' Social and Bowling Club. Thus, the glam rockers could paint on their make-up and attach their false eyelashes as if there were no such thing as a punk with a safety pin through his ear. And thus the respectable housewives could meet for their bridge evenings, and sing 'Jerusalem' at the Women's Institute meetings, without even being aware that in the pubs and clubs of the town's Barbary Coast there were men and women constantly hunting for carnal experiences.

Beresford would never have thought of what he did as 'hunting for carnal experiences' but if someone else had described it in those terms, he would, in all fairness, have had no objection to the label. Ever since he had lost his virginity – which was within weeks of his mother being admitted to the nursing home – he'd been driven to claw back the twenties he'd never had. He was not interested in a long-term relationship, and while he was happy to sleep with the same woman more than once (if she was willing, and was all that was available at the time) he didn't want even a short-term commitment. Of course, that meant there were nights when he'd been hoping to take a woman to his bed and instead went there alone, but that was the price he willingly paid for his independence.

It had been on some of these hunting trips that he'd noticed Tom Crawley. If they'd been targeting the same woman – two bucks drawn towards the one doe – he might have taken a closer interest in the other man at the time, but since Crawley had shown no interest in clashing horns, Beresford had simply stored him in the mental filing cabinet that many cops keep in a corner of their brains.

All of which explained why Beresford found himself in the Burning Bush, just after it opened its doors for business at half-past eleven.

The pub looked very different in the daytime, he thought. At night, with the garish blue lighting flashing on and off, and a jukebox so loud that it sent vibrations rippling through the floor, the Bush had an exciting and slightly dangerous edge to it. With the jukebox silent and sunlight leaking in through the windows, it looked like what it really was, a tired old boozer which only survived by serving as a pick-up place for people like him.

'Hello there, Colin,' said the man behind the bar, who was polishing the glasses.

'Hello, Pete,' Beresford replied.

Even Pete seemed different in the daytime, Beresford thought – less of the edgy bar keeper in a gangster film, and more of the cardigan-wearing barman in a soap opera.

'I should have thought this was a bit early for you,' the barman continued jovially. 'We don't get much totty in at this time of day.'

'I'm not here in search of a companion,' Beresford said. 'I'm wearing my police officer's hat today.'

'I never knew you were a bobby,' Pete said, suddenly starting to look worried. 'Look, if it's about that spot of trouble we had the other night, nobody robbed him in here, whatever he says. He was so pissed that my guess is he lost his wallet in the street.'

'Relax, it's not about that,' Beresford said. He took a photograph of Crawley out of his pocket and laid it on the counter. 'Do you know him?'

The barman examined the picture. 'His name's Tom something or other,' he said.

'His surname's Crawley,' Beresford told him.

Pete shrugged, as if that were information that he had not sought and did not need. 'I suppose it is, if you say so.'

'He's been murdered.'

'Has he, by God?'

'Didn't you read about it in the papers?' Beresford wondered.

'I hardly ever look at them. To tell you the truth, all that small print gives me a headache.'

'So what can you tell me about him?' Beresford asked.

'Nothing,' Pete replied.

'But he was a customer here, wasn't he?'

'Yes. So are you – and I didn't even know you were a bobby till you told me just now.'

Beresford sighed. 'Let's try it this way, then,' he suggested.

'What would you say about me, if somebody asked you? And don't worry – I want you to be brutally honest.'

'Well,' the barman said uncomfortably, 'I'd say you're always pleasant to everybody, and unlike some fellers who come in here, you haven't got deep pockets and short arms, by which I mean . . .'

'I know what you mean.'

'. . . that you're always willing to pay your way.'

'Give me more,' Beresford demanded.

'Well, you're always nicely dressed whenever you come in here, although, if you'll forgive me for saying so, Colin, your clothes do tend to look a bit old-fashioned.'

Now that was a shock, Beresford thought.

'But what am I like as a person?' he asked, trying to mask the hurt. 'What motivates me?'

'Well, since you did ask me to be honest with you . . .'

'Yes, I did.'

'. . . I'd have to say that the thing I've noticed most is that you seem to have your brains in your underpants,' the barman said. 'Not that there's anything wrong with that,' he added hastily. 'Most customers at that time of night only have one thing on their minds.'

'Right,' Beresford said, taking a deep breath, 'now talk about Tom Crawley in the same way as you've just talked about me.'

'Well, unlike you, he was one of them fellers who have deep pockets and short arms,' Pete said. 'You'd never see him buying a drink for himself, as long as there was someone else there to buy it for him. Still, you'd have to say, he did dress very nicely – very smartly.'

'And much more fashionably than me?' asked Beresford, who was still annoyed.

'Well, I think he probably spent a lot more on himself than you do,' the barman said. He held up his hands as if he was worried he might have caused offence. 'Not that there's anything wrong with cutting a few corners when it comes to sartorial elegance,' he added.

'And did he have his brains in his underpants, too?' Beresford asked.

'Well, yes, he did have – in a way.'

'What do you mean – in a way?'

'I'll put it like this,' Pete said, choosing his words carefully. 'He only started coming in here when the Ragman's Arms closed down.'

The Ragman's Arms had been the rendezvous point of the town's homosexual community until the brewery had decided to shut it, Beresford recalled.

'So let me get this clear,' Beresford said. 'Tom Crawley was a gay man, was he?'

'I don't know how happy he was,' said the barman, who appeared to be unfamiliar with the newly fashionable term, 'but he was definitely as bent as Dickie's hatband.'

The manager of the Whitebridge branch of Grindley's Bank was in his early fifties and was losing the battle against encroaching late middle age both on top of his head and around his waist.

He was wearing a tie with an elaborate heraldic design, which probably suggested to his average client that he had been either a member of an Oxford college or an officer in a prestigious Guards regiment. Kate Meadows, who, in a previous life, had rubbed shoulders with many scholars and soldiers, was not fooled. This man lacked the arrogant self-assurance to fall into either of those categories. What he actually was, she assessed, was nothing more than a member of the provincial bourgeoisie who had, within the circles of modest ambition, done quite well for himself.

He should be a doddle.

'The reason I'm here, Mr Foster, is that I'd like to have a quick glance at Tom Crawley's bank account,' she said, her deliberately casual choice of words making it seem as if it were a matter of no great importance.

The manager rested his clasped hands on his rounded belly.

'I'm afraid I can't allow that, not even when I'm asked by a charming young lady like yourself,' he told Meadows – and the condescending smile on his face said he fully expected her to be flattered. 'You see, we take our clients' confidentiality very seriously indeed.'

Flattered was not what Meadows felt. Annoyed or offended would have been much closer to the mark.

'You are aware, aren't you, that as well as being a "charming young lady" I am also a detective sergeant,' she said.

'Of course,' the bank manager replied. 'It is in recognition of that fact that I managed to squeeze in the time to see you in what, as you can imagine, is a very busy schedule.'

'And are you also aware that Tom Crawley has been murdered?'

'I most certainly am. How could I not be? It was in all the papers, Miss Meadows.'

'That's *DS* Meadows,' Kate corrected him. 'So if you know he was murdered and I'm a police officer, why can't I see the bank statement?'

'The executors of Mr Crawley's estate have instructed me not to make the bank details available without a warrant,' Foster said.

'Now that *is* interesting,' Meadows said.

'What is interesting?'

'You implied that you knew about Crawley's death because you read about it in the papers, but in actual fact, you knew because the executors of his estate had told you about it.'

'Ah!' Foster said, awkwardly.

'Ah?' Meadows repeated.

'The . . . err . . . truth is that I first learned about the murder in the papers, and *then* the executors told me about it.'

'Interesting,' Meadows said. 'And could I ask who the executors of the estate are?'

'They are a company called Arachnid Holdings.'

'Cute name,' Meadows said. 'The thing is, Mr Foster, I can get a warrant to look at the account, but that will take time, and in a murder inquiry, time is of the essence.'

'I'm sorry, but given my instructions there's nothing I can do until you do produce a warrant,' Foster said.

Meadows frowned. 'I like you, Mr Foster.'

'I like you, too Miss – Detective Sergeant – Meadows,' said the bank manager, looking as if he had known all along that that she would succumb to his charm eventually.

'And I worry about what the newspapers might do to you when they learn you've deliberately impeded a murder inquiry.'

'You wouldn't tell them that, would you?' Foster asked, starting to look worried.

Meadows laughed. 'Me? Of course not! I could never do anything so horrid to a nice man like you. But I'll have to file a report, you see, and I strongly suspect – though I can't prove it – that some of our filing clerks sell this kind of scandal to the papers.'

'Scandal!' Foster repeated, clearly shocked by her use of the word. 'It's not a scandal. Surely the newspapers will understand that all I'm doing is fulfilling my legal obligations.'

'I can see you don't know these people as I do,' Meadows said sadly. 'They are fiends.' She rolled this last word around in her mouth, making it simultaneously seductive and frightening. 'Once someone is drawn to their attention, they'll go back over his whole past, looking for one silly little mistake which they can blow up to giant proportions.'

It was a shot in the dark, but not *that much* of one, because everyone has something they'd prefer to keep hidden. Certainly it had had the right effect on Foster. Sweat was starting to form on his brow, his chin was wobbling, and the hands which had recently cradled his stomach now tapped nervously on the desk.

'I'd only need one quick peek,' Meadows said encouragingly. 'No one need even know it happened.'

'No, I . . .' Foster gasped. 'I'm sorry, but I simply can't.'

So he hadn't turned out to be such a doddle after all, Meadows thought. And it was easy to work out why, because however much she'd frightened him – and she really *had* done that – someone else had frightened him more.

At their usual table in the Drum, the rest of the team sat in silence while Paniatowski scanned the report which had been submitted by the Scene of Crime Officers.

When the chief inspector finished the report, and put it down on the table, she looked somewhat less than ecstatic.

'If any of you were pinning your hopes on the forensics cracking this case for you, then you're right out of luck,' she said. 'The only prints that the SOCOs found belonged to Crawley himself, and all the hairs recovered also look as if they belonged to the dead man.'

'How is that possible?' Beresford asked. 'We know that he threw parties in that flat. The people who attended must have left at least some evidence of being there.'

'It may have been weeks since he held his last party,' Meadows said, 'and Mrs Downes, Crawley's cleaner, will have paid the flat several visits since then.'

'But even so, to leave no traces at all . . .' Beresford protested.

'You haven't met the woman, sir,' Meadows said. 'I have.'

'Meaning what?'

'We were standing there, in the living room, with Crawley as dead as dead could be – his brains all over the carpet – and can you guess the first thing she said to me?'

'If you knew who killed him?' Beresford hazarded.

'If it would be all right if she could carry out her cleaning routine as normal. "I'll work around Mr Crawley," she told me. "I promise I won't touch him." The woman is a fanatic, and cleaning is her religion, so trust me when I say that if there ever were any clues, she'll have swept them up or polished them into oblivion.'

'I can ask the SOCOs to go over it again, if you're not happy, Colin,' Paniatowski said.

Beresford shook his head. 'No, if Sergeant Meadows says there's no point, then there's no point.'

'Right, so let's move on,' Paniatowski said. 'You talked to Giles Hatton this morning, didn't you, Jack?'

'Yes, boss.'

'Then tell us about it.'

Crane outlined his conversation with Hatton, including the incident of the girl in the doorway.

'Do you believe what he said about the girl?' Beresford asked.

'Yes, I think I do,' Crane replied. 'When most people lie, it's usually to put themselves in a better light, but the fact that Hatton turned his back on the girl in the doorway means he doesn't come out of the story looking particularly good.'

'That's one way of putting it,' Meadows commented. 'I'd say he came out of it looking a real arsehole.'

'Yes, I wouldn't disagree with you,' Paniatowski said.

'The thing is, from what my sources tell me, I think it's unlikely Crawley *would* have invited women to his parties,' Beresford said.

'And why's that?' Paniatowski asked.

'Because he was gay.'

Only a couple of years earlier, he'd have said 'queer' but Kate Meadows had expressed a strong dislike of the term, and now, as he used the more acceptable term, he noticed she was nodding approvingly.

'How reliable is this information?' Paniatowski asked.

'It was the barman of the Burning Bush who told me initially,' Beresford said, 'but I've since got confirmation from a couple more sources that I trust. And that got me thinking – maybe he was killed by his gay lover, like that writer, Joe something-or-other.'

'Joe Orton,' Crane supplied.

'That's right, Joe Orton. He was beaten to death, too. Then again, it's more than possible Crawley's murderer simply didn't like queers.'

'You mean "simply didn't like gays",' Meadows said sharply, clearly disappointed to hear him slipping back into his old ways.

'If they disliked him enough to kill him, they probably thought of him as a queer,' Beresford said.

'Fair enough,' Meadows said, looking, for once, a little disconcerted.

Paniatowski allowed herself a quick smile, because though she agreed that most of Meadows' jibes at Beresford were justified, it was nice to see Colin fight back once in a while.

'The other alternative might be that although he was gay, most of his guests weren't,' Crane suggested.

'It's possible, but unlikely,' Meadows said. 'Gays are like fetishists – they usually stick together and keep well clear of the straights.'

It didn't even cross the minds of Paniatowski, Beresford and Crane to dispute this. And why would it? Zelda (the night-time Kate) wore a purple wig, and carried whips in her leather bag – and possibly several other instruments for inflicting pain that it was best not to think about – and she knew more about the underground counter-culture than the rest of them combined.

'Maybe it wasn't a party for friends,' Crane suggested. 'Perhaps he was entertaining business associates.'

'Go on,' Paniatowski encouraged.

'And perhaps he knew his business associates didn't like gays, so he persuaded the girl to pretend she was his girlfriend.'

'Or maybe she didn't know she was supposed to pretend to be his girlfriend because he hadn't told her, and it was when she realized what was really going on that she decided to leave,' Beresford said.

'But Crawley pulled her back inside the apartment and persuaded her to stay,' Crane added.

'The big question that leaves unanswered is what sort of business Crawley could be involved in,' Paniatowski said. 'Was it something he started doing after he was fired? Or had he been at it even when he was a surveyor? And does it involve surveying?'

'We'd probably know the answer to all those things if the bloody bank manager wasn't holding out on us,' Meadows said, and told the team about her conversation with Foster.

'Well, as soon as you've got the warrant, you'll have all the answers you need,' Beresford said.

'You think so?' Meadows asked sceptically.

'Don't you?'

'No. What I think is that by the time I turn up with a warrant, all Crawley's records will have gone missing.'

'Why do you think that?' Paniatowski asked.

'Because somebody's got at the bank manager, and whoever he is, he frightens Foster more than I do.'

Beresford whistled softly.

'What's that supposed to mean?' Meadows demanded.

'It means that we didn't think it was possible that there was anyone more frightening than you, Sarge,' Crane said. 'It's a compliment,' he added hastily.

Meadows thought about it, and then a smile came to her face. 'Yes, I suppose it is,' she said.

'If Foster is being threatened, then you need to find out what he's being threatened with,' Paniatowski said.

'Could you spare me a team to keep him under investigation, sir?' Meadows asked Beresford.

'How many officers will you need?'

'I'd like it round the clock, so that would be three shifts with two men on each shift.'

'Will you authorize the overtime, boss?' Beresford asked Paniatowski.

'For two or three days, it shouldn't be a problem,' Paniatowski said. 'After that, the chief constable might start to dig his heels in.'

'I don't know what it is that somebody's holding over Foster's head,' Meadows said, 'but whatever it is, if it doesn't become obvious in a couple of days, it never will.'

'Right,' Paniatowski said, 'do you think there's still a possibility you might come up with a witness, Colin?'

Beresford shook his head. 'We'll keep looking, but my gut tells me that if there was a witness, we'd have found him already.'

'No witnesses and no forensics, so all we're left with is motive and opportunity,' Paniatowski said. 'Who had the opportunity? Probably half of Whitebridge – so what we need to home in on is a motive. I want all the residents of the James Hargreaves Building questioned, and if they've *already* been questioned, I want you to have them questioned again; I want you to dig as far into Tom Crawley's background as you can; I want you to find out who his friends were and who his enemies were; and if you can track down the girl who Giles Hatton saw in the apartment doorway, that would be the bloody icing on the cake.'

'What about you, boss?' Beresford asked.

'Me!' Paniatowski echoed. 'I'll keep on interviewing the people on Jordan Gough's hate list until I find out who has been sending him those nasty anonymous letters.'

'What if they don't really exist?' Meadows asked. 'What if he's just giving you the run-around just because he can? Have you thought of that?'

'Yes, I've thought of it,' Paniatowski admitted. 'And yes, I probably am wasting my time. But that's not what's important at the moment.'

'Your time isn't important!' Beresford exclaimed. 'Is that really what you're saying?'

'Yes, it is,' Paniatowski agreed. 'There's only one thing that matters at the moment, and that's catching Tom Crawley's murderer. And you can do that without me. You know you can. So who cares if I'm chasing my own tail, as long as it keeps the chief constable off your backs, and lets you get on with the job?'

They heard the phone behind the bar ringing, and were not in the least surprised when the landlord called across the room that there was a call for the chief inspector, because this had happened many times before, on many cases, right back to the days of Charlie Woodend.

Paniatowski stood up, and stepped into the corridor. The public phone was on the wall, halfway between the small mountain of stacked bottled beer crates and the ladies' toilets, and as Paniatowski reached it, it made a gentle tinkling sound to indicate that the landlord was transferring the call.

Paniatowski picked up the phone. 'Chief Inspector Paniatowski,' she said. 'Who is this, please?'

'It's Horace Markham,' said the voice at the other end of the line.

'Who?' she asked, puzzled.

The solicitor sighed, and gave into the inevitable. 'Spider Markham,' he said with resignation.

Oh, *that* Markham!

'How did you know I'd be here, Mr Markham?' she asked. 'Are you having me followed?'

Spider Markham chuckled. 'Of course not,' he said. 'The reason I knew you'd be there is because you're almost legendary for holding meetings with your team at the corner table in the public bar of the Drum and Monkey.'

'Then maybe I'd better think about changing my habits,' Paniatowski said – although they both knew it would take more than an oily solicitor to make her do that. 'So what do you want, Mr Markham?' she continued.

'I'm ringing you on behalf of my client to ask how your current investigation is going,' Markham told her. 'He is, as you will no doubt appreciate, most eager for the investigation to reach a satisfactory conclusion.'

'Let me make sure I've got this clear,' Paniatowski said.

'When you say you're ringing on behalf of your client, you mean you're ringing on behalf of Jordan Gough. Is that correct?'

'That is correct.'

'And he's expecting me to go running back to him with anything I find – as if I was no more than a bloody Golden Retriever?'

'No, no, you've got hold of the totally wrong end of the stick entirely,' Markham said with jovial reassurance. 'Mr Gough certainly doesn't expect you to go running back to him . . .'

'That's good, because if I thought he did . . .'

'. . . he expects you to come running back to me, and to drop whatever you've found at *my* feet.'

Paniatowski felt a lake of rage bubbling up inside her.

'I'm a detective chief inspector in the Mid-Lancs Constabulary, in case you've forgotten,' she said. 'I don't have to put up with this kind of crap – especially from a shyster like you.'

'Don't you?' Markham asked calmly. 'Mr Gough has already humiliated you once, hasn't he? You stormed out of his house, which was a grand dramatic gesture, but it all fell a bit flat when Mr Gough got the chief constable to make you go back. That must really have been a terrible blow to your pride and self-esteem.'

'I've been through worse,' Paniatowski said, unconvincingly.

'But at least that was only a *private* humiliation, which you can keep to yourself if you want to,' Markham continued, as if she had never spoken. 'Can you imagine what he could do to you if he really put his mind to it – how you would feel when he left you no choice but to grovel to him in *public*?'

'You can't threaten me,' Paniatowski said.

'But my dear Monika, I'm *not* threatening you,' Markham said. 'What I am doing is laying out your options for you. If you're a good little chief inspector and keep Mr Gough informed of the progress you're making in your investigation, then there'll be no need for any further unpleasantness.'

'Well, that is really very nice to know,' said Paniatowski, forcing herself to sound calm, but finding it hard to ignore the fact that her gut was erupting.

'And if you actually do catch the man who's been threatening my client, then Mr Gough will see to it that you get a great write-up in his newspaper.'

'Oh yes?'

'Indeed. He'll even make sure the *Telegraph* publishes a flattering photograph of you. And in addition, he'll recommend to your chief constable that you be promoted to superintendent – and if he recommends it, you can almost guarantee it will go through.'

'Let me tell you something,' Paniatowski said, 'if I thought my promotion prospects were dependent on a man like Jordan Gough, then I'd resign from the police immediately.'

'On the other hand, if you choose to be uncooperative . . . well, we've already discussed what might happen, haven't we?'

'Go screw yourself – and while you're at it, screw your lord and master Jordan-bloody-Gough,' Paniatowski growled.

It wasn't her wittiest riposte ever – not by a mile – but it was the best she could come up with at that moment, and having delivered it, she hung up.

For a moment, she stood staring at the wall next to the phone, and then – perhaps imagining for a second that it was Spider Markham's face – she made a fist of her right hand, and punched it as hard as she could.

She yelped as her knuckles made contact with the plaster, and she felt a shooting pain travel up her arm.

'Now that was a very stupid thing to do,' she told herself through clenched teeth.

She put her hand into her left armpit, hoping that, in some magical way, it would relieve the pain.

It didn't.

She'd lost control of herself, she thought, as she withdrew her aching hand again. She should never have allowed herself to do that, and it was important that there was no evidence of it having happened imprinted on her features when she re-joined her team in the bar – because the last thing they needed to know, when they were in the middle of a murder investigation, was that their boss had allowed herself to go off the rails.

She made her way gingerly to the ladies' toilets, and examined herself in the mirror. The woman who gazed back at her had mad eyes, framed by sunken sockets.

She took several slow deep breaths, and then examined herself again.

She didn't look much better, but at least now she was no longer a gorgon, she told herself, and the chances were that none of the team would even notice.

On the way back to the bar, she stopped and examined the spot on the wall she'd punched. There was a definite crack in the plaster, so at least she'd achieved something.

'Jesus, boss, what the hell happened to you?' Beresford asked, when Paniatowski re-joined the team at the table.

'I've no idea what you're talking about,' Paniatowski lied.

'Who was the phone call from?' Meadows probed.

'Spider Markham,' Paniatowski admitted. 'But it wasn't important.'

There was a finality about her words that persuaded the rest of the team not to push it, although they were desperate to know.

'So where were we?' Paniatowski asked.

'You were talking about the Gough case . . .' Crane began.

*'If you actually do catch the man who's been threatening my client, then Mr Gough will see to it that you get a great write-up in his newspaper . . . and he'll recommend to your chief constable that you be promoted to superintendent,'* Markham had told her. *'If you choose to be uncooperative . . . well, we've already discussed what might happen, haven't we?'*

'There is no Gough case,' Paniatowski said. 'The only serious crime that's been committed is the murder of Tom Crawley – and that's where I should be focusing my attention.'

'That must have been *some* phone call,' Meadows said softly.

'What was that you said, Sergeant?' Paniatowski demanded.

'Nothing,' Meadows said, 'or at least, nothing worth repeating. Welcome back, boss.'

# ELEVEN

Grindley's Bank stood on the corner of the High Street and Westgate. Unlike all the other banks in Whitebridge, which had abandoned their old-fashioned frontages for a new, shinier image, Grindley's had stuck with its reassuring conservative red sandstone. The bank had already closed to the public when Paniatowski and Meadows arrived at a quarter past four, but they had phoned ahead, and when Paniatowski rang the bell, the door was opened by a smartly dressed woman wearing a badge which labelled her as the chief cashier.

'Are you the police?' she asked.

'We are,' Paniatowski agreed, showing her warrant card. 'I'm DCI Paniatowski and this is DS Meadows.'

The chief cashier smiled. 'It's nice to see there are women in senior positions in the police force,' she said. 'I personally wish there were a few more female bank managers.'

'Then you'll have to learn to play dirty, like most of the men do,' Meadows said.

'Play dirty?' the chief cashier repeated.

'Would you like to see our search warrant?' Meadows asked.

'I suppose I should,' the chief cashier admitted, but she gave the document only the briefest of glances, then said, 'Would you like to come inside?'

Several of the employees looked up from their desks with frank curiosity about the new arrivals.

'This is my second visit, so I can probably find our own way to Mr Foster's office,' Meadows said.

'Mr Foster isn't in this afternoon,' the chief cashier told her. 'I've arranged for you to see Mr Brunskill, the assistant manager, instead. I hope that's all right for you.'

'It will have to be, won't it?' Paniatowski said, with ill grace.

\* \* \*

Mr Brunskill was in his early thirties, but had already started to develop the patrician air much favoured by large fish in very small ponds.

'Mr Foster knew we were coming, so why isn't he here?' Paniatowski asked, coming straight to the point.

'He had a business meeting with one of our best clients,' Brunskill said, 'and he couldn't really put it off. But I'm sure I can deal with any queries you might have, quite as well as he could.'

'Does it happen often?' Paniatowski asked.

'Does what happen very often?'

'Having a meeting with a client somewhere other than in the bank.'

'Well, no,' Brunskill said evasively.

'So how often *has* it happened? Five times? Ten times? As many as fifteen times?'

'To tell you the truth, it's such a rare occurrence that I can't actually remember the last time.'

'If I didn't know better, I'd say he was dodging us,' Paniatowski commented. 'Anyway, we're here to see Tom Crawley's bank statements, as indicated in this search warrant.'

Brunskill read the search warrant much more carefully than the chief cashier had done.

'Well, this does seem to be in order,' he said. 'I'll get one of my girls to bring it in.'

Oh dear, that was an unfortunate way to phrase it, Paniatowski thought, as she felt Meadows bridling beside her.

'Your girls?' Kate Meadows said innocently. 'How lucky you are that you can have your daughters working side-by-side with you.'

'Well, no, I think you misunderstand,' the assistant manager said. 'Both my daughters are still at school.'

'So it's not your daughters you're talking about. Then what else could you possibly mean?' Meadows mused. A sudden look of enlightenment came to her face. 'You're surely not telling me the bank allows you to bring your mistresses into the office, are you?'

'Sergeant Meadows is a bit of a feminist,' Paniatowski said, before Kate could really get into her stride.

'Yes, I'm beginning to appreciate that,' Brunskill agreed, showing signs of starting to sweat. 'I'll get one of my *staff* to bring the records in, shall I?'

'That really would be most kind of you, Mr Brunskill,' Meadows said sweetly.

The assistant manager picked up his phone and issued the instruction, and five minutes later a cardboard folder was delivered by a young woman who smiled broadly at Meadows – a clear sign that she'd been listening to the conversation from the other side of the door.

'Well, here it is,' Brunskill said, passing the file across his desk to Paniatowski.

Paniatowski opened the file. There didn't appear to be much inside.

'Where's the print-out?' Meadows asked.

Brunskill looked puzzled. 'I'm sorry, but you've lost me there.'

'The print-out from the mainframe computer in your head office,' Meadows explained.

Brunskill laughed. 'Oh, we don't have anything like that,' he said. 'We're not one of those big banks, like the National Westminster or Lloyds. Grindley's only has four branches. We keep our records in pretty much the same way as we did when we first opened our doors, one hundred and twenty-five years ago – and it seems to work rather well for us.'

Paniatowski flicked quickly through the three pages, which was all that the file contained. There had been regular payments in at the end of each month, which was when salaries were paid, though these had stopped once Crawley lost his job as a chartered surveyor. There were also standing orders for gas and electricity. And that was it.

'Have you looked at this yourself?' Paniatowski asked Brunskill.

The assistant manager shook his head. 'I don't deal with individual accounts any more. My remit is much more to do with long term . . .'

'Read it now,' Paniatowski said, handing it back to him.

Brunskill scanned the pages. 'It does seem rather thin,' he admitted.

'Thin?' Paniatowski repeated. 'The man lives in an expensive apartment and leads a lavish lifestyle. Where's the evidence of that here? And how is he able to pay for it, when he seems to have no money coming in?'

'Perhaps he's opened a new account with another bank,' Mr Brunskill suggested.

'There's absolutely no evidence in the documentation we found in his apartment that he has another bank account,' Meadows told him.

'Then I'm as mystified as you are. And I must admit that I am surprised that none of my gir . . . none of my staff . . . has drawn my attention to the lack of activity in the account. Someone certainly should have done, because it's the standard procedure which has been laid down for such circumstances.'

'Maybe nobody drew your attention to it because there was nothing to draw your attention to,' Meadows suggested. 'Maybe the account looked nothing like this until a few hours ago.'

Brunskill was horrified. 'You're not suggesting the account has been doctored, are you?' he asked.

'What do you think?' Meadows countered.

'Let me assure you that no one in this bank would ever dream of doing such a thing.'

'Perhaps you're right – but until I question your staff, we won't know for sure, will we?' Paniatowski asked.

'I'm afraid that isn't possible,' Brunskill said, with a new edge of defiance suddenly appearing in his voice. 'However, in the interest of maintaining the bank's good relations with the police, I am prepared to conduct my own internal inquiry, and if there's anything I think you should know about, I promise I'll contact you immediately.'

'Not good enough,' Meadows said. 'We need to interview all the staff ourselves.'

'I can't stop you from questioning them if that is what you want to do,' Brunskill said, 'but my primary duty is to protect the bank's good name, and with that in mind, I shall instruct the staff not to say anything.' He glanced up at the clock on the wall. 'And now, if you will excuse me, I still have a great deal of work to get through before I can go home for the day.'

\*       \*       \*

Paniatowski and Meadows were standing on the street, outside the bank. For perhaps a minute they stood in silence, watching the traffic go by as if it were the most interesting sight in the world.

Then Meadows said, 'Has the bastard really got us over a barrel, or can you see a way round it?'

'The bastard's got us over a barrel,' Paniatowski admitted. 'The search warrant gave us the right to see the bank records, but that was as far as it went. If the bank staff refuse to talk to us, there's nothing we can do about it.'

'We could pull them in for questioning,' Meadows suggested. 'Take them down to headquarters. After a couple of hours in the interview room, they might well feel inclined to talk.'

'And what grounds do we have for pulling any of them in?' Paniatowski asked. 'We think Tom Crawley's bank account has been doctored . . .'

'We *know* it's been doctored.'

'. . . but we have no way of proving it.'

'Brunskill's a prick of the first water, but I don't think he's actually part of any cover-up,' Meadows said.

'He probably hasn't been so far, but that's all about to change,' Paniatowski said. 'When he told us that his main concern was the bank's good name, what he was really saying was that if there's been a cock-up – and he now thinks there probably has been – it's his job to bury it.'

'So all we're left with is the possibility of finding some way to put the squeeze on Foster – who *is* already in it up to his fat sweaty neck,' Meadows mused. 'That makes it vital that one of the teams watching him comes up with something we can use.' She paused. 'Maybe I'll get more involved in the surveillance operation myself.'

'OK, but I don't want any corner-cutting – no bending of the rules in any way, shape or form,' Paniatowski warned.

Meadows grinned. 'You know me, boss.'

'Yes, I do know you,' Paniatowski agreed. 'And that's precisely what's worrying me.'

Normally, Bunny Slade considered himself far too classy to ply his trade at the gentlemen's public convenience in Corporation

Park, but since business had been slow that week, and since the places he usually operated in would not be busy for several more hours, he'd talked himself into breaking his own rules for once.

He had only been standing outside the toilet for a couple of minutes when his first potential client appeared. He was a young man, quite tall and slim, with the sensitive face of a poet.

Very nice indeed, Bunny thought, and if times weren't so hard, I'd do you for nothing.

But was he gay?

Well, there was only one way to find out.

He waited until the man drew level with him, then said, 'Excuse me, have you got a light?'

The man took a Zippo lighter out of his pocket, flicked it with his thumb, and held out the flame to Bunny.

Bunny did not move.

'Silly me,' he said. 'Here I am asking for a light when I seem to have forgotten my cigarettes.'

'I could give you one,' the man said, closing the lighter and reaching into his pocket for a packet of smokes.

Give me one! Bunny thought. Hmm, I'll just bet you could.

But aloud, he said, 'Don't bother about the cigarette, sweetie. Have you really come here to use the bogs?'

'What do you mean?' the young man asked, unconvincingly.

Bunny laughed, confident now that he was on the right track. 'Oh, I think you understand me clearly enough.' He had lifted his hand and touched his head. 'Do you like my hair?'

'It's very nice,' the other man said awkwardly.

'Yes,' Bunny agreed, 'I think a delicate shade of pink really suits me. But enough of this idle chit-chat. Do you want a bit of fun? And don't pretend you don't know what *that* means.'

The other man bit his lip uncertainly. 'How much?' he asked.

'Depends what you want,' Bunny replied. 'If all you're after is a quick hand job in the bushes, then it'll only cost you a fiver. If you want more than that, well, I'm open to offers.'

'The thing is, Bunny, I'm not a sodomite,' the young man said.

'Neither am I – I'm from Accrington,' Bunny answered. He

paused, and a worried look came to his face. 'Hang about, you called me by my name.'

'So I did,' the other man agreed.

'But I don't know you.'

'I don't know you either,' the other man said, 'but I can read a police record card.'

'You don't mean . . .' Bunny began.

'I certainly do,' the other man interrupted, and when his hand came out of his pocket again, it was holding a warrant card, not a packet of cigarettes. 'I am a police officer, and as cops always seem to say on the television, you're well and truly nicked, my son.'

It was as Arthur Gough was parking his car in front of his house that he noticed the grey-suited figure standing by his front door.

Oh Jesus, what did Cardoza want, he wondered.

He felt a strong urge to re-start the engine and drive off somewhere – anywhere. But what would be the point of that? It would be no more than a temporary reprieve from whatever Jordan had in mind for him.

He got out of his car and walked up the garden path on shaky legs. Cardoza did not move – didn't even seem aware of his approach – but Arthur knew the Portuguese was watching him every step of the way.

When he reached his front door, Cardoza reached into his pocket and produced an envelope. He handed it over to Arthur, then walked straight past him, down the path to the street. He had still not said a word.

Arthur opened the envelope and took out the single sheet of paper which had been inside.

It was a typewritten message.

Since you've been left on your own for a while, why don't you come round to my house at about seven o'clock for a bite to eat?

There was no signature.

He hadn't told his brother that Margaret had taken the children to stay with her parents for a few days, but he was not the least surprised that Jordan should know all about it.

He considered the note. How like Jordan it was to send him

what, on the surface, was a friendly, brotherly message, but to have his secretary type it and neglect to sign it, in order to make it clear what it actually was.

'Why don't you come round for a bite to eat?' it said, but it wasn't a suggestion, or even a request. Jordan had *ordered him* to be there at seven o'clock, and if he wasn't, his brother would find some ingenious and unpleasant way to punish him.

Mr Foster, the manager of Grindley's Bank, lived in a double-fronted detached house, which was just the sort of house that most people would expect a bank manager to live in. There was a garage at the side, and a small, neat garden in front, in which – as if he had deliberately chosen to live up to the cliché – Foster had placed a mock wishing well and several garden gnomes.

Meadows, who was sitting in her car at a discreet distance from Mr Foster's cosy home, was bored. She half-wished she smoked, because that might at least help to pass the time, but she didn't. She wondered if there was anything interesting on the radio, and decided there probably wasn't.

The tap on the window startled her, but not as much as the sight of Beresford looking in at her.

Meadows opened the door, and Beresford slid in beside her.

'What are you doing here, sir?' Meadows asked.

'I was just checking on my lads,' Beresford said. 'Except that there are no lads to be checked up on.'

'I sent them home,' Meadows said. 'There didn't seem to be much point in them being here, because it looks as if Foster's in for the night.'

'So why are you here?' Beresford wondered.

'It's not likely he'll come out again – but it is just possible.'

And when you've got not even the slimmest of leads, even a hundred-to-one shot starts to look good, she thought.

'We'll have to see what happens once Mrs Foster leaves,' Beresford said casually.

'You think she'll go out, do you?'

'I'm almost sure of it,' Beresford glanced down at his watch. 'In fact, she should be leaving in the next five or ten minutes.'

The Fosters' garage door opened, and a red Mini drove out.

As it passed them, Meadows saw that there was a middle-aged woman with tightly permed hair behind the wheel.

'How did you do that?' she asked.

'It's what is called "detective work", DS Meadows,' Beresford said complacently.

'All right, inspector, how did you know the butler was really an Albanian dwarf who once burned down a flea circus?' Meadows asked, hoping to mask her annoyance with a bit of off-beat humour.

'Mrs Olivia Foster is the sitting president of the Whitebridge and District Amateur Dramatic Society, and the society is holding its annual general meeting this evening,' Beresford said.

The garage door opened again, and a green Rover 3500 – Mr Foster's car – emerged.

'When the cat's away, the mouse takes the opportunity to go out on the razzle,' Beresford said.

'Do you want to get out of the car now?' Meadows asked.

'No,' Beresford said, 'I think I'll come along for the ride, if you've no objections.'

'Why should I object?' Meadows wondered.

Foster drove cautiously towards the centre of Whitebridge.

'Do you think he knows we're following him?' Beresford asked.

'No, he just naturally drives like my grandmother,' Meadows replied. 'Although thinking about it, that's not a good comparison at all.'

'Why not?'

'My grandmother used to drive like she was competing in the Le Mans 24 – and that was just on her estate. She used to scare the hell out of her tenants, and put one of her gamekeepers in hospital with a broken leg.'

They crossed the middle of town, and when they reached an area which might be described as one of the slightly less salubrious parts of Whitebridge, Foster pulled up in front of a two-storey brick building which had the words THE EXCELSIOR CLUB AND CASINO picked out in lights above its front door.

'That's one of Jordan Gough's businesses, isn't it?' Meadows asked.

'Indeed it is,' Beresford agreed.

As soon as Foster got out of his car, one of the two bouncers, who had been standing by the door, took his place behind the wheel and drove it away.

'Valet parking,' Beresford said. 'Our Mr Foster seems to be a valued customer.'

'Oh, this is so frustrating,' Meadows said.

'What is?' Beresford wondered.

'The fact that we need to know what he's doing in there, but we can't go in ourselves without alerting him to the fact that he's being followed.'

'You can't go in – but I can,' Beresford said. He opened the car door and stepped out. 'I'll be back,' he promised.

# TWELVE

The bouncer loomed up, and quickly blocked Beresford's entry to the club. He was a big feller with broad shoulders and slicked-back hair. From the way he balanced on the balls of his feet, it was obvious that street brawling was not an entirely alien experience to him.

'Sorry, but you can't go in there, pal,' he said.

'I'm a bobby,' Beresford told him, producing his warrant card.

'So you are,' the bouncer agreed. 'Is this the point at which you produce a search warrant?'

'No,' Beresford admitted. 'I don't have one.'

'Then I don't care if you're Lieutenant bleeding Kojak, you still can't come in.'

'Look, I'm not here on police business, it's more of what you might call a personal matter,' Beresford explained, trying his best to sound just a little desperate.

'Oh yeah? What kind of personal matter?' the bouncer asked.

'I think my fiancée is in there.'

'So what?'

'I think she might be with another man.'

'Then you should be more careful with her,' the bouncer said. 'And you're still not going in.'

Beresford squared his shoulders and balled his hands into fists. 'I *am* going in, and if you try to stop me, I'll flatten you,' he said.

The bouncer laughed. 'So you think you could take me, do you?'

'Maybe I could, and maybe I couldn't,' Beresford said, 'but I win whatever happens.'

'How do you work that out?' the bouncer wondered.

'Well, if it turns out I'm harder than you, I knock you down.'

'True,' the bouncer agreed.

'And if it turns out I'm not, I'll send some of the lads round here to arrest you for assaulting a police officer.'

'What seems to be the trouble?' asked a new voice.

Like the bouncer, the new arrival was wearing a dinner jacket, but his was of much higher quality, and had probably never been anywhere near a punch up.

'Who are you?' Beresford asked.

'I'm Gerald Dodd, the manager. And you are . . .?'

'DI Colin Beresford. I want to go inside to see if my girlfriend is cheating on me.'

'Look, inspector, people come here for a good time,' the manager said. 'The last thing they want is a scene.'

'You think that if I find her, I'll give her a bloody good hammering then and there, do you?' Beresford asked.

'I can't say it didn't cross my mind,' the manager admitted.

'You've got no worries,' Beresford assured him. 'I'd much prefer to deal with the pair of them later – when there are no witnesses around to see it.'

'Aren't you afraid that once you've kicked the shit out of them, they'll complain to the police?' the manager asked – and then he chuckled.

Beresford laughed, too. 'Oh, I don't think there's much danger of them doing that,' he said.

'You see, Sid,' Dodd said to the bouncer, 'scratch the surface, and policemen are just like us – real nasty bastards.'

'Could I go inside?' Beresford asked.

'Would you have any objection to me accompanying you?' the manager asked.

'None at all.'

'Then let's begin the grand tour.'

Bunny Slade looked up at the blonde woman who had just entered the interview room, and found himself wishing he had hair like hers.

'Hello, Bunny,' she said, sitting down.

'Are you the boss here?' he asked.

'That's what they tell me,' Paniatowski replied.

'Well, I've got a complaint,' Bunny said. 'That good-looking boy of yours arrested me for no reason.'

'Oh, I can't believe Jack Crane would ever do that,' Paniatowski said. 'And it's not as if this is the first time you've been arrested for soliciting, is it?'

'No, but this time I wasn't doing anything,' Bunny said.

'We both know that's not true, but to tell you the truth, I don't really want to charge you at all,' Paniatowski told him.

'Well then, why don't you just let me go?' Bunny suggested hopefully.

'I'd love to do just that,' Paniatowski told him, 'but I simply have to charge *somebody* today, or I'll start to look bad. Now if you could help me with one of my other cases . . .'

'What do you want to know?' Bunny asked.

Paniatowski slid Tom Crawley's picture across the table. 'Tell me about him,' she said.

'That's the feller that got himself killed in that posh flat,' Bunny said nervously. 'I didn't do it.'

Paniatowski smiled at him. 'Of course you didn't. You wouldn't hurt a fly, would you?'

'That's right,' Bunny agreed.

'But if I'm to tear up your arrest report, you're really going to have to tell me something about him that I don't already know.'

'And I won't be in trouble – whatever it is – will I?' Bunny asked cautiously.

'Not unless you've done something criminal yourself.'

Bunny nodded his head, gratefully. 'I haven't – so what *exactly* do you want to know?'

'Did Tom Crawley ever use male prostitutes?'

'How would I know whether he did or not?' Bunny asked.

Paniatowski sighed. 'Don't start making things difficult,' she said. 'You'd know because you're a male prostitute yourself.'

'I am not!' Bunny said, outraged. 'I am an entertainer.'

'All right, if that's what you want to call it, did you ever "entertain" Tom Crawley?'

'No!' Bunny said, and shuddered.

'You're acting like you were afraid of him.'

'I am not,' Bunny protested, unconvincingly.

'So what else can you tell me?'

'Nothing.'

'Oh well, I suppose I'd better call the sergeant and have you locked up in one of the dark nasty cells we've got downstairs for people who refuse to help us,' Paniatowski said philosophically.

'Wait!' Bunny pleaded.

'All right, I'm waiting. But I warn you, Bunny – my patience won't last forever.'

'You were right about me being afraid. But I wasn't afraid of him – I was afraid of his mate,' Bunny said.

'Would you like to explain a little more – so it finally starts to make sense?' Paniatowski suggested.

'There's a complete slag I know called Serge,' Bunny said. 'Serge! I ask you! What kind of stupid name is that?'

'You've got a good point,' Paniatowski said. 'You wonder why he doesn't call himself something sensible, like Bunny, don't you?'

'Well, exactly,' Bunny agreed. 'Anyway, this Serge spent some time with Tom Creepy . . .'

'His name was Crawley,' Paniatowski interrupted.

'I knew it was *something* like that. So he spent some time with this Tom *Crawley*, and then he got to thinking.'

'Thinking about what?'

'That this Crawley seemed to have plenty of money. So one day he followed him from his flat – which was nowhere near as nice as the one he was living in when he was murdered, by the way – and he found out that Tom worked for this firm of chartered something or other.'

'Surveyors. When was this?'

'It must have been nearly a year ago now. Anyway, this

chartered thingy-me-bob's business seemed a very strait-laced sort of place, and Serge figured out that if they knew Tom was having it off with a filthy beast like him, they'd immediately give him the boot.'

'So Serge started blackmailing Tom Crawley?'

'Yes, he did – the disgusting creature. I'd never do anything like that myself, but I guess some people just have no professional pride.'

'Is this where Crawley's friend comes into the story?' Paniatowski asked, masking her impatience – but only just.

'Yes, this is where his friend comes in,' Bunny said. 'And before you ask, the reason I know anything at all about this is because of what Serge told me when he came round to my place and begged me for some money.'

'So what did Tom's friend do?'

'He told Serge to get out of Whitebridge and never come back. He said if he saw him again, he'd kill him. That's why Serge needed the money from me – so he could get away.'

'So he obviously took the threat seriously.'

'You're not kidding. And wouldn't you – if he'd just cut the end of your little finger off?'

Jesus! Paniatowski thought.

'Did Serge know this man?' she asked.

'No, he said he'd never seen him before.'

'Did he tell you what the man looked like?'

'Yes, to be honest with you, he couldn't stop babbling about him. He said he was a big feller with a black moustache and swarthy complexion. According to Serge, he was some kind of foreigner.'

Dodd took Beresford to the nightclub first. A number of men sat hunched up at the bar, sipping their drinks with no apparent pleasure. A few couples were dancing lethargically on the pocket handkerchief sized dance floor to the music of a trio who sounded as if any enthusiasm they might once have possessed had been siphoned off years ago. And at the tables, other couples sat, striving to come up with things to say to each other and eventually giving up the battle.

'Do you see her?' Dodd asked.

'No,' Beresford replied. 'She's not here.'

They went to the casino next. The roulette wheel was being operated by two male croupiers, but the dealers at the three blackjack tables were all young, attractive women.

'The punters like to see women dealers,' Dodd said. 'They think they can run rings round them.'

'And can they?' Beresford asked.

Dodd snorted. 'Not a chance. My girls are very good at appearing to be panicked and out of their depth, but they've got nerves of steel and are as sharp as razor blades.'

In addition to the roulette wheel and the tables, there was a row of one-armed bandits, and a number of female punters, armed with plastic bags full of coins, were feeding them with quiet desperation.

'Is she here?' Dodd asked.

'No,' Beresford said.

Of the six snooker players in the games room, five had Ray Reardon haircuts, but were playing like Hurricane Higgins after a night on the whisky. There was no sign of any female admirers.

'Right, that's it,' Dodd said. 'Apart from my office and toilets, you've seen everything there is to see.'

'What about upstairs?' Beresford asked.

'There are no punters upstairs,' Dodd said.

'None?'

'None.'

'Are you sure about that?'

'Well, none who came here accompanied by a lady friend.'

'So it's a brothel, is it?' Beresford asked.

'You might call it that, if you were feeling uncharitable, but our solicitor, Spider Markham, would strongly disagree with you,' Dodd said. 'Look, I've been as cooperative as you could wish, haven't I?'

'Absolutely, you have.'

'So there's no cause to go giving me any grief, now is there?'

'There certainly isn't,' Beresford agreed. 'I'll be leaving now.'

'If you'd like a drink before you leave . . .'

'No, I'm fine.'

'Then I'll see you to the door,' Dodd said.

\*    \*    \*

Meadows was still sitting in her car, drumming her fingers impatiently on the steering wheel.

'Well?' she said.

'It was interesting,' Beresford replied.

'I want to know what went on in there,' Meadows said.

'I'm sure you do,' Beresford replied, thoroughly enjoying himself.

'What would it take for you to tell me?' Meadows asked. 'Would you like me to beg?'

'That would be nice,' Beresford admitted.

Meadows sighed. 'Oh, all right then. Please, please, kind Inspector Beresford, tell me what you found out in that sleazy establishment.'

'Well, I didn't find out who is putting the frighteners on Foster,' Beresford said. 'But since he wasn't actually on the ground floor of the club, he must have been upstairs, which means he has a fondness for visiting ladies of the night. I wonder if his wife knows about that.'

# THIRTEEN

At five minutes to seven, Arthur Gough reached the gates of his brother's mansion, and waited patiently for them to swing open. At seven o'clock on the dot, he was at the front door, waiting to be admitted.

He had expected to be met by José Cardoza, his brother's sinister shadow, but instead the door was opened by Lynn Adams, Jordan's cook/housekeeper.

Lynn was around thirty years old. She was a very attractive brunette, with what some people liked to call 'come to bed eyes'. There had been a time when Arthur had wondered if bedding Jordan had been one of her duties. But he didn't think that anymore, because he had reached the conclusion that Jordan had no interest in sex, and got all his kicks from making other people jump through the series of very unpleasant and degrading hoops he held out for them.

'Mr Gough wants you to join him in the library, Arthur,' Mrs Adams said, before turning on her heel and heading back to the kitchen.

So as far as she was concerned, Jordan was 'Mr Gough' and he was only 'Arthur', the visitor noted. And she had also made it plain that there was no need for her to extend any of the common courtesies to him, such as accompanying him to the library.

Had Jordan coached her to act like this – deliberately turned her into a weapon with which to hurt him?

It was possible, because there was nothing unpleasant or despicable that Jordan was incapable of.

But maybe it had nothing to do with Jordan at all. Maybe Lynn Adams' reaction was a natural one, merely reflecting reality as she saw it.

For God's sake, be honest with yourself, he thought angrily – if that is the case, she isn't reflecting reality as she sees it, she's reflecting reality as it actually *is*!

He made his way down the corridor, like a condemned man voluntarily walking towards his own execution.

The library, like the study, was full of expensive leather-bound books which Jordan Gough had never read, nor ever intended to read, and in the hearth a log blazed merrily – and unnecessarily – away.

And he hadn't done any of this because he felt insecure, Arthur thought. No, he had done it because he knew that other people would recognize it as being as fake as hell, and he would enjoy watching as they forced themselves to disguise this recognition for fear of offending him. It was all a parody, and the funniest thing about the whole business was that he could spend so much money on a joke that only he and his brother understood.

'Arthur, dear boy, how nice to see you,' Jordan said warmly.

And this again was a parody – part of the game he played – Arthur thought.

Well, he had had enough. He was not going to play that game anymore.

'I'm surprised you invited me tonight – especially since I was on that list you gave to DCI Paniatowski, of people who hate you,' he said.

'Well, you know the old saying,' Jordan replied. 'Keep your friends close, and your enemies closer.'

'But how can *you* do that, Jordan, when you *haven't got* any friends?' Arthur asked.

Jordan threw back his head and laughed. 'So you're showing a bit of spirit at last,' he said. 'I do like that, Arthur. Now let's see just how long it takes me to beat it out of you.'

He won't beat it out of me, Arthur promised himself. This time I'll be strong. This time, I'll stand up to him.

'We've hardly talked since you got back from Brazil,' Jordan said. 'So tell me, how was the trip?'

'How was the trip?' Arthur said. 'It was totally unnecessary – that's how it was. There was never any chance of me making the deal you sent me out there to make, and you knew that from the start.'

Jordan chuckled. 'You've caught me out, old boy – seen right through me, as it were. The truth is that I knew there wasn't much for you to do in the way of business in Brazil, but I thought you were looking a little peaky, and the change of scene would do you good.'

'So because you thought I was looking peaky, you sent me to a city in the middle of the Amazon jungle – a city so humid that you've barely had time to put your shirt on before it's drenched in sweat?'

'I admit it was a pretty poor choice on my part,' Jordan said. 'It would have been better if I'd sent you to Rio – but at least I meant well.'

'No, you didn't,' Arthur contradicted him. 'The reason you sent me to Brazil was because you wanted me to miss my wife's fortieth birthday party.'

Jordan's chuckle was even deeper this time. 'Caught me out again, old chap,' he said. 'But at least give me a little credit for not celebrating Margaret's fortieth by taking her to bed – because I could have done, you know, if I'd wanted to.'

He probably could have, Arthur thought miserably. He was in no doubt that Margaret loved only him, but Jordan had such a forceful inner power that if he'd really put his mind to it, she would probably have succumbed.

'You're beneath contempt,' he said aloud.

'If you hate me so much, why don't you do something about it?' Jordan suggested.

'Like what?' Arthur asked.

The sound of a gong being banged drifted down the corridor.

'It would seem that dinner is served,' Jordan said.

The rosewood dining table was covered with an immaculate white cloth. There was space around it to seat twenty, though only two places had been laid, and these were halfway along the table, and opposite each other. At either end of the long table there were candelabra, each with five candles burning. This, again, was probably Jordan's idea of a joke, Arthur thought.

Jordan walked straight to his chair and sat down, but before Arthur could do the same, his brother pointed to the sideboard, and said, 'There's the buffet. Fill a plate for yourself, and one for me.'

The sideboard was weighed down with delicacies. There was fresh salmon and foie gras, white truffles and delicate French cheeses, small quiches and sliced sausages.

He doesn't want any of this himself, Arthur thought. He just wants to demonstrate to me that though it's well out of my reach, he can afford it easily. And he knows that though I should refuse to eat it, I simply can't bring myself to turn down anything so good.

As he loaded the two plates, Jordan read the *Evening Telegraph* – *his* newspaper – which Mrs Adams had left by his setting, and it was not until Arthur returned with the plates, that he looked up and said, 'Well, what about the wine, man? It's there on the sideboard, just waiting to be served.'

The white wine, sitting in a bucket of finely crushed ice, was a Rothschild Réserve Spéciale Bordeaux. Arthur had no idea how much it had cost, but suspected that if he wanted a bottle himself, he would have to take out a second mortgage to pay for it.

'Come on, old boy – pour the wine,' Jordan called. 'Chop, chop!'

Arthur poured two glasses, and took them over to the table.

'A bit slow, but on the whole you did all that very well,' Jordan said. 'I'm thinking of employing a butler, and it just might be you. You'd do it, wouldn't you? Of course you would – if I ordered you to do it, you'd have no choice.'

'You wouldn't!' Arthur gasped. 'Even you wouldn't push me *that* far.'

'Well, we'll just have to wait and see what the future has in store for us,' Jordan said, enigmatically.

They ate their hors d'oeuvre in silence, and though Jordan hardly touched his, Arthur – much to his own disgust – polished off everything on his plate.

A little later than expected, the door opened, and Mrs Adams entered pushing a food trolley, holding two large steaks, a selection of fresh vegetables and a jug of pepper sauce.

She served both the brothers, and then said to Jordan, 'I'm awfully sorry to disturb you now, sir, but could I have a quick word in private?'

'But, of course,' Jordan agreed.

He stood up and walked to the door.

'Eat it up before it all goes cold, Little Brother,' he said with mock affection, over his shoulder.

Mrs Adams had said she only needed a quick word, and that proved to be the case. Jordan returned not much more than a minute after he had left.

'Time to tuck in,' he said, with fake heartiness.

He picked up the jug of sauce, and poured it generously over his steak.

'Don't you want some of this, dear brother?' he asked, still playing the considerate host.

Arthur shook his head angrily. 'Why do you always offer me some sort of hot or spicy sauce whenever you "invite" me to eat here?' he demanded.

'I don't know,' Jordan said, with fake innocence. 'Perhaps it's because I enjoy it so much myself, and I want you, my little brother, to enjoy it, too.'

'Liar!' Arthur said. 'You do it to remind me that I've got a delicate stomach – another gift from you – and I can't take that sort of thing.'

'Stop blaming it on me,' Jordan said, his tone now amused yet mildly rebuking. 'The reason you can't take pepper sauce is because it's a man-sized sauce – and you're not really much of a man at all, are you, Arthur?'

'There's more to being a man than being a bully,' Arthur said.

'Yes, there is,' Jordan agreed. 'There are many ways you can be a man – and you're a failure at all of them.' He paused for a moment. 'You really hate me, don't you?'

'Well, you've certainly given me enough grounds to,' Arthur admitted.

'Answer the question, you pathetic little worm!' Jordan bellowed.

'Yes, I hate you,' Arthur said.

'And you'd like to see me dead, wouldn't you?'

'Yes, I would,' Arthur agreed.

Jordan stood up with such sudden violence that his chair flew backwards. He glared across at his brother, then began to walk along his side of the long table.

Oh, my God, oh sweet Jesus, he's going to kill me, Arthur thought in a panic.

He knew he should make an attempt to defend himself – or at least try to escape – yet somehow it seemed pointless.

Jordan had reached the head of the table, and was turning.

You should have struck first – days ago, weeks ago! – a terrified, accusatory voice screamed in Arthur's head. You shouldn't have waited till now, because now is too late.

Jordan was towering over him. But instead of attacking his brother, he picked up Arthur's steak knife and pressed it into his hand. Then he knelt down beside the chair, with his back to Arthur.

'If you want me dead, then here's your chance,' he said. 'All you have to do is lean forward and slit my throat. I promise you, I won't resist.'

'I . . . I . . .' Arthur gasped.

'You . . . you . . . what?' Jordan mocked.

'What if Mrs Adams walks in?'

'Worried about witnesses, are you? Well, you needn't be – I've ordered her to go to her quarters and not come out again until she makes my breakfast.'

Despite all the other horrendous things that were going on, there was a tiny corner of Arthur's brain that found this shocking.

'You can't treat people like that,' he said.

'Of course I can,' Jordan said contemptuously. 'She works for me, and when I say jump, she jumps. But you don't give a shit about Lynn Adams anyway. You're just putting off the moment when you actually have to do something.'

'No, I . . .' Arthur protested weakly.

'It's easy,' Jordan told him. 'You put your left hand on my forehead and pull my head back. Then, with your right hand, you draw the knife across my throat. Even you couldn't bugger that up. So go ahead – just this once, show me you've got some backbone.'

'Why are you doing this?' Arthur asked.

'Go on! It will all be over in a couple of seconds.'

The knife fell from Arthur's hand, and landed on the floor with a loud clang which seemed to echo round the whole dining room.

Jordan stood up.

'I knew you hadn't got the guts to do it,' he said. 'You want me dead, but if you ever do decide to kill me, you'll choose to do it the coward's way.' He walked back to his own seat, much more calmly this time, sat down, picked up his knife and fork, and cut into his steak. 'Get out of my house, you maggot!' he said. 'I'm sick of the sight of you.'

And as Arthur slunk to the door, Jordan picked up a chunk of steak, smothered in pepper sauce.

6TH MAY 1981

# FOURTEEN

It had rained overnight. It had not been one of those heavy downpours which batter on the roof and hammer furiously against the window panes – the kind of rain loud enough to awaken the dead. No, this had been the gentler, pitter-pattering sort, a rain that seemed to be almost apologetic for intruding. And when the sun rose, it warmed the newly freshened air, and shone down on grass which was particularly lush at that moment. It was a morning that suggested optimism – a morning that promised new beginnings.

Lynn Adams did not feel optimistic, and had not expected to. Optimism was denied to her until her sentence was completed – and that still had two more years to run.

By a quarter past eight, she was in the kitchen, ready to prepare Jordan Gough's breakfast. The breakfast consisted of a glass of freshly squeezed orange juice, lightly chilled; two eggs, boiled for exactly four minutes; two slices of white toast, heavily buttered and cut into soldiers; and a large mug of PG Tips tea, with a lot of milk and three sugars. The order had never varied, and Gough expected it to be delivered to his bedroom at exactly eight thirty.

Mrs Adams had loved her late husband, and indeed there had been much about him to love. But he had had one great weakness, gambling on the horses, and it was not until he died – suddenly and unexpectedly of an embolism – that Lynn had truly come to appreciate the depth of his addiction. He had left behind crippling debts, and since both the bank account and the house were in his name alone, Lynn was facing the possibility of being thrown out onto the street, without a penny to her name. It was at this point that Jordan Gough came along, with his offer to settle all the debts, provided she agreed to work for him for five years.

It had seemed like a very generous offer at the time, and it was only later that she realized that paying her debts was no more than a nominal sacrifice to him, because most of them were owed to bookmakers that were part of Gough's empire.

On the whole, she did not mind the work, though there was one particular aspect of it – an aspect which was rapidly approaching – that she had hated from the start.

At eight twenty-seven, Mrs Adams picked up the breakfast tray and carried it up the wide sweeping staircase to the first floor. At eight twenty-eight, she placed the tray on the small, delicately carved table outside Gough's room, and steeled herself for what had to happen next.

She was wearing a white ribbed sweater, which she now removed and draped over the balustrade. Next, she removed her brassiere, and placed that next to the sweater.

The first time she had done this – had fulfilled this particular condition of her employment – she had truly hated it and wished herself dead, but now she mostly felt a sort of numbness.

She wondered why Gough made her do this. He had never come anywhere near to touching her, and now he hardly seemed to notice at all that she was topless when she brought him his breakfast. It was possible, she thought, that it was not so much the act of her undressing that excited him as it was the fact that he was making her do something he knew she found humiliating. Yes, that would certainly make sense. He enjoyed humiliating and belittling his brother, too, and had made a thorough job of it the previous evening.

She turned the door handle, then picked up the tray again.

Two more years, she told herself – two more years and I'll be free of this evil bastard.

She pushed open the door with her dainty right foot, and stepped into the bedroom.

'Here's your breakfast, Mr Gough,' she said.

But Gough was not there – and it was obvious that his bed had not been slept in.

Mrs Adams put the tray on the table next to the bed, and stepped out into the corridor. Her bra and sweater were where she had left them, and she put them on again. Then she looked around for some clue as to what might have happened.

'Mr Gough?' she called out. 'Where are you, Mr Gough?'

When there was no answer, she descended the staircase.

The last time she had seen Gough had been in the dining room, and that was where she found him now. He was on the floor, arms and legs akimbo. His mouth was wide open and so were his eyes, and there were blotches of crimson in the eyes, as if someone had dribbled red ink into them. Taking his face as a whole, he looked very much like a man who had been struggling for life – and lost.

Lynn Adams knelt down, and placed her index finger lightly on Gough's neck. It came as no surprise to her when she could not find a pulse.

Mrs Adams returned to the kitchen, and cooked herself an omelette – filled with the truffles left over from the previous evening – which she ate with relish. A cigarette, smoked in a leisurely fashion, aided her digestion, and when she had stubbed it out in the ashtray, she picked up the kitchen phone and dialled for an ambulance.

Louisa was working the night shift, and Reyes had an early morning doctor's appointment. So it fell to Monika Paniatowski to make the boys' breakfasts alone that morning, and as if fate had fickly decreed this would be a bad day for all detective chief inspectors with young children, Philip and Thomas had abandoned all notions of cooperation, and were putting on a master class of bloody-mindedness. Thus it was after nine – which meant she was already well behind schedule – when Paniatowski heard the phone ring in the hallway.

'I'll be back in a minute, boys,' she promised. 'Please try not to wreck the kitchen while I'm gone.'

She picked up the phone, and the voice on the other end said, 'Is that you, boss?'

She felt her stomach turn over, because if Colin Beresford was calling her at this time of day, it couldn't be good news.

'It's me,' she said. 'Let's hear it.'

'Jordan Gough's dead.'

Oh God, she'd expected the news to be bad, but did it really have to be *that* bad?

'Details!' she heard herself snap. 'Give me details.'

'According to the desk sergeant who called me, Mrs Adams,

the housekeeper, found him dead a little under an hour ago, and, as they always say on the telly, "Foul play is suspected".'

From the kitchen came the sound of the boys screaming at each other.

'There's no need for that,' Paniatowski called out.

'Sorry, boss?' Beresford said, mystified.

'I was talking to the kids,' Paniatowski explained. 'Who's at Gough's house now?'

'Half a dozen uniforms and the duty inspector, Jack Bates.'

The case could have been given a worse caretaker, Paniatowski thought, because while Bates was far from being an inspirational detective, he was at least a safe pair of hands.

'Mummy, Mummy, Philip's being really horrid to me,' Thomas shouted.

'Is the body still there?' Paniatowski asked.

'No, Doc Shastri's had it removed.'

'I want you up there – taking charge – right away.'

'Mummy!' Thomas screamed, louder than ever.

'When should I expect you at the crime scene?' Beresford asked.

A good question!

'That will depend on how soon Shastri can tell me what killed Jordan,' she said.

Although that, in turn, would depend on how soon she could relinquish charge of the twins to Reyes.

She hung up the phone and returned to the kitchen. She saw immediately that when Thomas had accused Philip of being horrid, he'd been no more than accurate, because not only had Philip been sick, but he'd then proceeded to rub the vomit in his brother's face.

'What do you think you're doing, Philip?' she demanded. 'How dare you treat your brother like that?'

Philip looked at his brother, then at his mother, then started to cry.

'It's not going to work, Philip,' Paniatowski said. 'You should know by now that Mummy's got a heart of stone.'

She folded her arms, to emphasize her point, and Philip stopped crying.

'I'm sorry, Mummy,' he said.

'You shouldn't be apologizing to me – I'm not the one with puke all over my face,' Paniatowski told him.

'Sorry, Thomas,' Philip said.

Paniatowski heard the front door click open, which could only mean that the US Cavalry – in the form of Reyes – had once again arrived in the nick of time.

When Mr Foster pulled into the car park behind the bank, he was shocked to see that the elfin detective sergeant was standing squarely in the middle of his designated parking spot.

'What, in God's name, are you doing there?' he asked, through the open car window.

Meadows smiled endearingly at him. 'I thought this was a rather good place for us to have a little chat,' she said.

'My secretary is in charge of my schedule,' Foster told her. 'If you want to see me, you'll have to book an appointment through her.'

'Is that what you say to all the girls?' Meadows asked innocently.

'Exactly what do you mean by that, sergeant?' Foster said, and though he was doing his best to sound justifiably outraged, he was actually starting to feel distinctly uneasy.

'For example, does your secretary book your appointments with the prostitutes down at the Excelsior Club?'

'That's a libellous thing to say!' Foster blustered.

'I think you mean slanderous,' Meadows said, with a smile. 'Libel is only when it's in writing, and since I've not had time to produce my report, it isn't in writing *yet*.'

Then she stepped aside, to allow the bank manager to drive into his parking spot.

'You've got it all wrong,' Foster said, getting out of his car and looking longingly at the back door of the bank. 'Yes, I admit I go to the Excelsior Club occasionally . . .'

'If it was only occasionally, I don't think the bouncers would park your car for you,' Meadows interrupted. 'That's a service that they reserve for their special customers.'

'Have you been following me?' Foster demanded.

'Well, I didn't see all this in my crystal ball,' Meadows replied.

'All right, so I'll admit I go to the club quite regularly, and I'm also willing to admit that, once in a while, I allow myself a modest flutter on the roulette wheel, though . . .' he laughed unconvincingly, '. . . I'd appreciate it if you didn't tell my wife that, because she doesn't approve of even moderate gambling.'

'Not bad,' Meadows said, almost admiringly. 'Not bad at all.'

'What are you talking about?'

'It was a nice touch to confess to something you weren't guilty of, in order to distract me from something you were,' Kate Meadows explained. 'You're a pretty good liar, Mr Foster, I'll give you that. Unfortunately for you, however, I'm something of an expert in the field.'

'You're making a big mistake,' Foster told her weakly.

'No, you're the one who'll be making a big mistake if you continue bullshitting me,' Meadows said sweetly, 'because I will give your wife – the queen of the Whitebridge and District Amateur Dramatic Society – a domestic drama all of her very own.'

'That's blackmail!' Foster said.

'Yes, it is, isn't it?' Meadows agreed.

'What do you want?' Foster asked.

'I want what I've always wanted – which is to see Tom Crawley's bank account.'

'You saw it yesterday. Brunskill showed it to you.'

Meadows reached into her pocket, took out her notebook, and flicked it open to a blank page.

'I've got your home phone number right here,' she lied. 'There's a phone box on the corner. It will take me no more than a minute to walk there, which means you've got about three minutes before your life is turned upside down.'

'You wouldn't phone her!' Foster gasped.

'No, I probably wouldn't,' Meadows agreed, as Foster's face almost collapsed with relief. 'After all, there's no real fun in that, is there?'

'Fun?'

'But telling her to her face is an entirely different matter. Seeing the shocked look when I tell her she's married to a real slug – now that's what *I* call entertainment.'

'You're a real bitch, aren't you?' Foster said.

'I certainly am,' Meadows replied. 'Do you talk to me, Mr Foster – or do I talk to your good lady wife?'

'All right, all right,' Foster said urgently. 'The original records of Tom Crawley's bank account have been destroyed.'

'By you?'

'Does it really matter who destroyed them?'

'By you?' Meadows repeated.

'Yes, damn it, by me.'

'I assume you didn't do it on a whim.'

'Well, of course I didn't.'

'So who asked you to do it?'

'I can't tell you that.'

'Can't – or won't?'

'I daren't tell you,' Foster said, and he seemed to be on the verge of bursting into tears. 'You don't know him. You don't know what he's capable of.'

'Who is "he"?' Meadows demanded, and when the bank manager said nothing, she continued, 'I could call on your wife right now . . .'

'Then do it, Sergeant Meadows,' Foster interrupted. 'Destroy my marriage, if you want to – but I still can't tell you.'

Whoever had scared him had made such a good job of it that nothing was going to make him come completely clean, Meadows thought.

'All right, you won't give me his name,' she conceded. 'But if you don't want me to tell your wife what you've been getting up to, you have to at least give me *something*.'

'I . . . I just can't.'

'If you choose the *right* thing – a bit of information I might have found out for myself, if I'd had the time – then nobody will have any reason to link it back to you,' Meadows said.

And possibly that was true, she thought.

But what if it wasn't?

Well, if you wanted to play with the big boys, you had to be prepared to take the consequences.

Foster's face was wracked with indecision, then he said, 'Tom Crawley spent a lot of money on travel.'

'That doesn't tell me much,' Meadows replied.

'I mean really *a lot* of money,' Foster said desperately.

'There are plenty of people who enjoy travelling,' Meadows pointed out. 'It's not a crime.'

'What you need to find out is *why* he travelled,' Foster said.

'And that will help my investigation, will it?'

'It will help it a great deal.'

Meadows nodded. 'All right, you're safe for the moment,' she agreed. 'But I need to know where he spent all this money. Was it at a local travel agent's?'

'That's something you'll have to find out for yourself,' Foster said. 'And when you do . . .' he clasped his hands together in supplication, '. . . when you do, please, please, remember that you didn't get it from me.'

He turned away from her, and started to walk towards the bank. After he had gone a few yards, he broke into an ungainly overweight trot, and Meadows had no doubt that if the bank had been further away, he would have been running by the time he reached the back door.

It was possible that what he had told her would be of absolutely no use to the investigation, Meadows thought, but it was perfectly obvious that Foster himself believed it to be important.

'Once more, the humble little Indian doctor has worked miracles and come up with a result for you in an almost impossibly short time,' Shastri said, as Monika Paniatowski entered the doctor's office at just after midday.

She was in one of her playful moods – if you could call Shastri's particular kind of macabre humour playful – Paniatowski realized. And once the doctor *was* in this mood, it was best to let it run its course, because both impatience and anger would only result in her slipping into a state of serene mystic calm, from which she might not emerge for hours.

And anyway, given the nature of her bloody business – and her willingness to go the extra mile for the police on any investigation – she was surely entitled to her little quirks.

But I wish she'd get straight to the point just this once, Paniatowski thought, because if this *is* a murder, then it isn't just *any* murder – it's one I've been involved in even before it happened.

'I am a methodical woman,' Dr Shastri said, 'so unless there is a pressing reason for a different approach, I always start at the top and work my way down. So the first thing I discovered about our friend here, when I sliced the top of his head off, was that he was dying.'

Paniatowski gasped. 'Are you saying that he was still alive when you started your post-mortem?'

Shastri laughed, with that gentle laugh of hers that so resembled the ringing of small temple bells.

'Of course he wasn't still alive,' she said. 'I am a trained doctor, and making sure my subject is dead, even before I switch on my dinky little electric bone saw, is standard procedure for me.'

'You did that deliberately!' Paniatowski accused.

'Did what?' the doctor asked innocently.

'You know what – explaining things in just the sort of way that you knew would shock me.'

Shastri laughed again. 'Alas, you have caught me out in my little joke. Shall I be serious now?'

'That would be nice,' Paniatowski agreed.

'Mr Gough had a brain tumour, which I am almost certain was inoperable, and though it did not kill him this morning, it would probably have done so in the next three or four months – at the latest.'

'Did he know he was dying?'

'He would certainly have been aware that something was wrong. He would have suffered from headaches and lapses in concentration . . .'

'I saw him do that! I bloody well saw him do it,' Paniatowski said.

She remembered how Gough had broken off in the middle of his story about Chippie Cousins, and gone into a sort of trance. And when he came out of the trance again, he seemed to have no idea he had been talking about the woodwork teacher.

'. . . headaches and lapses in concentration,' Shastri repeated, 'but he may not have known just how serious it was. He certainly did not ask his local doctor about it, because I checked, and Whitebridge General has no record of ever carrying out a brain scan on him.'

'So what did kill him?' Paniatowski asked.

And she was thinking . . . please make it natural causes, please make it natural causes.

'He stopped breathing,' Shastri replied. 'But it is what caused him to stop breathing that is of interest.'

'And that is?'

'Mr Gough was poisoned – and that poison led to paralysis and eventual suffocation.'

It still didn't necessarily have to be murder, Paniatowski told herself. There was still a slim chance that he could have poisoned himself accidentally. Or – though it seemed unlikely from what she knew about the kind of man he was – maybe he had committed suicide.

'You are wondering if it could have been an accident or suicide,' Shastri said, reading her mind.

'Yes.'

'There was no note, was there?'

'No, there wasn't. Or, at least, there was none that my officers have been able to find so far.'

'Most people who kill themselves leave a note. And they usually leave it somewhere it can be found right away.'

'Yes, they do,' Paniatowski agreed.

'They choose a place which is comfortable in which to die – the floor of the dining room is certainly not that – and they usually take a drug which will send them to sleep before it kills them. I cannot think of any case in which the victim took a poison which would leave him conscious – and struggling for breath – as a prelude to his death.'

'Accidental poisoning?' Paniatowski asked, hopefully.

'If it had been rat poison, or some drug that is fairly easily available, then I might be willing to consider accidental poisoning as a possibility. But this is much more exotic.'

'So what is it?'

'I will need to send it to a specialist laboratory for confirmation, but I suspect, from the simple tests I have been able to carry out myself, that it is the secretion from a member of the Dendrobatidae family.'

'The what?'

'It is more commonly known as the poison dart frog.'

'How do you come to know about something like that?'
Paniatowski wondered.

'Ah, the man who my parents had arranged for me to marry
was a brilliant – one might even say obsessive – toxicologist.
He regarded discussion of the poison dart frog as suitably light
conversation over the teatime scones and crumpets.'

For a moment, all Paniatowski's worries were brushed aside,
and replaced with a burning curiosity about Shastri's life before
she arrived in Whitebridge.

'You didn't marry him, did you?' she asked, though she knew
she shouldn't have.

'Would you like to hear more about the poison dart frogs or
not, my dear Monika?' Shastri asked.

'Yes, please, I would,' Paniatowski replied meekly,
recognizing a justifiable rebuke when she heard one.

'They exist mainly in Colombia, though some have been
found in Brazil,' Shastri said. 'The native tribes used them to
poison the darts in their blowpipes. Often they would boil the
frogs, although with the more venomous ones, it was sometimes
only necessary to stick a dart in their backs.'

'Are they only found in South America?' Paniatowski asked.

'Yes.'

'There are none in zoos or private collections in England?'

'There may be, but once they are removed from their natural
habitat, they usually lose their toxicity.'

'So the poison must have come directly from South America?'

'That would be my guess.'

'When was the poison administered?'

'Given his probable time of death, and subtracting from that
the time it should have taken the poison to work, I would esti-
mate it was administered at around eight o'clock last night,'
Shastri said. 'The poison was probably in his evening meal. I
would guess – and this can only be a guess – that the murderer
put the poison in the pepper sauce which accompanied the
steak.'

'Would it have been a quick death for Gough?' Paniatowski
asked.

'Suffocation never takes more than a few minutes,' Shastri
said. 'But unless he was unconscious – and there is no reason

why he should have been until the final stages – then it will have been a very frightening death.'

So whoever had killed Gough must have hated him so much that he really wanted him to suffer, Paniatowski thought.

Jesus, it might still be just after noon, but already this had not been a good day!

If there had been such a thing as an aristocracy within the local legal circles, then Hadleigh Chase would certainly have been included in it. He had been educated at a public school which, though it was not Eton or Harrow, was still held in moderately high regard. He had attended the same Oxford college as his father had, and, also like his father, had spent three years there without being rusticated. And, at the end of it all, he had joined the family firm of Chase, Godwin and Chase, Solicitors and Commissioners for Oaths. It was a good business with a strong, if uninspiring, reputation, and Chase was used to dealing with the crème de la crème of Whitebridge society.

The man sitting opposite him at that moment was not the crème de la crème – he wasn't even the semi-skimmed milk – and he'd only been allowed through the door because he was Jordan Gough's brother.

Chase rocked slightly in his seat – which he knew always looked impressive – and said, 'So what can I do for you?'

'I've just been with the police to the town mortuary, where I was asked to identify my brother's body,' Arthur said.

'Good God, is Mr Gough dead?' Chase said.

'Mr *Jordan* Gough is,' Arthur said, the anger more than evident in his voice. 'But he's not the only Gough, you know – I am Mr *Arthur* Gough, and I am still very much alive.'

'Yes, yes, of course,' Chase said smoothly. 'I meant no disrespect. How did your brother die, Mr Gough?'

'The police didn't say,' Arthur Gough said. His tone was dismissive, as if it really didn't matter one way or the other. 'The reason I'm here is because I want to know when I can get my hands on the money.'

It was always the same, Chase thought, with a tinge of regret. Whether they were in deep mourning for their loss, or couldn't give a damn about the dear departed, their main focus was on the will. You had to view the whole process with wry amusement, he supposed, because the only alternative was to give up completely on humanity.

'What money are we talking about here, Mr Gough?' he asked, determined to make the snivelling little rat work for the piece of information he thought he wanted – but would hate once he had it.

Arthur Gough sighed with mock exasperation. 'What money? My brother's money, of course!'

'So you're assuming that you're his heir, are you?' Chase asked.

'It's more than an assumption. I know I'm his heir – because he bloody well told me himself.'

What Jordan had actually said was, *'If I die, you'll inherit most of my estate, Arthur. You'll be a rich man. You and your family can have a wonderful life. The only problem is that to get all that, you have to survive me – and with your weak chest and delicate stomach, that's not a likely prospect, now is it?'*

Yes, the inheritance had been one more thing Jordan had used to torture him with. But that had backfired, hadn't it, because now that his brother was dead, it was all his, wasn't it?

'So when *do* I get the money?' he asked impatiently.

'I'm afraid I really couldn't say,' Hadleigh Chase told him.

'Couldn't say?' Arthur repeated. 'Why couldn't you say? You are his solicitor, aren't you?'

'For most matters, yes, but not this one,' said Chase, who was finding the other man increasingly obnoxious, and so was starting to rather enjoy his obvious discomfort. 'As laid down in your brother Jordan's will, the executor of that will is another solicitor – one who has no connection with this office.'

'Could you tell me his name?'

'Certainly. It's Mr Horace Markham.'

'Are you sure of that?' Arthur gasped.

'Absolutely sure,' Chase confirmed. 'I drew up the will myself.'

And at every stage of the proceedings, I did my best to talk Jordan Gough out of it, he thought.

'But Spider Markham is a crook!' Arthur said.

Yes, and that's precisely *why* I was against it from the start, Chase reminded himself.

But you never agreed with civilians in matters of this nature, because when anyone in the profession was under attack, your immediate instinct was to circle the wagons.

'Mr Markham is a colleague of mine, and is recognized by the Law Society as such,' he said coldly.

'What if I said I wanted you, not him, to run things?' Arthur asked. 'Could you become the executor then?'

'I could not, nor would I wish to,' Chase said. 'It would be completely unethical to even attempt it.'

'If I said I'd double your fees . . .'

'We have no more to discuss, Mr Gough,' Chase said firmly. 'I wish you good morning.'

Under normal circumstances, he would have reached across the desk to shake hands, but now all he did was to pretend to become absorbed in some papers that lay in front of him.

Arthur Gough sat there for perhaps half a minute, then stood up and slunk over to the door.

'Oh, there is one more thing, Mr Gough,' Chase said.

'Yes?'

'You have all my sympathies.'

'Look, if you say there's nothing you can do, I suppose I have to accept that,' Arthur replied.

'You misunderstood me,' Chase told him. 'You have my sympathies because there's been a death in your family.'

'To tell you the truth, I'd much rather have your congratulations,' Arthur Gough said.


# FIFTEEN


The uniformed constable posted on the gate of Jordan Gough's mansion saluted as Paniatowski drew up in her car. She hated being saluted at the best of times, and on this day of all days, it only served to make her dark mood even darker.

Beresford met her at the front door of the mansion.

'I've got men searching the grounds, though I'm not entirely sure what it is we're looking for,' he said.

Neither am I, Paniatowski thought.

If Gough had been stabbed or shot, they might hope to find his assassin's discarded weapon, but what kind of evidence would a poisoner leave behind him?

'Are the SOCO team here?' Paniatowski asked.

'Yes, boss. They've dusted the dining room and kitchen for prints and fibres, and now they're working their way through the rest of the house.'

'Where are all the staff?' Paniatowski said.

'Actually, there are only two permanent staff, because most of the chores around the house are done by contract workers,' Beresford told her.

'And who are they?'

'One of them is a Portuguese feller by the name of José something.'

'I've met him.'

'But he's away, according to Mrs Adams.'

'She's the cook, isn't she?'

'That's right.'

'Where is she at the moment?'

'I've asked her to confine herself to her sitting room.'

'Good,' Paniatowski said. 'Let's go and talk to her.'

Mrs Adams' suite was on the ground floor, in the right-hand corner. The sitting room, which was the only access to the rest of the suite, had a window which looked out over the forecourt.

It stood in marked contrast to the parts of the house she had seen previously, Paniatowski thought. In the study, to take just one example, the emphasis of the interior design had been on display and opulence – all heavy wood and ancient leather. This sitting room contained two armchairs which were not expensive, but seemed to be of good quality. The coffee table, too, was a triumph of taste over flashiness, and the magnolia walls were bare, save for two photographs of a man who would have been dashingly handsome but for a rather weak chin.

Mrs Adams herself was wearing a white ribbed sweater. She had long elegant fingers, and between two of them she was holding a Turkish cigarette.

'Do you feel up to talking, Mrs Adams?' Paniatowski asked.

'Yes,' the other woman replied.

'Because if you'd prefer to leave it until the shock's worn off . . .'

'I'm not in shock,' Lynn Adams said. 'My father was a rubber planter in Malaya, and I was brought up on his estate until I was old enough to go to boarding school in England. This was during the State of Emergency, when the communists were trying their damnedest to take over. Although I was only a child, I was taught how to use a pistol, and no one in the family ever travelled anywhere without being heavily armed.'

'I see,' Paniatowski said.

'I'm not sure you do, entirely. The point is that when you have that kind of upbringing, you soon get used to looking death in the face. And usually, because the rebels wanted to make an example of anyone collaborating with the British, the bodies of our workers that I saw back then had been mutilated, which means they looked a great deal more horrific than what I saw this morning.'

'There's something that's been puzzling me,' Paniatowski admitted.

'What is it?'

'Why was it only this morning that you found the body? Why didn't you go back to clear the dishes last night, and find him then?'

'I wasn't allowed to do that.'

'What do you mean?'

'Once I had cooked the meal, Gough had no further use for me, and he told me I was finished for the day. When I am off duty, I am expected to be here, in my quarters.'

'Nowhere else in the house?'

'No. He said that I have everything I need here – this sitting room, a bathroom,' she pointed an elegant finger at one of the doors, 'a small kitchen,' pointing again, 'and a bedroom – and he expected me to stay here.'

'I find that hard to believe,' Paniatowski said.

'Why?'

'Because it's so restrictive – so unreasonable.'

Mrs Adams laughed. 'That's precisely the point,' she said. 'You demonstrate you have power over people by making them do things they wouldn't choose to do themselves – in other words, by restricting their freedom. By confining me to this – admittedly comfortable – prison, Jordan Gough was doing just that.'

'Mr Gough didn't die of natural causes,' Paniatowski said. 'He was murdered. Did you know that?'

Mrs Adams smiled. 'With all the policemen banging about around the house, I'd already worked that out for myself,' she said.

'Was anyone else here last night?' Paniatowski asked.

'Yes, Jordan's brother, Arthur – but he left in the middle of the meal, shortly after I'd served the main course.'

'I thought you said you came straight to this room after you'd served the meal.'

'I did.'

'Then how do you know he left.'

'Look out of that window, and you will see where his car was parked. I was looking through the window last night, and I saw him get into it and drive away.'

'And you're sure it was him?'

'Definitely.'

'So then were only the two of you here?' Paniatowski asked.

'Yes.'

'No one else came in?'

'No.'

'How can you be so sure of that? Couldn't someone have sneaked in without you noticing it?'

'No, that would be impossible,' Mrs Adams said. 'Mr Gough had had some death threats, and so he'd taken the precaution of updating the house's security. All the doors and windows have electronic locks, and the moment Arthur Gough had left, Jordan activated them from the central control panel.'

'How do you know that, if you were in here?'

'I heard the lock on my window click closed, which means all the other locks closed up, too. No one could have got in – not even someone as resourceful as José Cardoza.'

'What made you mention him?'

'When you think of something nasty happening, you automatically think of José.'

'Jordan Gough was poisoned,' Paniatowski said, with all the flourish of a magician pulling a rabbit from his hat.

'Given what I've already said about no one being able to get into the house, I suspected it had to be something like that,' Mrs Adams said, seeming distinctly unimpressed.

'And taking into account all the circumstances you've just outlined, aren't you worried that I might suspect you of the murder?' Paniatowski wondered.

'You may well suspect me, but I didn't do it, and I had no reason to kill him. It was quite the reverse, in fact – I very much wanted him to stay alive.'

'Were you in love with him?'

Mrs Adams laughed. 'In love with him?' she repeated. 'Can you see *yourself* falling in love with him?'

'That's not an answer to my question,' Paniatowski said.

'Like most people who came into contact with Jordan Gough, I thoroughly despised him,' Mrs Adams said.

'And yet you very much wanted him to stay alive? Why was that?'

'I was considerably in debt to him,' Mrs Adams said. 'He agreed to write those debts off, but only if I worked for him for five years. I have a contract which states just that. But I have only worked for him for three years, and so I still owe his estate the money.'

'You seem to be taking this very calmly,' Paniatowski said.

'As I told you earlier, I faced death in the face from a very young age – I take everything calmly.'

'If I told you that we believe Gough was poisoned by the pepper sauce that you made for him, what would you say?' Paniatowski wondered,

'I would say that I did not put any poison in the sauce. I might also add that after I had served the sauce, Jordan Gough and I left the room, which means that Arthur Gough was alone with the jug of sauce.'

'To your knowledge, did Arthur Gough bear his brother any ill will?' Paniatowski asked.

'He wanted him dead, if that's what you mean,' Mrs Adams said.

'And why would he wish that?'

'You'd need an hour or two to hear the whole story, but if you're in a hurry, I can just give you the highlights,' Mrs Adams said.

'All right,' Paniatowski agreed. 'Let's start with the highlights.'

'Jordan made Arthur's life as unpleasant as he possibly could. He gave him all kinds of jobs to do which were utterly pointless – and made sure Arthur knew just how pointless they were. He was always humiliating Arthur in front of other people. And he took real joy in putting a strain on Arthur's marriage. For instance, when Arthur's wife was just about to celebrate her fortieth birthday, Jordan ordered him to go to South America, and . . .'

'Hold on,' Paniatowski said. 'Exactly where in South America did Jordan send him?'

'I think it was Brazil,' Mrs Adams said.

Robbie Holland, the editor of the *Whitebridge Evening Telegraph*, was not a man with burning ambition. Though many journalists would have regarded editorship of the *Telegraph* as no more than a stepping stone en route to far greater things, he was more than happy to view it as a pinnacle that he had been quite surprised to reach, and from which he could comfortably view the rest of the world until the day that he retired.

He had been promoted to editor shortly after the previous holder of the post – who'd had several clashes with the new owner of the *Telegraph* – had been sacked. Some of his friends and colleagues had warned him that he was being handed a poisoned chalice, and that Jordan Gough would force him to do things he found personally repugnant. But it hadn't worked out like that at all. Most of the time, Gough had allowed him to run the paper as he saw fit, and if the proprietor did occasionally intervene – to commission an article praising one of his other businesses or to push a piece in favour of the police – well, that was fine. After all, why shouldn't Jordan Gough make the general readership aware of the services offered by another of his enterprises? That could almost be regarded as a public service. And as for saying nice things about the police – well, it was always wise to stay on the right side of the forces of law and order.

The death of Jordan Gough troubled him, because it created uncertainty. Who knew what would happen next? Perhaps the new owner would be much more 'hands on' than Gough had been. Perhaps he would insist that his editor come up with exciting new initiatives, which was a very unsettling thought indeed, because 'new' and 'initiative' were two of Holland's least favourite words.

Thus, he was already in a state of some anxiety when the phone on his desk rang – and though he did not realize it yet, things were just about to get a great deal worse.

'Mr Holland?' asked the voice at the other end of the line. 'This is Horace Markham. I'm Mr Gough's solicitor.'

'Oh yes?' Holland said, non-committally.

'I take it you have heard that Mr Gough is dead.'

'Yes, I was informed by my source at the mortuary, and the police have just confirmed it. Naturally, we're all in a state of shock here . . .'

'I'm the executor of Jordan Gough's estate, and until the will is submitted for probate, it falls on me to perform certain duties,' Markham interrupted. 'For this reason, I think we need to meet.'

Oh dear, Holland thought.

'Well, as you can imagine, you've caught me at a really bad time,' he said, 'As upsetting as Mr Gough's death has been to all of us here, we still have a job to do, and at the moment we're still working on what the appropriate editorial response should be.'

He paused, to give the solicitor time to say that yes, he could quite see that, but there was only silence at the other end of the line.

'Perhaps we could have dinner together sometime next week,' he continued, shakily. 'Shall we say seven o'clock next Tuesday, at the Trocadero Grill? The paper will, of course, pick up the tab.'

'You appear to be very free with dishing out the paper's

money,' Spider Markham said coldly. 'And what I have to say won't take long. I'll be round in half an hour.'

'I'm afraid that will be quite impossible. We have an editorial conference at that time,' Holland said, trying to sound brisk and efficient, but aware that he wasn't even getting close. He took a deep breath. 'If you'd like to talk to my secretary, I'm sure she can find a time which would be mutually conven—'

'Half an hour,' Markham said curtly – and rung off.

Holland pushed his chair back a little, and rested his feet on his desk. He should have found the action of marking out his territory both comforting and reassuring, but somehow he didn't.

'So what do you think, Colin?' Paniatowski asked, as they stood at Gough's front door, watching the search team scour the grounds.

'Odds are that Arthur Gough did it,' Beresford said. 'He had the means – he'd been to Brazil, where, presumably, it was possible to buy this poison. He had the motive – by all accounts, he hated his brother. And he had the opportunity – there were only two of them at the table when Jordan was poisoned.'

'But don't you find it just a little too neat and tidy?' Paniatowski wondered. 'And would Arthur Gough have poisoned his brother when he must have known he'd be the obvious suspect?'

Beresford shrugged. 'Murderers are not always the most logical of men,' he said. 'And, if he didn't do it, who did?'

'Lynn Adams. She says she has no motive, but do we believe her? And she had even more opportunity than Arthur to poison Jordan. Besides, I distrust people who volunteer information I've not yet got around to asking for.'

'What have you got in mind?'

'She was at some pains to point out to me that after she'd served the meal, she and Jordan left the room for just long to enough to allow Arthur to poison the pepper sauce. That sounds to me like a definite attempt to pin the whole thing on Brother Arthur.'

'Or maybe she was simply trying to deflect the blame from herself because she was innocent,' Beresford suggested.

'Anyway, what about the means? Where would she lay her hands on a South American poison?'

'She could have got it through José Cardoza,' Paniatowski said. 'He's from Portugal, so maybe he knows people in Brazil – a lot of Portuguese have relatives there. And remember, he was Jordan Gough's right-hand man – his bodyguard. Ever since Jordan started receiving death threats – and in the light of what's happened, I think we can assume he *was* telling us the truth about that – he's kept José almost constantly by his side. So where was he last night?'

'Maybe there was something important that Jordan needed him to do,' Beresford suggested.

'We only have Lynn Adams' word that he *wasn't* there. And is it likely that Jordan Gough would have had the man who was on his hate list round for dinner, when his bodyguard wasn't there to protect him?'

'You've seen how this brain tumour of his caused him to lose his concentration,' Beresford said. 'Maybe it had got worse, and he'd completely forgotten that his life had been threatened.'

'Or maybe he simply put his trust in his bodyguard, never realizing that José and Lynn were conspiring to kill him.'

'You got my head spinning,' Beresford confessed.

'I'm feeling a little dizzy myself,' Paniatowski said.

'So what are we going to do?'

'We're going to attack it from all fronts. Lynn Adams says she's got a contract with Gough which states that if she doesn't complete five years' service, she's still answerable for all her debts – I want you to find out if she's telling the truth. You also need to ask José Cardoza where he was last night, and check out his alibi. And get a search warrant for Arthur Gough's house.'

'And what will you be doing, boss?' Beresford asked.

'Me?' Paniatowski said. 'I'll be back at headquarters, doing my best to deflect all the flak that will be flying our way.'

Spider Markham had announced he would be at the *Evening Telegraph* offices half an hour after his phone call with the editor, and he lived up to his promise – or perhaps it would be more accurate to call it his threat – by arriving right on time.

Robbie Holland greeted him enthusiastically, and, trying to overlook the fact that shaking hands with Markham was rather like grabbing hold of a dead fish, led the solicitor into his office. There, laid out on his desk, was the dummy front page for that day's edition of the paper.

Tragic Death of Jordan Gough.

It is with great sadness that we report the death, in suspicious circumstances, of Jordan Gough, the owner of this newspaper. Mr Gough was a public benefactor on a huge scale, and there are very few charities in this town which have not received his help and support.

Speaking this afternoon, the mayor of Whitebridge, Councillor Andrew Mathers, said, 'This town is the poorer for his passing. He was, indeed, an admirable man and a role model for future generations.'

The whole page had a black border running round it.

'We think we've managed to hit just the right note,' Holland said, looking at Markham for signs of approval.

The solicitor opened his slim leather briefcase, extracted a single sheet of paper, and laid it on Holland's desk.

'You can forget all that,' he said. 'This is what I want on the front page. It will need photographs to accompany it, but you must have plenty of them in your archives.'

Holland frowned. 'We really have worked rather hard to produce the front page I've just shown you,' he said.

Markham tapped the sheet of paper impatiently with his index finger.

'Read it,' he said.

Holland did not like conflict, and thus had become quite good at suppressing any emotions which might result in a face-to-face confrontation, so it was with some surprise that he noted he was becoming irritated.

'Look here, Mr Markham,' he heard himself say, 'you can't just come in here and . . .'

'But I can,' Markham interrupted him. 'I am the sole executor of the will, I can do anything I wish to. Besides, if you read the article, I think you'll agree it would have been what Mr Gough wanted.'

Holland read the article, and the further he got into it, the more his horror grew.

'But . . . but this is virtually a declaration of war,' he spluttered.

'Ah, I was worried about hitting the right tone, but from your reaction, I appear to have been spot on,' Markham said.

'Mr Gough would never have approved of this,' Holland protested. 'He was a great supporter of the police.'

'Yes, he was, but then he was murdered, and I suggest that would have changed his perspective somewhat,' Markham replied. 'Perhaps I shouldn't say this about a client – even a deceased one – but he was not a nice man. He would certainly have wanted revenge, and this article is intended to assist in that process.'

'I have to live in this town,' Holland said, 'and I'm certainly not going to take responsibility for publishing something like this.'

'In that case, you can collect up your personal possessions and get out,' Markham said.

'You can't do that.'

'I can,' Markham contradicted him. 'As I said earlier, until the estate is settled, I can do what I damn well please. So will you publish it, or not?'

'I'll publish it,' said Holland, defeated.

Paniatowski had anticipated that there would be some flak flying around at headquarters, but she had never anticipated anything like this.

From the moment she entered the front door, she was made to feel like a pariah. The smile that the clerk on the reception desk gave was wan at best. When she met other officers on the corridors, they refused to meet her eyes, and their hellos were mumbled. And several people who were clearly intending to take the lift backed away when they saw she was going to use it.

It wasn't hatred she was sensing, she thought, as she travelled up to the top floor. It wasn't even that her colleagues wished to shun her. They were simply embarrassed, because they had heard what had happened, and just didn't know what to say to her. And she supposed she couldn't blame them for that – if she were in their shoes, she wouldn't know what to say, either.

There was no such evasion from Mrs Crow, the chief constable's secretary, who looked her straight in the eye. And why shouldn't she? She was not a fellow officer, but a civilian, as detached from the life and rhythms of the force as the Isle of Wight is from mainland England. And besides, she was rumoured to have ice water, rather than blood, running through her veins.

'The chief constable is out, Chief Inspector,' she said, 'but he told me to ask you to wait.'

Paniatowski took a seat.

'Do you know where he is?' she asked.

The secretary threaded a fresh sheet of paper into her typewriter.

'No,' she said.

'Well, do you know when he's likely to be back?'

'I haven't a clue,' Mrs Crow told her, and began typing.

'Could I at least have my hearty breakfast now?' Paniatowski wondered.

Mrs Crow stopped typing. 'Your what?' she asked.

'My hearty breakfast,' Paniatowski repeated. 'You know – the condemned man ate a hearty breakfast.'

'I have no idea what you're talking about,' said Mrs Crow, before continuing the assault on her keyboard.

It was going to be very hard to find the silver lining in this particular dark cloud, Paniatowski thought.

It was over an hour before Baxter returned, and when he did the first things that Paniatowski noticed about him were that he had a worried look on his face and a copy of the *Whitebridge Evening Telegraph* under his arm.

'Could you step into my office, please, Chief Inspector,' he said in a voice entirely drained of emotion.

'Of course, sir,' Paniatowski replied.

'I've just been in a meeting with the police authority, and

they're not at all happy,' Baxter said, once they were sitting down and facing each other across his desk.

'Is it Jordan Gough's murder that's upset them?'

'What do you think?'

'But how did they find out about it so quickly?' Paniatowski wondered.

'I take it from that comment that you haven't seen the first edition of the *Evening Telegraph* yet,' Baxter said.

'No, as a matter of fact, I haven't.'

'Then perhaps you'd better look at it now,' the chief constable said, sliding the newspaper across the desk. 'You shouldn't have any trouble finding the article I want you to read, because it takes up the entire front page.'

The first thing Paniatowski saw was a photograph of herself. She couldn't say precisely when it had been taken, but it was obviously at a moment when she was feeling very stressed, and it made her look both worried and helpless.

That was not good – but the article was even worse.

Jordan Gough In Memoriam

Jordan Gough was the publisher of this newspaper. It was his purpose in life to see that the *Telegraph* served both the community and the truth, and in both he was more than successful.

He served the community in many other ways, too. As president of Whitebridge Rovers FC he made sure that the club offered the fans the cheapest tickets in the north-west. He was the patron of many local charities, and donated to a number of others anonymously. He never asked for anything in return except the rights and privileges afforded to all citizens, yet one of the most important of these rights – the right to sleep safely in his bed – was denied to him.

When Jordan Gough received several death threats, he informed the police, and was interviewed by Detective Chief Inspector Monika Paniatowski. DCI Paniatowski assured him that she would investigate the threat thoroughly, but after conducting a couple of half-hearted interviews, she seemed to lose interest – leaving the man who had threatened Jordan Gough a clear run at carrying out his evil intentions. And now Jordan Gough is dead

– murdered – and our town is made all the poorer for his passing.

The police have failed him, and this newspaper thinks the police in general – and DCI Paniatowski in particular – should answer for it.


'Well?' Baxter asked.

'Well what?' Paniatowski replied.

'Is the article right? Did you conduct a couple of half-hearted interviews and then lose interest?'

It wasn't as simple as that, she thought. She'd never been enthusiastic about an investigation which she was convinced was leading nowhere, but until Spider Markham had rung her at the Drum and – in effect – issued her with instructions, she'd at least been prepared to go through the motions.

'Well?' Baxter asked.

'I devoted as much time as I could spare to what seemed to me to be an improbable threat,' Paniatowski said awkwardly.

'But it wasn't an improbable threat, was it?' Baxter asked. 'Because Jordan Gough *is* dead, and somebody *did* kill him.'

'You didn't seem to take it seriously, either,' Paniatowski said.

'Didn't I?' Baxter asked. 'Funnily enough, I have the distinct impression that after you came back from Gough's house prepared to drop the investigation, I ordered you to continue with it.'

'Yes, you did,' Paniatowski agreed. 'But that was a purely *political* decision. On a policing level, you didn't really think that Gough was in any danger at all, did you?'

'No,' Baxter agreed. 'But then I was only seeing the whole thing from a distance. You, on the other hand, were close to the ground.'

'So this is it, is it?' Paniatowski demanded. 'You're throwing me to the wolves.'

Baxter shook his head – rather sadly, she thought.

'You should know me better than that,' he told her. 'When the press interview me, I'll say that you had no reason to consider it a serious threat, and neither did I. I'll also say I still have complete confidence in you, and that I'll be keeping you on the case.'

'You'll meet a lot of resistance over that decision,' Paniatowski said.

Baxter laughed bleakly. '*You're* telling *me*. I've already had to fight the police committee. And most of my senior management team won't exactly be over the moon about it, either.'

'You could lose a lot of the good will you've built up during your time as chief constable.'

'I'll lose most of it. There'll be very few officers under my command who will ever really trust my judgement again.'

Paniatowski realized she was almost in tears.

'I'm sorry for doubting you, George,' she said. 'Listen, I don't want you to sacrifice yourself for me. Go ahead and throw me to the bloody wolves – I'm a big girl and I can handle it.'

'I've made my decision,' Baxter said firmly.

This really was the old George Baxter she'd once known, she thought, and for the thousandth time, she wished that, back then, when they were sleeping together, she could have learned to love him as he deserved to be loved – and as he had loved her.

'If I don't solve Gough's murder I'm finished,' she said.

'Yes, you are.'

'And even if I do solve it, there's a seventy-five per cent chance it won't be enough to save my career.'

Baxter smiled grimly. 'Is that what you think? I'd have put it closer to ninety-five per cent myself,' he said.

'If that's what you calculate, then please don't throw yourself on the bonfire after me, like some kind of demented nineteenth-century Hindu widow,' Paniatowski begged, 'because it will all be for nothing.'

'Aren't you rather mixing up your metaphors?' Baxter asked, chuckling. 'First I'm a callous sleigh driver, and now I'm a grieving widow.'

'It's not funny, George,' Paniatowski said. She was furious, though she had not yet quite decided whether most of her fury was aimed at herself or at Baxter. 'We're talking about your career, here – a career which you told me just yesterday was the only thing that gave any meaning to your life.'

'Oh, that was just talk,' Baxter said airily, 'you should ignore it.'

'Please, George, think again,' Paniatowski said. 'Like you said, even if I lose everything else, I've still got my kids.'

'I'm doing what I have to do,' Baxter told her. His face became a perfect mask. 'Thank you, Chief Inspector, that's all. You're dismissed.'

'George . . .'

'You're dismissed *now*.'

Paniatowski bowed her head. 'Yes, sir,' she said.

# SIXTEEN

José Cardoza glared at Paniatowski and Beresford across the table in Interview Room B.

'They tell me this is a free country, but it does not feel like that to me,' he said.

'Do you have a complaint, Mr Cardoza?' Paniatowski asked.

'Yes, I have a complaint.'

'Then by all means tell us what it is.'

'I was returning to my house . . .'

'By which you mean Jordan Gough's house?'

'Does it amuse you to interrupt me?' Cardoza asked.

'No,' Paniatowski told him. 'I just want things to be clear.'

'In Portuguese I would say *"minha casa"*. That means the place where I live, but I will agree that what I was returning to was *Sr Gough's* house.'

'Thank you, you've made that perfectly clear now, and you can carry on,' Paniatowski said.

Cardoza smiled. 'Do you think I don't know what is going on?' he asked. 'I was a policeman myself, back in Portugal . . .'

'So we've heard.'

'. . . and when I was interrogating suspects, I would always correct them over the little things. It would confuse them – and that was when they would start making mistakes.'

'But we're not going to confuse *you*, are we, Mr Cardoza?' Beresford asked. 'You're much too smart for that.'

'I would also let my suspect think that he was smarter than I was – which is what you are trying now,' Cardoza said.

Paniatowski sighed. 'Oh, for God's sake, get on with making your complaint,' she said.

'I saw all the police cars outside parked outside,' Cardoza said. 'I asked the sergeant what was going on, and he said he had orders to bring me here, so that you could interrogate me. This is my complaint – that an innocent man can be dragged here against his will.'

'You do know that your boss has been murdered, don't you?' Paniatowski asked.

'Yes, your sergeant told me.'

'But you didn't know before then?'

'How could I have known?'

'I have to say, you don't seem very upset about his death,' Beresford told Cardoza.

Cardoza shrugged. 'I am not like your English pansies – your fairy boys. I am a Portuguese man. We do not show our feelings.'

'You don't even seem very surprised,' Paniatowski said.

'He had had many death threats, and then somebody killed him. How surprised should I be?'

'What I don't understand is how you, as his bodyguard . . .'

'I was not his bodyguard. I was his personal assistant. I only say this because you want things to be clear.'

'All right, I don't understand how you, as his personal assistant, could have left him alone overnight when you knew his life was in danger.'

'The only two people he saw were his brother and his house-keeper. The brother does not have the stomach for murder, and it was not in Sra Adams' interest to kill him.'

'And yet he is dead,' Paniatowski pointed out.

'I am as surprised about it as the *Evening Telegraph* says that you are,' Cardoza told her.

'Hang about,' Beresford said. 'You're claiming that you knew nothing of the murder until you got to the house, aren't you?'

'That is correct.'

'So you hadn't seen an *Evening Telegraph before* then, and

you've been in police custody *since* then. So how do you know what was in the newspaper?'

'Perhaps your sergeant told me that also. Maybe he has a big mouth.'

'You can't even be bothered to lie convincingly, can you?' Beresford asked, getting angry.

Cardoza shrugged again. 'It does not matter what I say, or how I say it,' he told the inspector. 'You cannot prove anything against me – because there is nothing to prove.'

'Where were you last night?' Paniatowski asked.

'I was in Accrington.'

'And what were you doing there?'

'I was visiting my cousin.'

'Does this cousin of yours have a name and address?'

'Yes – everyone has a name, and most people have an address.'

'Just what we needed – a sociopathic comedian,' Paniatowski groaned. 'Would it be too much trouble to give us your cousin's name and address, Mr Cardoza?'

'Of course not. His name is Jeronimo Ferreira, and he lives at 16 India Mill Road.'

'Did you stay overnight?'

'Yes.'

'Why would you do that, when it would have only taken you fifteen or twenty minutes to drive back to Whitebridge, where you could have slept in your own bed?'

'I did it because I chose to do it,' Cardoza said. He stood up. 'And now, unless you charge me with something, I am going to leave. Are you going to charge me?'

'You can go,' Paniatowski said.

'I *am* going,' Cardoza said haughtily. 'But it is because I want to, not because you have given me your permission.'

'So what did you make of all that?' Paniatowski asked, when the Portuguese had left the room.

'I know India Mill Road,' Beresford said. 'It's nothing but a terrace of old two-up, two-down weavers' cottages, so the question we have to ask ourselves is why any man would choose to spend the night in those cramped conditions if he didn't have to.'

'And your answer is?'

'He did it to establish an alibi.'

Paniatowski nodded. 'That's what I think, too. Did he play any role in the murder?'

'I don't know,' Beresford admitted, 'but if he did, I think it was in partnership with Mrs Adams.'

'I agree,' Paniatowski said. 'He neither likes nor trusts the only other possible suspect – Arthur Gough. And more to the point, Gough not only doesn't trust him, he's scared of him.'

'And Cardoza might well have the hots for Mrs Adams,' Beresford said, 'I know I have.' A look of horror came to his face. 'What I mean is, I *would have* the hots for her if she wasn't part of the investigation.'

'Good, I'm glad we've got that clear,' Paniatowski said dryly. 'Here's what we do next. Jack Crane goes to Accrington to check out José Cardoza's alibi; you take some of your team and raid Arthur Gough's house the moment the magistrate has signed the search warrant; and I'll see if I can establish that Cardoza has a Brazilian connection who could have supplied him with the poison.'

'What about Meadows?' Beresford asked.

'Sergeant Meadows will be following a lead on our other murder. You remember that one, Colin – feller with his head bashed in in the James Hargreaves Building?'

The shop was called Blue Bird Travel, and it had as its logo – unsurprisingly – a bluebird on the wing.

Meadows gave the shop window a cursory glance. There were several posters on display. Two of them were pictures of historic buildings – venerable and worthy cultural icons, no doubt, but unlikely to quicken the pulse of the average Whitebridge holiday traveller in search of sun and sangria. The remaining posters – all of which seemed to have improbably well-muscled men and bikini-clad girls with hourglass figures relaxing on sandy beaches while palm trees swayed in the background – would be much more to local taste.

'*Tom Crawley spent a lot of money on travel,*' the bank manager had told her, once she'd backed him into a corner from which there was no escape.

'*That doesn't tell me much.*'

*'I mean really* a lot *of money . . . And what you need to find out is* why *he travelled.'*

This didn't feel like the sort of place where Crawley would spend a lot of money, Meadows thought, which meant that coming here at all was probably a complete waste of time – but the thing was that in police work you could never afford to dismiss a lead, because the chances were that if you did, it would turn out to be the one lead that mattered.

When Meadows opened the door, a small bell issued a tinkling warning. The three young women sitting behind their respective counters – a brunette, a bottle blonde and a redhead – looked up in eager anticipation of earning some commission.

Meadows held up her warrant card. 'Sorry to disappoint you, girls, but I'm not a customer.'

The women sank back into their seats, disappointed.

'But you could help me solve a very big crime,' Meadows said, by way of compensation.

The news perked the three women up – not as much as the possibility of money for a new pair of shoes or a night on the town would have perked them up, but at least somewhat.

Meadows produced a photograph of Tom Crawley. 'I need to know if you've ever done business with him,' she said.

'He looks like the feller who got his picture in the paper on account of being murdered,' the brunette said.

'That's right,' Meadows confirmed. 'So was he a customer of Blue Bird Travel?'

'No, worse luck,' said the bottle blonde.

'What do you mean – worse luck?' demanded the brunette.

'Well, you know,' the bottle blonde said evasively.

'No, I don't know,' the brunette said.

The bottle blonde shrugged. 'My boyfriend's always saying that I've got a really boring job. Can you imagine the look on his face if I could say to him, "Well, as a matter of fact, Tony, I was the one who sold the ticket to the murder victim"?'

'You're just sick,' the brunette said.

'And you're just jealous because *I* don't need a padded bra,' the bottle blonde countered.

Meadows slapped a hand down hard on the counter before this discussion could go any further.

'Have any of you sold this man a ticket of any kind?' she said in a voice which would have stopped a rampaging rhino in its tracks.

'I haven't,' the redhead said, speaking for the first time.

'Me, neither,' said the brunette.

'I've already told you I haven't,' said the bottle blonde, sulkily.

'Thank you for your time,' Meadows said. 'And if I come across any homicidal maniacs who need plane tickets, I'll be sure to recommend you,' she told the bottle blonde.

Well, that was one travel agent's crossed off her list, she thought, as she opened the door.

One out of the twenty-seven in the Whitebridge area.

Only twenty-six to go!

The factory hooter announced the end of the day's work, and the men began to stream out. First came the young and fleet of foot, eager to get away – apprentices and men not long out of their apprenticeships, who still lived at home with their mums and dads, but spent most of their free time fishing in the canal or down at the pub. Next came the main body of workers, middle-aged family men heading for home out of habit, but without any real enthusiasm. Finally, there were the stragglers, mostly men approaching retirement, who had given up hurrying anywhere long ago.

'That's him,' said the personnel manager.

He was pointing at a stocky man with an olive skin, who was walking slightly apart from the rest of the workers.

'I'll handle it from here,' Crane told him.

He waited until the stocky man had drawn level with him, then said, 'Mr Ferreira?'

'Yes?' the Portuguese replied, in a voice that seemed a combination of alarmed and haunted.

Crane produced his warrant card. 'If you don't mind, I'd like to have a talk to you.'

'I have done nothing wrong!' Ferreira protested. 'I work hard. I pay my taxes. And I do not fight.'

'I'm sure you're a model citizen,' Crane said. 'But it's not you I want to talk about – it's your cousin José.'

Ferreira was definitely looking worried now. 'Whatever bad thing he does, I don't help him,' he said.

'I'm sure you didn't,' Crane said reassuringly.

He was getting nowhere fast with this encounter, he realized, and he needed to come up with something to change the dynamic of the meeting.

'There's a pub around the corner called the Crown and Anchor,' he continued. 'Do you know it?'

'Yes.'

'Is it a good pub?'

'It's all right,' Ferreira said non-committally.

'Then why don't we pop in there now, and I'll buy you a drink?' Crane suggested.

Jeronimo Ferreira took a sip of his pint of bitter and said, 'In my country, the police do not buy beer for men like me.'

'How would you describe a man like you?' Crane asked.

Ferreira shrugged. 'A hard-working man,' he said. 'Not very clever, but honest. How you describe *yourself*?'

Crane grinned. 'Someone who tries to be both a policeman and a poet – and is not sure he's much good at either.'

'You *look* more like a poet than a policeman,' Ferreira said.

'Thank you – I think,' Crane replied. 'Your cousin says he was with you all last night.'

'He was,' Ferreira confirmed. 'He come to my house at six o'clock. I say to him, "But it is not Thursday."'

'Why did you say that?'

'Thursday is pay day.'

'And he comes to collect money off you,' Crane said, remembering José Cardoza's other cousin, the gardener at Gough's mansion.

'Yes, he come to collect money,' Ferreira confirmed. 'He lend me money to come to England, but I must pay him back – I must pay him back a lot more than he give me.'

'But last night he didn't come for money?'

'No. He say he is just visiting me. He had never visited me before. He sit on my sofa watching television. My wife is getting very nervous.'

'Is she frightened of him?'

'Of course she is. So am I. If you were not a policeman, maybe you would be frightened of him too.'

'Yes, maybe I would be,' Crane admitted.

Ferreira gave him a long searching stare. 'I like you,' he said, finally.

'I like you,' Crane said – and meant it. 'So did he stay there on the sofa all night?'

'No. At seven and a half he say we should go to the pub. I want to go to the King's Head. It is quiet. But José say no, we must choose a pub where there are many people, so we go to the Green Dragon.'

'And you were there until what time?'

'Ten o'clock – that is when we get thrown out.'

'Why did you get thrown out?'

'José have an argument with the barman.'

'What about?'

'About nothing! The barman is a nice fellow who does not want to offend anybody. There is no reason for José to fall out with him.'

But there probably was a reason, Crane thought. Cardoza may well have staged the argument in order to ensure that the other people in the pub remembered that, when Jordan Gough was being poisoned, he himself was several miles away.

'So then what did you do?'

'We go back to my house. José say he is tired. He say he will sleep in my bed and I must sleep on the sofa. He say my wife may sleep in the bed with him if she want to. She sleep on the sofa with me, but there is not much room, and we do not sleep very well. In the morning, José leave.'

But he didn't drive directly back to the Gough mansion, did he, Crane thought. He waited until the police had searched the house and questioned Mrs Adams before putting in an appearance.

'Thank you for your help, Jeronimo,' he said.

There was something more he wanted to say, but he knew it would be unprofessional (and might possibly damage his career) to say it. Thus, a smart, educated young man like him would be wise to keep his mouth firmly shut.

'Have I really been a help?' Ferreira asked.

To hell with being a wise man!

'You've been a great help, and I hope that by the end of the week your cousin will be behind bars,' he said.

Ferreira lifted his pint glass off the table.

'So José may go to gaol,' he pondered. 'What is it that you English say at such times? Ah yes – I'll drink to that!'

# SEVENTEEN

Arthur Gough took a while to answer the summoning knock on the front door of his semi-detached house, and even when he did eventually get there, he took some time to draw back the bolts.

Once the door was opened, he squinted at his caller, as if trying to focus properly.

'It's Inspector Beresford,' he said finally, with a hint of self-congratulation in his voice. 'What can I do for you, Inspector Beresford?'

'I have here a warrant to search this house, Mr Gough,' Beresford said.

This new information obviously required some more processing, and for perhaps twenty seconds Gough turned it over in his mind.

Then he said. 'Sorry, I can't possibly allow that.'

'You have no choice in the matter,' Beresford told him.

Gough put a hand on each of the door jambs, effectively blocking the way.

'You come in here over my dead body,' he said, slurring his words slightly.

'Look, sir, it's obvious you're drunk . . .' Beresford began.

'Drunk! Who's drunk? Nowhere near drunk. Just having a little celebration, that's all.'

'. . . and I'm prepared to grant you some leeway because of it, but if you don't start cooperating soon, I shall have to have you forcibly removed,' Beresford said, in measured tones.

The message finally appeared to sink in, and Gough dropped his arms to his sides.

'All right, you can come inside if you must, but you won't find anything,' he said sulkily.

'I think it would be best if you and me went into the lounge, so we don't get in the way of the search,' Beresford said, taking hold of his upper arms and steering him backwards down the hallway.

The lounge told its own story, Beresford thought. It was clean, and it was cared for, but it had been furnished on the cheap, and was as different to Jordan Gough's mansion as a broken-down mule is to a sleek young racehorse. It was obvious that Jordan had been keeping Arthur on a tight financial leash – and probably getting great satisfaction from doing it.

Arthur Gough slumped down in one of the armchairs. He seemed much calmer now they were inside.

'Would you like a drink, Inspector?' he asked, pointing to the expensive bottle of malt whisky, which was sitting on the coffee table.

'Well, you certainly seem to have money to burn,' Beresford said.

For a moment, the remark seemed to puzzle Arthur Gough, then he said, 'Oh, you mean the whisky.'

'That's right,' Beresford agreed.

'Just yesterday, I'd never have thought of buying anything that cost this much,' Gough said candidly. 'But this morning I went to see my brother's solicitor, to confirm what I already knew.'

'Which was?'

'That Jordan has left me almost everything he had. I'm going to be a rich man – a *very* rich man. Do you know how long it would take to spend a few million pounds, even if you were trying your hardest?'

'Quite a while, I would imagine,' Beresford said.

'Quite a while,' Gough agreed, echoing him in the way that drunks often do echo whoever they're talking to. He picked up the bottle and looked closely at it, as if he was still finding it hard to believe that anything that good was actually there in *his* lounge. 'Anyway, you never said whether or not you wanted a drink,' he slurred.

'I'll pass,' Beresford told him.

'Please yourself,' Gough said indifferently. 'Don't mind if I have one, do you?'

'It's your liver,' Beresford said.

Arthur Gough poured himself a glass of whisky with all the infinite care of a man attempting to prove that – all appearances to the contrary – he was really quite sober.

'Sorry if I was rude to you when you turned up unexpectedly at the door like that,' he said.

'Think nothing of it,' Beresford told him.

'No, I'd like to make it up to you,' Gough said. 'How do you like the idea of a couple of tickets for the director's box the next time the Rovers play at home?'

'I think I'll pass on that as well,' Beresford said.

'That's twice you've turned me down,' Arthur Gough said, starting to get angry again. 'You seem to have forgotten that I'm a man of consequence now, and that means you should treat me with the proper respect.'

A detective constable entered the room.

'You're wanted upstairs, sir,' he said.

'You stay with Mr Gough,' Beresford told him, as he headed for the door. 'And remember, he's a man of consequence now.'

Another constable was waiting for him on the landing. 'I think you ought to see what we've found in the lavatory cistern, sir,' he said.

The top of the cistern had already been removed, and looking down into the tank Beresford could see a plastic bag containing some kind of white powder.

'Do we know what the powder is?' Beresford asked.

'I'm putting my money on it being poison,' the constable told him.

'Me too,' Beresford said. 'Take it out of the tank and put it in an evidence bag.'

Monika Paniatowski had met Inspector Armando Silva of the Brazilian Polícia Civil at an international conference on policing in Geneva, and perhaps because their backgrounds had been so very different – and yet in some ways so similar – they had got on extremely well.

He had been born in a village that was so small it did not

even feature on the map, he had told her. It had been a poor place, too – so poor that none of the bands of brigands who roamed freely in the province had ever considered it worth plundering. At the age of twelve he had left his home forever, and walked the several hundred miles which separated the miserable hamlet from the city of Rio de Janeiro. Once he reached the big city, he had worked hard, taking whatever jobs were offered to him, and at the same time completing his high-school education.

Paniatowski, in turn, had described the life that she and her mother had led in war-torn Europe – how they had been forever on the run from one army or another, and how she had eventually been taken to England by a stepfather who had abused her.

'And now we are both fine, and it is as if those things never happened,' he had said, when she'd concluded her tale.

'Yes, now we are both fine, and it is as if those things never happened,' she had repeated.

But she had not been sure if either of them had believed it.

Silva had joined the police at the age of nineteen, and twenty-five years later had risen to the rank of inspector.

'I will go no further,' he had confided, as they shared a bottle of vodka. 'I am an honest man, you see – and in Brazil no one really trusts an honest man. But,' he had shrugged, 'I enjoy my work and would hate to spend my life behind a desk, so where I am now is fine with me.'

When they parted, he had promised that he would visit her in England, and she had promised that she would visit him in Brazil, but they had not been particularly surprised when neither of those things happened. There had been no telephone calls, and no Christmas cards, either. But after their nights of drinking and soul-baring, Paniatowski was still expecting a warm reception when she rang him out of the blue.

She was not disappointed.

'So you have a crime you want me to solve for you,' Silva said.

'I am currently conducting an investigation in which I think it is just possible you may be a little help,' Paniatowski said, smiling as she spoke, and knowing that he was, too.

'So what is your problem?' Silva asked.

'I am investigating a man called José Cardoza,' Paniatowski told him. 'He's Portuguese, but I think there might be a Brazilian connection.'

Silva said nothing, and Paniatowski could sense a sudden chill coming down the line.

'Armando?' she said.

'It is a common name,' Silva said cautiously. 'Several of my drinking companions are called Cardoza, as are half a dozen men I have arrested. Do you have a photograph of him?'

'Yes,' Paniatowski said.

'Then fax it to me, and I will get back to you later.'

The fluorescent lighting in the police interview room wouldn't flatter anyone, but it was particularly merciless with someone who looked as totally wrecked as Arthur Gough did.

Gough's face was unnaturally pale, his skin was drawn tightly across his cheekbones, and his left eye flickered like a strobe light. He did, however, seem to have sobered up, Beresford thought, a process which had no doubt been aided by the shock of being arrested.

'I'll ask you again, Mr Gough – what's the white powder we found in your bog?' Beresford said.

Gough shifted awkwardly in his seat.

'No comment,' he said.

'Is it a poison?' Beresford wondered. 'Is it what killed your brother?'

'He wasn't my brother,' Gough said, with a sudden flash of anger.

'Your stepbrother, then.'

'He wasn't that either – he was just some snivelling little bastard that my stupid parents took pity on.'

Beresford sighed. 'All right, have it your own way. Was the powder we found in your bathroom used to kill Jordan Gough?'

'No comment.'

'Look, if you cooperate now, it will stand you in good stead when you go to trial,' Beresford said persuasively. 'On the other hand,' his voice hardened, 'if you leave it until tomorrow morning, we won't need your cooperation anymore, because by then we'll have a report from the lab.'

'I want to see my lawyer,' Arthur Gough said.

Oh well, at least he'd tried to get the sod to talk, Beresford told himself.

'I shall need the name and telephone of your lawyer,' he said.

'I don't have his telephone number, but his name is Spider Markham,' Gough told him.

It was a good three-quarters of an hour before Inspector Silva rang Monika Paniatowski back.

'As I suspected, I know your Cardoza very well,' he said, in a voice heavy with either anger or sadness – and perhaps both. 'He was here for two or three years. He ran a string of prostitutes, and also a protection racket. I suspect him of blackmail as well, but all these things are nothing in comparison to what he did to Bianca Ramos. It is not a pretty story. Shall I tell it to you?'

'Yes, please.'

'Bianca was one of his whores. Like me, she came from a poor background, and also like me, she wanted to better herself. She secretly took sewing lessons, because she hoped that when she was good enough, she could get a job as a seamstress. But José found out, and decided to make an example of her, so his other whores would not be tempted to do the same. He took his razor to her, and then dumped her on the street, next to the garbage cans. But he was careless, and several people – good people – saw him doing it.'

'What happened to the girl?'

'She was rushed to hospital. The doctors did all they could, but she died anyway. There were seventy-four slash wounds on her body.'

'Didn't you arrest him?'

'I wanted to, but he had disappeared. I thought he must have gone to some other city – this is a very big country, and it is not too difficult for a man to hide – but now you say that he is in England, so he must have been smuggled out on a ship. Are you going to arrest him?'

'I'm hoping to.'

'Please do. I was with Bianca when she died, and it has always haunted me that I let him get away with it.'

'Now you know where he is, couldn't you put in a request to have him extradited to Brazil?' Paniatowski asked.

'It would be my dearest wish, but sadly there is no extradition treaty between Britain and Brazil.'

There was an odd sound on the other end of the line, which Paniatowski thought could almost have been a sob.

'Don't let him get away with whatever he has done in your country, Monika,' Silva continued. 'Put him in gaol. Do it for me.'

Arthur Gough sat in the interview room gazing down at his hands. He had never really looked at them before, he thought – never regarded them as anything more than convenient grabbing tools on the ends of his arms. And yet when you took a moment to study them, you began to appreciate how well engineered they were – how cunningly everything fit together.

They were . . . they were . . .

Jesus, I'm going mad, he told himself.

And why wouldn't he be going mad? Anyone finding themselves in his situation would go mad.

The door of the interview room opened, and the constable on duty said, 'Your solicitor is here.'

Spider Markham walked into the room, and sat down at the table.

'Thank you, constable,' he said. 'You may go now. And by the way, I'm *a* solicitor, not *his* solicitor.'

'What the hell did you mean by that?' Gough demanded, once the officer had gone.

'Exactly what I said,' Markham replied. 'I was your brother's solicitor for certain matters while he was alive, and now that he is dead, I am the solicitor who is acting as his executor. What I am definitely not is *your* solicitor.'

'Then I'll hire you now,' Arthur Gough said.

Spider Markham chuckled. 'You couldn't possibly afford me, Mr Gough,' he said.

'What do you mean?' Gough asked. 'Of course I can afford you. I'm my brother's principal heir. I must be worth millions.'

'No,' Markham corrected him. 'You are not worth millions – the estate is worth millions.'

'It's the same thing.'

'No, it isn't – not until all the legal procedures have been completed.'

'But as executor, there's nothing to stop you using my future inheritance as the basis for taking out a loan with which to pay your fees, is there?'

'There's a great deal to stop me,' Markham said. 'I have been entrusted with the care of the estate. I can't be seen to abuse my position by using it as collateral for a loan from which I will benefit personally.'

The man was as bent as a corkscrew, and could find his way round any objections if he really wanted to, Gough thought. So why was he being so difficult now?

'I'll tell you what I'll do,' he said, trying not to seem desperate. 'If you help me now for free, I'll pay you a hundred thousand pounds once I get my hands on Jordan's money. Think about it, Spider – a hundred grand is a lot of money.'

'Yes, it is,' Markham agreed. 'But what bothers me, you see, is that I don't think I'd ever get it.'

'You trust me, don't you?'

'Frankly, no, but that's not the problem. What concerns me is . . .'

'Oh, for God's sake, put it down in writing and I'll bloody sign it.'

'The problem with that is, your promise may not be worth the paper it's printed on.'

'That's bollocks!' Gough protested.

'You seem to be assuming that, in the end, you will get your brother's money,' Markham said.

'Well, I will, won't I?'

'Not necessarily,' the solicitor said, with what could only be regarded as a smirk. 'In this country, you cannot profit from crime, so if you are found guilty of killing Jordan, you will get nothing.'

It was only when you were sitting alone at the table in the Drum and Monkey that you really started to appreciate how much the team meant to you, Jack Crane thought.

It couldn't last forever, of course. One or more of them might get promotion and move on, and the magic circle would be broken. But while he did have it, he'd be a fool not to cherish it, because though it had its faults – God, it had its faults! – there was nothing quite like it, nor ever would be again.

The door opened and Colin Beresford walked in.

'Are the others on their way, sir?' Crane asked.

Beresford shook his head. 'We've arrested Arthur Gough, but it seemed like a bad idea to question him anymore tonight, so the boss has gone home.'

'And DS Meadows?'

'Your guess is as good as mine. You know what Meadows is like.'

Oh yes, he knew what she was like, Crane thought. She was a very difficult woman to keep track of, and when she did turn up, it was usually when you were least expecting it.

'So tell me about Arthur Gough,' Crane suggested.

Beresford described the raid on the house and the discovery of the mystery white powder, and Crane, for his part, told the inspector about his interview with Jeronimo Ferreira.

'The problem is that none of it hangs together,' Beresford said. 'Cardoza and Gough can't have been working together, because they knew they couldn't trust each other. But if, instead, Cardoza and Mrs Adams are the murderers, what's Gough doing with the white powder? And if Gough carried out the murder on his own, why did Cardoza go to such trouble to establish an alibi in Accrington?'

'I'll tell you what's bothering me,' Crane said, 'why did the murder take place at the house at all?'

'I'm not sure I know what you mean,' Beresford admitted.

'We only have three possible suspects – Cardoza, Gough and Mrs Adams. Isn't that right?'

'Yes,' Beresford agreed, 'because if the killer had been someone else, he couldn't have poisoned the pepper sauce without Mrs Adams seeing him.'

'So the *actual* murderer – whether it was Mrs Adams or Gough – must have known that he or she would be one of our two prime suspects, because nobody else could have done it.'

'Whereas if Jordan Gough had been hit by a car, or shot by a sniper, the murderer could have been anybody in Whitebridge – or from even further afield,' said Beresford, catching on.

'So why would either of them take the risk?' Crane asked.

'This whole investigation could go tits up,' Beresford said gloomily.

Yes, Crane agreed silently, and he was thinking that the magic circle was already starting to come apart.

It was half-past ten when Paniatowski got home. She had expected that everyone would have already gone to bed by then, and was surprised to see that though the upstairs was in darkness, the downstairs was still brilliantly – maybe even excessively – illuminated.

The minor mystery was explained when she was met by Louisa at the front door.

'Why are you burning so much electricity, girl?' Paniatowski asked, trying to keep her tone as light as the hallway was. 'Are you trying to ruin me?'

'I wanted it to be welcoming, Mum,' Louisa said. 'Why don't you come on through to the kitchen?'

What Paniatowski really wanted to do was go to bed, but she was too tired to argue, so she followed her beloved adopted daughter down the corridor and into the back room.

'Sit down, Mum,' Louisa said, with a breeziness which was very obviously forced.

Paniatowski sat, and looked around her. The two of them had spent so much time in this kitchen over the years, she thought. It was here that she had inexpertly made cakes – most of which had stubbornly refused to rise – for little Louisa. Here that they had had their discussions – some might call them arguments – about Louisa joining the police instead of going to university. And now here they were again – a knackered chief inspector and a bright young cadet with her whole future ahead of her.

'I've made you cabbage rolls,' Louisa said.

'You shouldn't have,' Paniatowski protested. 'You have enough to do already.'

'I wanted to make them,' Louisa said.

'I'm not hungry,' Paniatowski told her.

'So what was the last thing you ate – and when did you eat it?' Louisa demanded.

Paniatowski thought about it. 'I'm not quite sure,' she admitted.

'You must eat *something*,' Louisa insisted.

Behind her, the oven pinged. Louisa opened it and took out the dish of cabbage rolls. She transferred them swiftly and efficiently to a plate, and placed the plate in front of her mother.

'Just eat one,' she pleaded.

As the aroma of the cabbage rolls rose and seeped into Paniatowski's nostrils, she discovered not only that she was hungry, but that she was starving. She sliced into one of the rolls and popped some into her mouth. As the mixture of cabbage, ground sirloin, rice and mushrooms teased her taste-buds, she felt herself start to relax.

She had been a very young girl when she left her homeland, and had spent most of her life in Whitebridge, where Lancashire hotpot and meat pies were considered part of an essential food group, and tripe and onions was regarded as a gourmet treat. And yet Polish food like this could still induce a feeling of well-being in her that no other cuisine could.

Which, of course, was why, on this night of all nights, Louisa had chosen to cook it for her.

'You've heard, haven't you?' she asked.

'Heard what?' Louisa asked innocently.

'That I've cocked things up.'

'I've heard you've made an arrest.'

Yes, she had, but George Baxter had been quite right that it was too late. Jordan Gough had asked for help, and she had not taken him seriously. She'd told herself that the reason she had done nothing was not because of personal dislike, but because it had seemed improbable that anyone had been trying to kill him. Yes, that *was* what she told herself, but she was no longer completely convinced. Nor would many other people be, so arresting his murderer would not be enough, and even catching Tom Crawley's murderer, too – assuming that was possible – would not save her.

She looked down her plate, and discovered that despite her earlier protests, she had polished off all the cabbage rolls.

'Thank you for this, Louisa,' she said.

'No need to thank me,' her daughter told her. 'It's the least I can do for my dear old mum.'

Dear *old* mum!

'When I arrived at the crime scene, yesterday, this young bobby rushed forward and opened the car door for me,' she told Louisa.

'So what?'

'I was annoyed at the time, but I didn't quite know why. Now I think I do. What got my goat was that he opened the door for me not because I was a chief inspector, and not even because I was a *female* chief inspector – but because I was old enough to be his mother. How awful is that?'

'It's not awful at all,' Louisa said. 'For heaven's sake, don't go writing yourself off yet. You've still got a good ten or fifteen years' policing left in you.'

Ten or fifteen years! She knew Louisa was trying to make her feel better, but it just wasn't working. The girl was right, of course, looking at it objectively. Anything beyond that and she would be keeping her warrant card next to her old-age pension book. Even so, ten or fifteen years! – it seemed like an awfully short time.

But that was all irrelevant, anyway. A few days earlier, it would have been possible to talk about another ten or fifteen years. Not anymore – not after the Jordan Gough murder.

She probably wouldn't be dismissed from the force, but it would be made quite plain to her that she had no alternative but to resign.

What would she do then?

She could get a fairly high-level job in security easily enough, but that would mean moving away from Whitebridge to some-where much bigger, like Manchester – or even London. And though this was nothing but a former mill town – covered in over a hundred years of industrial grime and struggling to find a role in a changing world it still did not quite understand – she knew it would break her heart to go.

'You'll get through this, Mum,' Louisa said.

'Course I will, love,' Paniatowski agreed.

But neither of them really believed it.

7TH MAY 1981

# EIGHTEEN

Distant thunder had been rolling ominously for most of the night, and Paniatowski's bedroom had occasionally been lit by the pale-yellow glow of lightning searing its way through the helpless sky.

Now it was morning, and threatening black clouds hung overhead. As Paniatowski was driving to work, it started to rain. At first, it was just a gentle drizzle – no more than a prelude of the trouble to come – but by the time she arrived at police headquarters, the full fury of the storm had finally reached Whitebridge, and the skies were emptying.

She dashed towards the back entrance of the station, her briefcase held over her head for protection, and as she dodged the newly formed puddles, she couldn't help recalling that this was just the sort of weather in which the doomed heroes of tragic fiction met their sticky ends.

Arthur Gough looked as rough as Paniatowski felt.

'I didn't sleep at all last night,' he said, reading her expression.

'Before we begin, Mr Gough, I should remind you that you're entitled to have a solicitor present,' Paniatowski said.

'I have no money,' Gough said. 'My brother arranged matters so that I was constantly in need of a handout. I was like a dog, begging for its supper, each and every day.'

'If you can't afford a solicitor, one will be provided for you,' Paniatowski said.

'Legal aid,' Gough said, spitting out the words as if they were a curse. 'Jordan always says – always said – that if something is free, it's not worth having.'

'Jordan is dead,' Paniatowski pointed out, 'and it's time to come out from under his shadow. Let us get you a solicitor.'

Arthur Gough folded his arms decisively. 'I'm done with taking charity,' he said.

Paniatowski sighed. 'All right, if that's the way you want to play it. Mrs Adams says you've recently been to Brazil. Is that true?'

'Yes.'

'Where did you go?'

'Manaus. It's a city in the Amazon jungle.'

'And why did you go there?'

Gough laughed bitterly. 'Do you want the reason I was *supposed* to be there, or the reason I was *actually* there?' he asked.

'Both,' Paniatowski told him.

'The supposed reason was that Jordan was thinking of importing Brazil nuts – which is insane, because there's already a well-established market and supply chain, and any newcomer who tried to muscle in would be crushed like a bug.'

'And the real reason?'

'One of Jordan's little games was to find an excuse to take me away from my wife and children at times of celebration. He's sent me to all kinds of places – Coventry, Cornwall, Glasgow – but this was my wife's fortieth birthday, which was a really big event, so he wanted me as far away from it as possible. I think the reason he chose Manaus was because he thought that somewhere in the middle of the Amazon jungle was bound to be unpleasant.'

'And was it?'

'It was hot and sticky, and there seemed to be thousands of biting insects, but I didn't have anything like as bad a time as he imagined I would. I considered that a victory – only a small one, you understand, but in my position, you take what you can get.'

'Forgive me, Mr Gough, but I'm still finding the whole idea of Jordan sending you to Brazil as part of a spiteful game rather difficult to swallow,' Paniatowski said.

'After everything you've learned about him so far, you shouldn't have any difficulty at all,' Arthur Gough told her. 'His whole life was powered by a sense of grievance and the urge to strike back for what the world had done to him. And the closer you were to him, the more he wanted to hurt you.'

'What did you do in Manaus?' Paniatowski asked.

'I went to a couple of meetings with Brazil-nut producers, but they had no real interest in dealing with me, especially on the terms Jordan had instructed me to offer.'

'Did you buy anything while you were in Manaus?' Paniatowski asked.

'I don't know what you mean.'

'Did you, for example, buy the powder we found in your house – perhaps under the impression that it was some kind of tribal medicine?'

'Did I buy the poison that killed Jordan, you mean,' Arthur Gough said angrily.

'Yes,' Paniatowski agreed. 'That is what I mean.'

'You're making a big mistake treating me like this,' Arthur Gough said, in a voice that was almost a scream. 'When you let me go – and you *will* have to let me go – you'd better look out, because once I get my hands on Jordan's money, I'll make you pay for the way you've humiliated me.'

A look of horror came to his eyes, and he covered his face with his hands.

'Oh God, what's happened to me?' he moaned. 'Jordan's turned me into himself. It's his final revenge.'

'Jordan's dead,' Paniatowski said. 'You can't blame him. It's time to take some personal responsibility.'

Arthur Gough lowered his hands, and she could see that he was crying.

'I'm sorry I spoke to you like that,' he said. 'But I didn't kill Jordan. You have to believe me. *Please* believe me – I'm begging you!'

'If you're not responsible, how do you explain the fact that you left just before Jordan took the poison? Because on the face of it, it looks very much as if you wanted to get as far away as possible before he went into his death throes.'

'I left because he ordered me to leave,' Arthur Gough said.

'The problem is, the only person who could confirm that is Jordan, and he's dead.'

'So what are you suggesting? That when I saw Jordan was about to take the poison, I said I had to leave?'

'You must admit, that is a possibility.'

'Do you seriously think I would have dared to tell Jordan I

was leaving?' Arthur Gough asked. 'I didn't *want* to be there, but I went anyway – because he *told* me to – and I would only leave when he told me I could leave.'

The door opened, and Crane entered.

'This is from the lab,' he told Paniatowski. 'You said you wanted to see it as soon as possible.'

Paniatowski scanned it, then looked across the table at Gough.

'Arthur Gough . . .' she began, in a toneless, official voice.

'Oh Christ, no!' Gough sobbed.

'. . . I am arresting you for the murder of Jordan Gough . . .'

'Please, don't!'

'. . . you do not have to say anything, but anything you do say may be taken down and used in evidence against you.'

Although she still had another twelve travel agents to visit, Meadows had almost reached the point at which she felt that if she saw one more poster of smiling young people on a beach, her head would explode.

This one was called Sunshine Travel, and unlike the others she'd visited, it was not in a prime commercial location, but on a side street which could almost have been called an alley. It was smaller than the others inside, too, and though the middle-aged woman behind the counter had a badge pinned to her ample bosom which announced that she was the supervisor, there didn't seem to be any other staff for her to supervise.

Meadows delivered her usual spiel, and instead of replying that she'd never seen the man in the photograph before, the 'supervisor' said, 'Yes, he was a very regular customer. I'm going to miss him.'

'Are you sure it's him?' Meadows asked.

'Oh yes, I'm not likely to forget someone who spent as much money here as he did, now am I?'

'So when you saw in the paper that he'd been murdered, why didn't you inform the police?' Meadows wondered.

The woman looked at her blankly. 'I saw no reason to,' she said. 'I bet the supermarket where he did his grocery shopping didn't contact you, either.'

'That's a good point,' Meadows conceded. 'What did he buy from you?'

'He bought airline tickets,' the woman said. 'To Rio de Janeiro. That's in Brazil.'

'I know it is,' Meadows said.

'But it's not the capital, as many people seem to think. The actual capital is Brasilia, which is in the highlands, and . . .'

'Do you have any record of his transactions?' Meadows interrupted.

The woman looked vaguely offended, as if she suspected the sergeant was questioning her competence.

'Of course I have records,' she said. 'I'm famous for my meticulous record-keeping. Would you like to see them?'

'If you wouldn't mind.'

The woman stood up and walked over to her filing cabinet.

As Meadows watched her, the word 'Brazil' kept bouncing around and around her brain.

Arthur Gough had been to Brazil, the poison used to kill Jordan Gough had originated from Brazil, and now, it seemed, the victim of a quite distinct murder also had a Brazil connection. It could all be a coincidence, of course, but the longer she was a detective, the more Meadows learned to distrust coincidence.

The travel agent returned with a buff-coloured folder. 'Here you are,' she said. 'I think you'll find it all in order.'

Meadows read through the file.

'Mr Crawley seems to have travelled to Brazil about once every six weeks,' she said.

'That's right,' the travel agent agreed.

'And if I've got this right, he also booked three other tickets, one for Iris Borges, another for Sara Espindola, and a third for Iris Lopes.'

'Yes.'

'Yet though he always bought a return ticket for himself, he bought one-way tickets – Rio de Janeiro to Manchester – for the women. Have I got that right?'

'You have.'

'But in order to keep coming to England, they'd have to keep returning to Brazil, wouldn't they?'

'I suppose they must have.'

'So how did they get there?'

'I imagine they flew.'

'And they didn't book their tickets with you?'

'No, definitely not.'

'Didn't you think that was odd?'

The travel agent was beginning to look distinctly uncomfortable. 'I suppose you could say it was a *little* odd,' she conceded.

'But you didn't ask Mr Crawley about it?'

'No.'

'Why not?'

The travel agent suddenly seemed to find the backs of her own hands fascinating. 'It didn't occur to me,' she mumbled.

'I don't like being pissed about,' Meadows said.

The travel agent looked up. 'I beg your pardon!'

She was doing her best to appear outraged, but only came across as sounding scared.

'I don't like being pissed about,' Meadows repeated. 'You're an intelligent woman, and you do keep meticulous records. It must have occurred to you.'

'The business has been going through a very rough time,' the travel agent confessed. 'To be honest, about the only thing that was keeping us afloat was Mr Crawley's custom, and I didn't want to annoy him by seeming too inquisitive.'

Which was probably why Crawley had chosen to use a back-street firm tottering on the verge of bankruptcy, rather than one of the bigger companies on the High Street where he could probably have negotiated himself a better deal, Meadows thought.

Jack Crane would later claim that he was in the Prince Albert Bar of the Royal Victoria Hotel that early afternoon because that was where his gut feelings had told him he *should* be. That was a lie, told to spare him the ridicule that one of his colleagues would undoubtedly have heaped on him if he'd told the truth. The simple fact was that he felt a sudden craving for an extremely dry sherry – a taste he had acquired during his years at Oxford – and had chosen the Prince Albert Bar both because it had the best selection of sherries in Whitebridge, and because in a posh place like that, there was virtually no chance of running into professional Northerner Colin Beresford, who considered pints of best bitter to be the only appropriate drink for a man.

He was savouring his schooner of amontillado when the door opened and Giles Hatton walked in.

Crane felt his heart sink. He had no wish to talk to the bloody man, especially since – as was evident from his gait – Hatton had already had quite a lot to drink. Unfortunately, Hatton had spotted him, and made straight for him.

'Hello, Jack,' he slurred. 'Well, this is a surprise. What's a humble copper like you doing in a fancy place like this?' And then, without leaving even a second's gap for Crane to answer his question, he continued, 'I've just come away from a very successful – and very liquid – business lunch.'

'That's nice for you,' Crane said, and, with some regret, knocked back – rather than savoured – the remainder of his sherry. 'Anyway, I'd love to stay and chat with a fascinating man like you, but unfortunately I've got a previous appointment.'

'As a matter of fact, I've been hoping to run into you for a couple of days,' said Hatton, making it obvious that the sarcasm had gone right above his head. 'Lemme . . . lemme buy you another drink, Jack.'

'I really do have to go,' Crane said.

But Hatton had no intention of letting him leave yet.

'You really upset me the other day,' he said. 'You suggested I was some kind of pervert.'

Crane looked longingly at the door. Hatton had something he wanted to get off his chest, and Crane realized that if he tried to leave now, the other man would almost certainly try to stop him. Of course, it would be easy enough to push him away, but given the state he was in, Hatton would probably collapse onto the floor. And Crane really didn't want that kind of scene.

'You must have misunderstood me, Giles,' he said. 'I never called you a pervert.'

'Not in so many words, no,' Hatton admitted. 'But when I said that the girl I saw coming out of Tom Crawley's flat was probably nothing more than a whore, you looked at me like I was a maggot.'

That's because you *are* a maggot, Crane thought.

'As I explained at the time, you may have been right about

what she was, but since I wasn't there myself, I couldn't possibly know one way or the other,' he said, in a placatory voice.

'Like a maggot,' Hatton repeated. 'But it turns out that I was quite right – and you were quite wrong.'

'What are you talking about?'

'I'm a member of the Excelsior Club,' Hatton said. 'Have you been there?' He shook his head. 'No, of course you haven't, because it's a very exclusive establishment.'

'It's a seedy nightclub,' Crane said.

If Hatton had been paying attention, he would probably have been offended by the remark, but he was way past that stage.

'Anyway, they have hostesses upstairs for any gentleman who feels like some entertainment,' he continued. 'I don't normally use the service myself – I can usually talk most girls I fancy into my bed without having to pay for it – but I'd been working hard, and I thought, "Why not treat yourself?"'

'Is there some natural conclusion to this tale, or do you just intend to drone on forever?' Crane wondered.

'So I went upstairs, and there she was – the girl I'd seen in the doorway to Tom Crawley's apartment.'

'Are you sure?'

'Yes, I'm sure. I never forget a nice pair of tits.'

'Did you ask her about it?'

Hatton laughed. 'Course I didn't. I wasn't up there to talk. I asked her name – which was Beatriz – and then I set about getting my money's worth. Anyway, the point is, I was quite right, and you, Mr-First-Class-Honours, Mr Smart-Arse-Detective-Constable, were quite wrong.'

'I wouldn't talk quite so loudly if I were you,' Crane advised.

'And why would that be?'

'Well, that reporter might have overheard you.'

'What reporter?' Hatton asked, starting to sound alarmed.

'That reporter,' Crane said, pointing to a man in a pin-striped suit who he'd never seen before.

'If he's a reporter, he's only from the local rag, surely,' Hatton said, and though he was attempting to appear unconcerned, his words were framed with a jagged edge of unease.

'No, as a matter of fact, the man doesn't work for the *Evening Telegraph* at all,' Crane replied. 'He's in Whitebridge because he's visiting his mother, but his base is in London. He's got a job writing a gossip column for some glossy magazine. I think it's called the *Tat*-something.'

'The *Tatler*?' Hatton asked, his horror growing.

'Yes, that's right.'

'But Cassandra reads the *Tatler*! And – Jesus – so do all her friends! Do you think he heard what I was saying?'

'From the way he turned his head in our direction when you started talking about prostitutes, I'd say I'm almost sure he did,' Crane lied.

Hatton put his head in his hands. 'Oh God, what I am going to do?'

'You could try praying,' Crane said helpfully.

There was an air of anticipation in Paniatowski's office – a feeling that, finally, they had stopped banging their heads against a brick wall and might actually be getting somewhere.

'According to the tickets issued by Sunshine Travel, the same three women took a flight from Rio de Janeiro to Manchester once every six weeks,' Paniatowski said. 'Does anyone think it really *was* the same three women?'

'No,' Beresford said, speaking for the rest of the team. 'It was three different women using the same three fake passports.'

'And why do we think they were brought to England?'

'To work as prostitutes,' Meadows said.

'Now we know that one of these women was seen in the doorway of Tom Crawley's apartment by Giles Hatton, and that she seemed to be there against her will,' Paniatowski continued. 'We also know, again according to Hatton, that the same woman is working as a prostitute in the Excelsior Club.'

'Which was owned by the late, unlamented Jordan Gough,' Meadows pointed out.

'And let's not forget that José Cardoza, who was Gough's right-hand man, ran a prostitution ring in Brazil,' Paniatowski said. 'Do we think that Cardoza was helping to run this prostitution ring, too?'

'Given that it operates out of Gough's club, it would be surprising if he wasn't,' Jack Crane said.

'Now, the big question,' Paniatowski said heavily. 'Does all this have anything to do with Tom Crawley's murder?'

'Again, it would be surprising if it didn't,' Beresford said. 'We now know that Crawley and Cardoza were probably running an illegal racket together, and Cardoza is known to be a violent criminal.'

'So what was Cardoza's motive?' Paniatowski asked.

'It could be one of a number of things,' Beresford said. 'Crawley could have got greedy and demanded a bigger cut, for example.'

'Crawley might have been creaming money off the top,' Meadows suggested.

'Or possibly Cardoza may have decided to cut out the middle man and take over the recruiting in Brazil himself,' Crane chipped in.

'You can forget that last one,' Paniatowski said. 'Cardoza is wanted for murder in Brazil. He wouldn't dare go back there. Otherwise, I agree with you. Cardoza is our prime suspect. In fact, I'd put it even more strongly than that – he's the only one that makes any sense.'

'But we can't prove a damn thing,' Meadows said. 'We've no witnesses and no forensics, and he'll have set up an alibi we can't break, like the one he had on the night Jordan Gough was murdered.'

'That's a point,' Crane said.

'What is?'

'Why did he *need* an alibi for the night of Gough's murder, when we now know that Arthur Gough was the killer?'

'Shall we try and avoid getting distracted?' Paniatowski suggested, sounding irritated. 'In case you've forgotten, it's Tom Crawley's death we're investigating at the moment.'

'Fair enough,' Crane said.

'Do any of you have an idea about how we might advance the investigation?' Paniatowski asked.

'I think it might be a good idea to talk to this girl – Beatriz,' Jack Crane said.

'And how do we go about that?' Beresford asked. 'Do you think we can just roll up to the front door of the club, and say we want to question Beatriz?'

'No, that wouldn't work,' Paniatowski said. 'The second we make it official, whoever is running the club will be on the phone to Spider Markham, and after that, the only words we'd get out of her would be "No comment".'

'Even if they allowed us to speak to her, she wouldn't say anything, because she'd know *they* knew we were questioning her – and were probably listening in to it – and she'd be terrified that if she said something they didn't like, they'd probably do unspeakable things to her after we'd gone,' Meadows said.

'So what's the alternative?' Beresford asked.

'We send someone in pretending to be a client, and he questions Beatriz once they're alone together,' Meadows said.

'It can't be me,' Beresford replied. 'They know who I am, because I was there the other night.'

'They probably would, and even if they didn't, they'd be suspicious of you from the start,' Meadows said.

'Why is that?' Beresford demanded. 'Is it because I'm so obviously just a thick bobby?'

She hadn't meant quite that, but, as a matter of fact, he was not a million miles off the mark, Meadows thought.

'No, no, it's not that at all, sir,' she said aloud. 'It's just that they'd see right away that you're not the kind of man who *ever* needs to pay for a woman.'

Clever! Paniatowski thought, hiding her smile behind her hand.

For his part, Beresford tried not to look too pleased, but the swelling of his chest gave him away.

'Thanks very much,' he said.

'What we need is someone who can act the part of a callow virgin,' Meadows said. 'Do you know anybody like that, Jack?'

Crane nodded. 'I'll do it,' he said.

'Wait a minute,' Paniatowski warned. 'Before you go rushing headlong into this, have you considered the risk?'

'What risk?' Crane asked.

'There's a chance you might get searched going in, so you can't take a radio, or even a whistle, with you. And it doesn't matter how many officers we've got on the street, once you pass through that door, you're on your own.'

'I can handle it,' Crane said firmly.

'We know that at least *one* violent bastard – Cardoza – is involved with this ring, and there may be more. If one of them decides to slit your throat or cave your head in, we'll catch him, and I'll see to it personally that he's banged up forever. But that's not going to be much consolation to you when you're dead.'

'I want to do it,' Crane insisted.

Paniatowski looked at her sergeant for guidance.

'Even the baby of the team has to leave the nest eventually,' Meadows said. 'And I think that if you give Jack the chance, he'll soar like an eagle.'

Paniatowski sighed. 'You're right,' she agreed. 'Fine, Jack, show us what you can do.'

# NINETEEN

The carpet warehouse had two obvious advantages. The first was that it overlooked the Excelsior Club, and the second was that it had a back entrance, through which Paniatowski and Meadows had entered, unobserved, just before night fell.

Now, looking out through the narrow window, they had a clear view of the entrance to the club, illuminated by the streetlights, and of the bulky man in a dinner jacket who was standing beside it.

'There he is!' Paniatowski said.

And there he was indeed. Detective Constable Jack Crane – in a new suit, purchased hurriedly from the best tailor in Whitebridge – was approaching the club with an awkward gait.

About ten yards from the club, Crane came a halt, stood indecisively for about half a minute, then crossed over to the opposite side of the road. When he drew level with the Excelsior, he walked straight past the club, though he did keep nervously glancing at it.

'What's he doing?' Paniatowski hissed worriedly.

'He's getting into the part,' Meadows said.

'What does that mean?'

'He's role-playing. It will make things easier for him when he does eventually try to get into the club.'

'Are you sure about that?' Paniatowski asked, unconvinced.

'I'm sure,' Meadows said. 'I'm an expert at role-playing – or at least, Zelda is.'

Ah yes, Zelda, Meadows' alter ego, with her whips and her leather corsets and God alone knew what else.

Crane came into view again, walking in the other direction, and once again he walked past the club.

'Isn't he overdoing it now?' Paniatowski asked anxiously.

'No, not at all,' Meadows assured her. 'He's playing it just right.'

A good nightclub bouncer could handle any trouble that arose with speed and ruthless efficiency, but a *very good* bouncer could spot trouble in advance, and head it off before it ever reached the breaking-bones stage.

Sid Mottershead prided himself that he was at the top of the second category, which was why, as he stood in the doorway of the Excelsior Club, his eyes were constantly scanning the street.

For the last five minutes he had been watching a man who was pacing up and down on the other side of the road.

He was a youngish feller, probably in his mid-twenties, the bouncer thought. And from the way he held himself, it was obvious that he was nervous – very, very nervous.

Another two minutes passed before the young man seemed to find the courage to actually cross the street and approach the club. Even then, when he came to a halt in front of the bouncer, he seemed to be struggling for words.

'Could I . . . could I go in?' he asked.

Mottershead ran his eyes up and down the other man. The suit was new, and a cut above the average, the leather shoes had certainly not been purchased from any High Street chain-store shoe shop in Whitebridge.

'I'm sorry, sir, but this is a private members' club,' the bouncer said.

The young man nodded. 'I know that. But I've got this friend, Giles, and he said that as long as you were willing to pay the membership fee, you were pretty much guaranteed to be accepted.'

'Is the Giles that you're talking about Mr Giles Hatton, by any chance?' Mottershead asked.

The young man nodded with relief. 'Yes, yes, that's right. He told me he came here quite a lot.'

Indeed he did, Mottershead thought. Hatton was a real tosser, who might talk like a gentleman but had the appetite – and manners – of a randy old goat. Still, his money was good, and no doubt this young man's would be too.

'I'll tell you what I'll do for you,' he said, dropping his voice to a confidential tone, though there was no one else there to hear them. 'Slip me a fiver, and I'll introduce you to the manager. Now I'm not promising anything, mind, but he just might agree to let you join.'

'Thank you,' the young man said gratefully.

Mottershead made no move.

'Shall we go in then?' the young man asked, with barely concealed impatience.

'You're forgetting my commission,' the bouncer said.

'Oh course, how stupid of me,' the young man replied. 'You said five pounds, didn't you?'

'Did I? That was a mistake. What I meant was a tenner,' the bouncer said. 'You've no problem with that, have you?'

'Well, I . . .'

'Because if you do have a problem, then maybe we'd just better forget the whole thing.'

'No, that's fine,' the young man said hurriedly.

He took out his wallet and peeled off two five-pound notes from what looked like a pretty thick stash.

'Can we go inside now?' he asked.

'Yes,' the bouncer agreed, wishing he'd asked for fifteen pounds, 'we can go inside now.'

'He's in,' Meadows said.

They'd discussed the matter thoroughly – looked at it from all angles – and decided that infiltrating someone into the club was the only way to achieve their aims, Paniatowski reminded herself.

And the operation was going as planned – which was a good thing.

Yet there was a part of her which wished it hadn't worked – that the bouncer on the door had seen right through Crane's act and sent him away with a flea in his ear.

She had never put any member of her team in this kind of danger before, and the fact that Crane had accepted the risk, and gone in willingly – almost like a lamb to the slaughter – didn't make her feel even the slightest bit better.

Maybe Louisa – who was only a few years younger than Jack – might find herself in a similar situation soon, because, like Crane, she would jump at the chance to prove herself.

'Relax, boss,' Meadows said.

'I don't want anything to happen to Jack,' Paniatowski said. 'This will be my last case, before they make me resign, and I don't want to leave the force with the knowledge that it was my decision that sent a young man to his death.'

'He'll be fine,' Meadows said. 'Look at me. I was undercover for nearly a year, and I'm still here.'

It should have been comforting, but it wasn't, because she was the indestructible Kate Meadows, and Jack was . . . Jack was a boy, and she should never have sent him in there.

Gerald Dodd stood in the cramped foyer, watching the nervous young man fill in the application form.

Dodd was not a violent man by nature. That was not to say he didn't think violence had any part to play in his world – in many cases it was a handy shortcut to achieving your aims – but he felt no urge to become directly involved himself, which was why he employed muscle-bound thugs like the gorilla on the door.

It was fair to say he'd had a varied career, one that included car theft, burglary and blackmail, but he had never enjoyed any of it as much as he enjoyed being the manager of the Excelsior Club.

The young man had completed his application, and handed it over for inspection.

'Peter Smith,' Dodd read. 'Now there's a novelty, because most of our members are called *John* Smith. Is it your real name?'

'Well, yes, it is,' said the young man, blushing. 'I didn't know we were allowed to use false names.'

'Are you related to Sir William Smith, the Whitebridge brewery owner?' the manager asked.

'No, I . . . He isn't my father, if that's what you're thinking. In fact, I've never heard of him,' replied the young man, turning even redder.

'Well, this all seems in order,' Dodd said. 'Have you got your membership fee handy?'

Crane reached into his wallet.

'Fifty pounds seems like a lot of money,' he said.

'Well, this is an exclusive club,' Dodd told him. 'Of course, if you can't afford it, or would rather not pay it . . .'

'No, no, that's fine,' said Crane.

He fumbled with his wallet, but finally managed to detach the necessary fifty pounds.

The manager first counted the money and then held it up to the light to check that it was real.

'So now you're a member, Mr Smith,' he said. 'This calls for a celebration. Why don't you go into the bar and order yourself a bottle of champagne? Or perhaps you'd prefer to pay a visit to our gaming room.'

'I . . . err . . . I don't gamble at all, and I'm really not much of a drinker,' Crane stuttered.

'I see.' The manager smiled knowingly. 'In that case, perhaps you would like to go upstairs and meet one of the young ladies.'

'Yes, yes, I think I would like that.'

'I believe that Helga, who comes from Germany, is free at the moment,' the manager said. 'If you'd like to follow me . . .'

'No, no, I don't want her,' the young man protested.

'I can assure you she is a charming, well-endowed young lady who is regularly checked for infection by a qualified doctor,' the manager said, his voice hardening.

'Oh, I've nothing against Helga,' Crane said quickly. 'I'm sure she's charming. It's just that Giles – that's my friend, Giles Hatton . . .'

'Yes, we know Mr Hatton quite well here.'

'He said there was a girl called Beatriz that I really must try.'

'Let me explain the way things work here, Mr Smith,' Dodd said firmly. 'Old and valued clients can choose who they see, but new boys like you are expected to take what they're offered. I promise you, you will like Helga. In fact, you'll probably ask for her next time you come.'

'It has to be Beatriz,' Crane said obstinately.

It wasn't a good idea to give in to the punters, Dodd told himself, because they started to think they were in charge, rather than you. On the other hand, this little plonker was Sir William Smith's son, and seemed terrified at the idea his father might find out where he'd been, so he would almost definitely be open to a little gentle blackmail once he'd done the dirty deed.

'I wouldn't normally bend the rules, but since it's you, Peter, I think I can arrange it,' he said.

Crane looked around the cramped lobby – as if to check that no one was watching – then reached into his inside pocket for his wallet. 'Do I pay you now, or after I've finished?' he asked.

Dodd clamped his hand on the young man's arm, and forced it back towards his chest.

'Listen to me, sunshine,' he hissed, 'you don't pay us anything.'

'But I thought . . .'

'If you enjoy the young lady's company, then of course it would only be right to give her a present before you go. But you give it to *her* – not to anybody else. Do you understand what I'm saying?'

'Yes, I think so,' Crane replied. 'Do you think you could let go of my arm now, because it's really starting to hurt.'

'Of course,' the manager agreed, relaxing his grip. 'By the way, in case you're not clear about what sort of gift you should leave behind, I'd suggest anything less than twenty-five pounds would be considered a pretty poor show.'

The girl was sitting on the bed when Crane entered the room. She was wearing a dress which looked as if it could be shed at a moment's notice, and dark stockings. She smiled at him, but it was the sort of smile a woman might produce only if she was frightened of the consequences of not smiling.

'I'm Jack,' he said. 'Are you Beatriz?'

'Yes, I am,' the girl replied.

Well, she seems to speak some English, let's hope she can read it as well, Crane thought, as he handed her his notebook, opened at the right page.

The girl read what he had written.

I AM A POLICEMAN. I WANT TO HELP YOU. CAN THEY HEAR WHAT WE SAY OUTSIDE?

Beatriz nodded, and handed the notebook back to him.

'I don't want to have sex with you just yet,' Crane said, for the benefit of the hidden microphones. 'Would it be all right if I just sat down here on the chair and looked at you?'

'Yes,' the girl said, 'you can do what you like for half an hour, but then you must go.'

Crane wrote, ARE YOU BEING HELD HERE AGAINST YOUR WILL?

The girl studied the notebook, and replied, I DONT UNDERSTOOD WHAT YOU SAY.

Crane thought for a moment, then wrote, ARE YOU A PRISONER HERE, OR CAN YOU LEAVE WHEN YOU WANT TO?

I AM PRISONER, the girl wrote.

AND DO THEY TREAT YOU BADLY? Crane asked.

THEY HIT ME IF I DO NOT DO WHAT THEY SAY, the girl answered.

He'd heard more than enough to justify a police raid, Crane decided. All he had to do now was to make the prearranged signal, which was to switch the lights on and off three times in rapid succession.

He felt a sudden surge of relief, and realized that he must have been more worried than he'd thought he was.

Well, there was no need to worry now, because the whole thing was all over, bar the shouting.

He walked over to the window and drew back the thick orange curtain which covered it.

And that was when he saw that the whole thing wasn't all over at all.

Meadows lowered the night-vision binoculars, and turned to Paniatowski.

'We may have a problem,' she said ominously.

'What kind of problem?' Paniatowski asked, as her stomach began churning over.

Meadows handed her the binoculars. 'Just take a look at the top floor,' she said.

Paniatowski raised the glasses and did a sweeping search. 'Three of the windows are boarded up,' she said.

'Of course, they could just be store rooms,' Meadows said, though she did not sound entirely convinced.

Yes, they could be, Paniatowski thought – or they could be the prostitutes' rooms, in which case the boarding was there to deny them any kind of access to the outside world.

But it would be denying Crane access, too!

'Do you think we should go in now?' she asked Meadows.

'We could,' the sergeant said cautiously, 'but without the signal from Jack, we don't have any justification for raiding the place.'

'We'll find all the evidence we need inside,' Paniatowski said.

'You can't be sure of that,' Meadows cautioned. 'They may have moved Beatriz on by now. And even if we do find something, the evidence will probably be thrown out of court because the search was illegal.'

She was right, Paniatowski thought. If they went in now, they might ruin their chances of saving all the girls who'd already been trafficked from Brazil, and those who might be trafficked in the future. But if they delayed, Crane could well suffer the same fate as Tom Crawley.

'How long has Jack been in there?' she asked.

'About twenty minutes,' Meadows told her.

'We'll wait another ten, and if Crane hasn't found a way to contact us by then, we're going in.'

Crane stared at the boarded-up window, and wondered what the bloody hell he should do next.

If he went downstairs and told the manager he had finished, he'd probably be allowed to leave.

But that would mean deserting the girl, and if anything happened to her between him leaving the club and returning mob-handed – and it could, easily, if the management suspected something was wrong – then he knew that he would never forgive himself.

He could try and smuggle Beatriz out of the club with him, but that sort of thing only worked in romantic novels.

Well, then, there was nothing for it but to stick to the original plan.

He tapped the boarded-up window gently with his knuckles. It was only hardboard – but it was thick hardboard. If he'd had a claw hammer, he could have prised it off in less than a minute, but foolishly, he had not thought to bring one with him.

He looked around the room for a suitable substitute, even though he knew before he even began that DIY kits were not a common feature of prostitutes' bedrooms.

He reached into his pocket, and pulled out his Swiss army knife.

A Swiss army knife!

What kind of weapon is that? he asked himself.

The only one you have, you idiot, another part of his brain answered.

He forced the strongest blade on his knife between the hardboard and the window frame.

'What are you doing?' Beatriz asked, alarmed.

Crane raised his finger to his lips to signal that she should be silent, but her panic was increasing by the second.

'What are you doing?' she asked for a second time.

'Don't worry,' Crane told her soothingly, aware that microphones were probably picking all this up. 'Everything is going to be all right, Beatriz.'

One corner of the hardboard was free of the window frame, but there were at least nine other nails still holding them together.

'They will punish me for this,' Beatriz moaned.

'It's not you who's doing it,' Crane said, prising a second nail free of its hole. 'It's me.'

'They will hurt me,' Beatriz said. 'That will hurt me very bad. And they will hurt you, too.'

If they *were* monitoring this, they would know by now that something had gone seriously wrong, Crane thought, attacking another nail.

\*     \*     \*

Meadows had the binoculars trained on the upper windows of the Excelsior Club. Paniatowski was pacing the floor of the warehouse, and occasionally taking a deep drag on the cigarette she was holding in her right hand.

'How long has it been since I said we'd wait ten minutes?' Paniatowski asked.

Meadows glanced down at her watch. 'It's been five minutes, boss,' she replied.

Paniatowski gasped. 'Are you sure it's been as little as that?'

'Yes, boss.'

Christ, it felt like a century!

Crane heard the sound of someone running along the corridor, and knew he was in deep shit.

Beatriz was sitting on the bed, with her head in her hands, sobbing, 'They are coming,' she gasped. 'They are coming.'

'Hide behind the bed,' Crane said. 'I will protect you.'

Brave words, he thought – but he was not entirely sure that he could even protect himself.

The door burst open, and Sid Mottershead, the bouncer he'd bribed earlier, was standing there.

'What the bloody hell do you think you're doing?' Mottershead demanded.

There seemed to be little point in continuing to pretend he was a green young punter, Crane decided.

'I'm a police officer, and if you've got any sense, you'll turn right round and walk out of here,' he said.

'You little shit!' Mottershead bellowed. 'You got in here under false pretences. You've made me look a complete fool.'

'Seriously, with what's going to happen in a few minutes, being made to look a fool should be the least of your worries at the moment,' Crane said.

Now that really was clever, he thought, the moment the words were out of his mouth. Acting like a smart-arse and antagonizing a bouncer – who hurts people for a living – was almost a stroke of genius.

Mottershead rushed across the room, and before he'd even come to a complete standstill was throwing a punch at the detective constable. Crane had already dropped his knife, and now he quickly sidestepped, and counter-attacked with a blow to Mottershead's jaw.

It was a very good punch – better, even, than the one which had won him the university middleweight boxing championship.

His knuckles felt as if they'd been struck by an express train, and the impact of the blow sent reverberations through his whole being.

But it had even more effect on Mottershead. His feet left the ground, and his body flew backwards for several feet, before landing with a sickening thud on the floor.

He'd never have launched such a careless attack if he hadn't been in a blinding rage, Crane thought, massaging his bruised knuckles with the palm of his uninjured hand, so maybe antagonizing him had been the smart move after all.

There was no sound of anyone else approaching, and Mottershead – still lying on the floor and groaning softly to himself – would be out of action for at least a few more minutes. Crane bent down and retrieved his Swiss army knife, and attacked another nail in the hardboard.

He had prised two more nails free when the noise behind him – a series of grunts, some of which were high-pitched, others which sounded much deeper – distracted him.

He turned around. Mottershead was still on the floor, but now Beatriz had stood up and was kicking him in the groin.

'He hurt me, and now I hurt him,' she said, by way of explanation.

That seemed fair enough, Crane thought.

He returned to his task. Half the hardboard was now free of the window frame, and that should be enough. Ignoring the throbbing in his knuckles, he took hold of the freed part of the hardboard with both hands and pulled it away from the window. For a couple of seconds, the hardboard creaked in protest, and then it came away so suddenly that Crane almost lost his balance and joined Mottershead on the floor.

He turned around, stepped over Mottershead, and walked over to the light switch. He switched off the lights, counted to three, then switched them on again. He did it twice more – switch off the lights, count to three, switch them on again;

switch off the lights, count to three, switch them on again.

'That's it!' Meadows said. 'That's the signal.'

Paniatowski flicked a switch on her radio. 'Go, go, go!' she said – and noticed that her hands were trembling.

A dozen police officers – some in uniform and some in plain clothes – appeared out of nowhere and sprinted towards the club. The door had been locked and bolted the moment Gerald Dodd had realized that something had gone seriously wrong in Beatriz's room, but the hand-held battering ram, wielded by the anchorman of the police tug-of-war team, soon reduced it to splinters and sawdust.

Dodd stood at the far end of the lobby, doing his best to look like an outraged respectable businessman.

'Do you have a warrant to enter these premises?' he demanded.

'Nope,' said Colin Beresford happily.

'Then I must protest in the strongest possible terms. This is a respectable business and . . .'

'No, it's not,' Beresford interrupted him. 'It's a sleazy knocking shop. And if I was you, pal, I'd keep my mouth buttoned in case I said something that might be used against me.'

Beatriz was sitting on the bed again, and Crane was looking out of the window.

'What is happening?' the girl asked.

'The place is being raided.'

'Then I am safe?'

'Yes, you're safe.'

'And José cannot hurt me anymore?'

'No, he can't.'

Beatriz stood up, walked over to Crane, and flung her arms around him.

'You are my hero,' she said into his chest.

How about that? Crane thought. I've never been anybody's hero before.

\*    \*    \*

Helga had blonde hair and wide, inviting eyes. An earlier, more judgemental, generation might have called her a brazen hussy, and that, Paniatowski suspected, was part of her appeal to the men who'd 'visited' her at the Excelsior Club.

'I am not used to being treated in this manner,' she said, in carefully enunciated English. 'In Hamburg, where I usually conduct my business, prostitution is regarded as a profession like any other.'

'So what are you doing in Whitebridge?' Paniatowski asked.

'It is a working holiday. I stay at the Excelsior Club for two months, and then I will go and see some of your sights – the Lake District, Stratford-on-Avon and Windsor Castle, for example.'

'Are you free to come and go as you chose?'

'Within reason, yes I am.'

'What does "within reason" mean?'

'I am expected to fulfil the terms of my contract, which means I must be present and available in the club in the evening.'

'You have a *contract*?'

'Naturally, I have a contract. I would never have left West Germany without one.'

'Tell me more,' Paniatowski encouraged.

'There was an advertisement in a newspaper in Hamburg for temporary work at the club, and I applied.'

'Who else works with you?'

'There is a Scottish girl called Rosie. Sometimes, when we are not working, we go out together.'

'What about Beatriz?'

'Who?'

'The girl from South America.'

'I did not see her.'

'And why was that?'

'She did not leave her room.'

'Do you mean, she *didn't* leave her room, or she *wasn't allowed* to leave her room?'

Helga shrugged. 'I did not ask, and I was not told.'

'Was Rosie on a temporary contract as well?'

Helga laughed. 'No, Rosie is a common whore, not a career

woman. She is what you call a freelance, which means she was paid by the customer. But she, too, was soon to leave.'

'And why was that?'

'Because there are only three rooms, and the club was expecting new mules.'

'New *what*?'

'Mules. That is what they call the girls who come from Brazil. I don't know why they call them that – they certainly don't *look* like donkeys.'

8TH MAY 1981

# TWENTY

Paniatowski had spent a fitful night, tossing and turning in her lonely bed. She told herself it was because of the storm – which had raged all night, sometimes in the distance, like a whispered ugly rumour, sometimes directly overhead, like the roaring of an angry god – but she really knew that it wasn't that at all.

The team had already solved one of the murders they had been presented with – Arthur Gough was in the holding cells, waiting to be transferred to the nearest remand centre. By the end of the day, they would have solved the second, too, because they had Gerald Dodd and José Cardoza in custody, and one or the other was bound to crack eventually, and give them all the evidence they needed to make a second arrest.

And then?

Once it was all over she would hand in her resignation, because there was at least a little dignity in resigning, rather than waiting to be pushed.

She was surprised to find her daughter sitting at the kitchen table, dressed in her civilian clothes.

'I thought you were on the early shift this week,' she said.

'I was,' Louisa agreed, 'but I had a few days' leave coming, and I thought I'd take them now.'

'Why have you done that?' Paniatowski asked.

Louisa shrugged. 'I just felt like it,' she said.

That was a lie, Paniatowski decided. The real reason Louisa had taken her leave was so that she could be around to help her mother deal with the trauma of losing a job that had almost become a part of her.

She took both of Louisa's hands in hers.

'I wish I could be as good a mother to you as you've been a daughter to me,' she said.

For a moment, Louisa's expression froze, and then an awkward grin appeared on her face.

'All we need now is some mournfully sweet strings playing in the background, and we'd have all the makings of a perfect soap opera,' she said.

Paniatowski smiled, sadly. 'And now I've embarrassed you,' she said, 'and I'm very sorry.'

Louisa gazed down at the table. 'Go to work, Mum,' she said. 'Go to work – and give 'em hell!'

This was not the last time she would make this journey, she thought, as she drove towards police headquarters, because detective chief inspectors didn't just disappear overnight. Once her resignation had been accepted, there would be several meetings and de-briefings before the whole process was completed. So it wasn't the last time – but it was the last time it would be of any real importance to anyone.

She switched on the car radio. The disc jockey could have put on any of a thousand records, but the one he had chosen was 'I Will Survive', by Gloria Gaynor.

'Are you taking the piss?' Paniatowski shouted at him, as she reached forward and changed stations.

Beresford, Meadows and Crane were already waiting for her in her office, but there was a notable absence of the enthusiasm – the buzz of excitement – that usually accompanied this stage of the investigation, because they all knew that by successfully concluding it, they would be ringing the team's death knell.

'Gerald Dodd and José Cardoza are represented by the same solicitor, boss,' Meadows told her.

'And I'm guessing that would be Spider Markham,' Paniatowski said.

'It is. What do you want us to do – point out to Markham that there's a conflict of interest, and get him to drop one of them?'

'Yes,' Paniatowski said, but a moment later, she shook her head. 'No, cancel that. Keep it as it is for the moment, because I think we can use that conflict of interest to our advantage.'

Crane and Beresford both looked mystified, but Meadows grinned.

'Oh, I get it,' the sergeant said. 'Very clever, boss! Which of us do you want riding shotgun on you in the interview?'

'None of you, because I won't be conducting it,' Paniatowski told her. 'I'm giving it to you and Jack.'

After all, she thought, you're going to have to handle things alone very soon, so you may as well start now.

'Well, gentlemen, I expect the first thing you would like to know is why I'm the one conducting this interview, and not DCI Paniatowski,' Kate Meadows said to the two men sitting on the opposite side of the interview table.

'Don't say a word,' Spider Markham told Gerald Dodd.

'The answer is simple enough,' Meadows continued, as if she thought they really *did* want to know. 'It's because it's the big-game hunters like the chief inspector who get to go after the kings of the jungle, and the small fry like me are left to deal with the snakes and monkeys.'

'You see what she's doing, don't you, Gerald?' Markham asked. 'She's trying to make you feel like you're not worth shit, and your only chance is to do everything she tells you to.'

'Mr Markham's got your number all right, sarge,' said Crane. 'He's far too smart for you.'

'Shut up, Jack,' Meadows snarled.

Markham laughed. 'This is a most amusing double act, but don't you think the good-cop/bad-cop routine is just a little old-fashioned?'

'Now he's rumbled us both,' Crane commented wryly.

'Since you've already been cautioned, I'd like to ask you about the prostitution ring you've been running, Mr Dodd,' Meadows said.

'My client will not be answering any of your questions,' Spider Markham told her. 'However, he has prepared a statement, which he would now like to read out to you.'

'I'm listening,' Meadows said.

Dodd put the piece of paper he'd been holding in his hand on the table, and smoothed it out.

'As manager of the Excelsior Club, I had at my disposal three upstairs rooms which I soon realized I could offer as accommodation. I did this mainly for philan . . . philan . . .'

'Philanthropic,' Markham supplied.

'. . . philanthropic reasons,' Dodd continued, 'though I did hope to make a bit of money out of it myself. I rented these rooms to three young women who said they were in need of accommodation. I accept it was wrong of me to do this without informing my employer or his legal representative. I thought at the time that they were decent honest girls, but I have since learned that they used the rooms for the purpose of prostitution. I now regret that I was not more careful about screening the women I accepted as tenants.'

Dodd finished reading, and fixed his eyes on a point in the wall high above Meadows' head.

'Beatriz tells quite a different story,' Meadows said. 'According to her, she met Tom Crawley in Rio. He was very charming. He offered her a job as an au pair, and promised that if that worked out, he would help her get a grant so she could study to be a nurse. Then, just before she and the other two girls got on the plane, he persuaded them to swallow balloons full of cocaine.'

'I had nothing to do with the drugs,' Dodd protested.

'So the only thing you were involved in was the prostitution, then?'

'I never said that.'

'You would have thought that having got the girls to transport potentially lethal drugs in their stomachs, Crawley and his gang would have considered they'd done enough, and found them the au pair jobs they'd originally been promised, wouldn't you?' Meadows asked.

'My client has no comment to make,' Markham said.

'Yes, that's what you would have thought,' Meadows continued, 'but that would be overlooking the fact that the gang were loathsome human beings – if they were even human at all. So what did actually happen was that Crawley locked the girls in his fancy, sound-proofed apartment for three days, and over those three days, they were raped by at least five men. Then they were taken to the Excelsior Club by José Cardoza. He said they were to work as prostitutes, and that if they caused him any trouble, he'd kill them.'

Markham laughed dismissively. 'The girl is making it all up,' he said. 'And you can't really blame her. After all, if she can convince you she was forced into it, then it's not her who has committed the crime – it's somebody else. So tell me, do the other two girls who flew over with her confirm her story?'

'We haven't found them yet,' Meadows admitted.

'Oh really?' Markham asked. 'And why is that, do you think?'

'You know why,' Meadows said. 'They were moved on to other brothels. But when we track them down – and we *will* track them down, because somewhere in the club, there'll be records of where they'd gone – they'll confirm Beatriz's statement.'

'Let's forget what may or not happen in the future,' Markham suggested. 'All you've got at the moment is two completely opposite statements – one of them made by my client, and the other made by a foreign whore.'

'You're not quite right there,' Meadows said. 'It's true that at the present moment we've only got Gerald's and Beatriz's statements, but DCI Paniatowski is talking to Cardoza even now – the big-game hunter dealing with the big game, remember – and within half an hour, Cardoza will have made a statement which drops you right in it, Mr Dodd.'

'That's a lie,' Markham said. 'If Paniatowski really was questioning José, I'd be . . .'

He stopped, abruptly.

'What was that, Mr Markham?' Meadows asked.

'Nothing,' Markham said.

'You were about to say that if DCI Paniatowski was questioning Cardoza, you'd be there. In other words, if it came to a choice between Gerald here and José, you'd go for José every time.'

'They're trying to confuse you, Gerald,' Markham said. 'It's perfectly possible for me to represent you *and* José, because I would never allow them to question both of you at the same time.'

'You're beginning to have your doubts about Spider, aren't you, Gerald?' Meadows asked.

'I insist you return my client to the cells,' Markham said.

Ignoring him, Meadows turned to Crane. 'Tell me, Jack, if you were a solicitor working for two clients charged with the same thing, which one would you work the hardest for?' she asked.

'I think I'd work hardest for the one with the most money,' Crane said.

'Or . . .?'

Crane made a show of thinking about it.

'Or the one I was most frightened of,' he said finally.

'So if the choice was between Dodd and Cardoza . . .?'

'I'd pick Cardoza every time.'

'I've already asked you to stop this interview,' Markham said. 'If you won't return my client to the cells, then I at least need time to confer with him.'

'Is that what you want, Mr Dodd?' Meadows asked. 'Because you do know that your solicitor's other client – José Cardoza – is trying to fit you up for Tom Crawley's murder, don't you?'

'You never told me that!' Dodd said to Markham.

'I didn't tell you because it's not true. She's just trying to con you into saying something you shouldn't.'

'I had nothing to do with Crawley's murder,' Dodd said to Meadows. 'I didn't even know about it until it was all over.'

'Don't say any more,' Markham urged his client.

'Listen, if Joey's trying to pin the murder on me . . .' Dodd began.

'I've already told you he isn't. Turning suspects against each other is one of the oldest tricks in the book,' Markham said. 'Even an idiot like you should know that.'

He knew it was a mistake the moment the words were out of his mouth, but it was too late to take them back.

'Who are you calling an idiot?' Dodd demanded.

'You should be nice to your solicitor, Mr Dodd,' Meadows said. 'After all, he's on your side.' She frowned. 'Or is he?'

'I don't want you representing me no more,' Dodd told Markham.

'Gerald, be sensible,' Markham pleaded.

'You heard him,' Meadows said. 'He doesn't want you representing him anymore. I'd like you to leave now, Mr Markham.'

'And if I don't?' Markham asked, folding his arms defiantly.

'You may correct me on this – because, after all, you are a

smart lawyer and I'm only a thick bobby – but if you refused to go I believe I'd be within my rights to use an element of physical compulsion to make you go,' Meadows said sweetly.

Markham stood up, and walked reluctantly over to the door. 'If you don't want me representing you, then for God's sake get another solicitor, Gerald,' he said, as a parting shot.

Meadows waited until she heard the sound of his footsteps retreating down the corridor, then said, 'You could get another solicitor if you wanted to, Gerald.'

'I'm bloody well going to,' Dodd replied.

'But your new solicitor will be going head-to-head with your old solicitor, each one trying to pin all the blame on the other one's client,' Meadows pointed out. 'And the question you have to ask yourself is – could I afford as good a lawyer as Markham?'

'What am I to do?' Dodd moaned.

'What you could do is work with us,' Meadows said. 'Give us something we can use, and we'll ask the judge to go easy on you.'

'You mean, if I cooperate I could walk away from all this?' Dodd asked hopefully.

If he'd been watching Meadows' eyes he'd have seen them flash with rage, but he wasn't looking at her, and when she spoke again, her voice was gentle and moderated.

'Oh, dear me, no,' she said. 'You've been a very bad boy, and you're certainly going to have to serve some time. But it won't be anything like as long – or as hard – as if you don't help us.'

'What do you want?'

'For starters, I need the addresses of all the other clubs that the girls who worked in the Excelsior were sent to.'

'That shouldn't be a problem.'

'Good. Next, I need to know who killed Tom Crawley.'

'That was Joey.'

'You're sure?'

'He couldn't stop bragging about it to me.'

'Why did he kill Crawley?'

Dodd shrugged. 'Chances are, they had an argument about money.'

'Can you prove that he killed Crawley?'

'Well, no, not exactly.'

Meadows sighed exasperatedly. 'You're a real disappointment to me, Gerald,' she said.

'I've told you all I know,' Dodd whined.

'Well, it's not good enough,' Meadows said coldly. 'Think of something else.'

Dodd frowned with concentration, then he said, 'I could tell you about that white powder that you found in Arthur Gough's toilet cistern.'

'How do you know that's where we found it?' Meadows asked.

'Well, that's where I put it, isn't it?'

Paniatowski looked at her team. All their faces were complete blanks, which wasn't good, but was still a hell of a lot better than the expressions of desperation they were doing their best to mask.

'So Gerald Dodd is given a package containing the poison and the front-door key of Arthur Gough's house, and is told by Cardoza that while Arthur is having dinner with his brother, he is to hide it in the cistern,' Paniatowski said. 'What does that tell us?'

'It tells us that we've probably arrested the wrong man,' Crane said.

'And that Cardoza obtained the poison and organized the murder, and Mrs Adams carried it out.'

'She knew she was bound to fall under suspicion, but she wasn't too concerned, because Cardoza had told her he would frame Arthur for the murder,' Beresford added.

'So have we got enough evidence to arrest her?' Paniatowski asked.

Meadows shook her head. 'We know that Arthur didn't commit the crime, but we can't prove it,' she said. 'And we know that Mrs Adams did commit the crime – and we can't prove that, either.'

'One of us needs to question her again, and hopefully this time she'll make a slip that will give us something to work on,' Paniatowski said. 'Where can we find her?'

'She's still at Gough's place,' Meadows said.

'She's still at the *crime scene*?' Paniatowski exclaimed.

Meadows shrugged. 'It's not a crime scene anymore. Forensics have given it the all-clear.'

'Even so, what kind of woman stays somewhere there's so recently been a murder?' Paniatowski asked.

'A woman with a clear conscience?' Beresford suggested.

'Or a woman with no conscience at all,' Meadows said tartly.

'I think you're the right person to talk to her, Colin,' Paniatowski decided. 'You can use your famous charm on her.'

'And if she tries to talk you into her bed, resist,' Meadows said.

'That's about as funny as a wet weekend in Clitheroe,' Beresford told her. He turned to Paniatowski. 'Who should I take with me, boss?'

'Don't take anyone,' Paniatowski told him. 'It shouldn't seem like an interrogation. I want her to feel at ease – because maybe then she'll lower her guard.'

'Who is going to interrogate Cardoza?' Meadows asked.

'I will,' Paniatowski said.

'In that case, can I tell you about an idea that's occurred to me?' Meadows said.

'Of course.'

'Well, I've been thinking about the fact that there's no extradition treaty between the UK and Brazil,' Meadows began.

She laid out her thoughts for the rest of the team to pull apart, and when she'd finished, Paniatowski said, 'It will need a bit of tweaking, but it might just give us some leverage.'

# TWENTY-ONE

When Mrs Adams answered the door of Jordan Gough's mansion she was wearing a cotton apron which, in Inspector Beresford's opinion, clung very fetchingly to her fine breasts.

'I'm in the middle of making my famous hunters' stew,' she said. 'Would it be all right if we talked in the kitchen?'

'I'm happy with that,' Beresford said.

She led him down the corridor into the kitchen, which had oak beams on the ceiling, and a large open fireplace with a meat spit dominating one wall.

'It's all fake, of course, but Jordan Gough loved it,' she said, waving her hand dismissively around the room. 'He had about as much class as a second-hand toilet brush.' She pointed to a high stool. 'Why don't you sit down there?'

Mrs Adams returned to the stove and stirred the contents of a pan which had just begun to bubble.

'Another few seconds, and I would have been too late,' she said.

'I beg your pardon?'

'It would be fatal to let the vegetables turn brown.'

'Ah!' Beresford said.

She was a very attractive woman, he thought, and it was such a pity that she was a cold-blooded killer.

The aroma from the pan drifted across the room. He thought he could detect garlic, onion and cabbage, but he was sure there was more to it than that.

'Are you expecting company?' he asked.

'No,' she said, 'but I like to eat well, even when I am alone. I have a hearty appetite.'

I'll bet you do have a hearty appetite, Beresford thought – and not just for food.

'Tell me about the pepper sauce that you served Jordan Gough just before he died,' he said.

Mrs Adams picked a glass of red wine, and drizzled it into the pan. Then she began to stir again.

'This wine is necessary to loosen any bits of food or flour that may have stuck to the bottom of the pan,' she said. 'Was it the pepper sauce that was poisoned?'

'Yes, we think it was.'

'A good choice,' Mrs Adams said.

'I beg your pardon,' Beresford said, for the second time.

'Some cooks make pepper sauces which are so bland they are almost tasteless. Mine have fire and spirit. And Jordan Gough was very fond of it that way. In fact, he often said that of all the things that I cooked, he considered my pepper steak my masterpiece. That's why, on that particular evening, when my first attempt didn't taste quite right, I threw it away and started again. It made dinner a little late, but I knew he would prefer that to a sauce that simply didn't pass muster.'

'Did anyone but you have access to the sauce before you took it through to the dining room?' Beresford asked.

'Wait one moment,' Mrs Adams said. She began to add to the mixture in the pan from a number of small jars she had lined up next to it. 'Bay leaf, basil, marjoram, paprika, salt, pepper, caraway seeds and cayenne pepper,' she explained. 'You might think you could omit one of them, but you would be wrong. I suspect they are rather like the clues you collect during your investigation – they all have their part to play, and if one was missing, it would not be the same.' She turned up the heat. 'In answer to your question, there was no one else in the kitchen, and from the moment I began the pepper sauce to the moment I took it through, I never lost sight of it.'

And so you are condemned by your own words, Beresford thought.

José Cardoza entered the interview room with a swaggering arrogance he must have developed when, as a secret policeman in Portugal, he'd had the power of life and death in his hands.

'Where is your solicitor, Mr Cardoza?' Paniatowski asked.

'I told him to crawl back under his stone.'

'Now why would you have done that?'

'He told me that Gerald Dodd will make a deal with you. He said I should make a deal myself.'

'And so you should.'

'I do not make deals with *putas*!' Cardoza said.

'If you wish to engage another solicitor, we can wait until he arrives,' Paniatowski told him.

Cardoza sat down. 'I do not need a lawyer to handle a woman,' he said.

'Very well,' Paniatowski agreed. 'Let's get down to business, then. I have a couple of murders I need to clear up, and I'd like you to confess to them.'

'*Two* murders? What do you mean?'

'I should have thought it was obvious – Tom Crawley's murder, and Jordan Gough's murder.'

'But it was Arthur who killed Jordan.'

'No, it wasn't. The main evidence against Arthur was that some of the poison used to kill his brother was found in his house, but now we know that you got Gerald Dodd to plant it there, because he told us so himself.'

'Dodd has no spirit,' Cardoza said in disgust. 'No spine.' He paused. 'You have no proof I killed Tom Crawley.'

'That's true,' Paniatowski agreed.

'Why should I confess?'

'Because serving a prison sentence for murder in England is much easier than serving one in Brazil.'

'That is true, of course. Brazilian prisons can be terrible places, even for a hard man like me,' Cardoza conceded. 'But you see, I am not in Brazil . . .'

'I know you're not.'

'. . . and you cannot send me back there, because Britain has no extradition treaty with Brazil.'

'You're right, of course,' Paniatowski admitted. 'So you won't confess?'

'Of course not.'

'Then we'll just have to get you for living off immoral earnings and intimidation – because that, we *can* prove.'

'And how long would I go to prison for?' Cardoza asked, with a sneer. 'Three or four years? That is nothing to a man like me. And when I am released, I will still have all the money that Mr Gough gave me.'

'Actually, I was thinking you might serve less than that,' Paniatowski said. 'I was thinking that if I speak up for you in court, you might get away with as little as a year.'

'Why would you do that?' Cardoza asked suspiciously.

'In order that justice might be served as quickly as possible,' Paniatowski told him.

'You make no sense.'

'It's simple, really. If you serve a prison sentence, even a short one, I will have grounds for requesting that you be deported to your country of origin. What do you say to that?'

'If you want me to beg, you will be disappointed,' Cardoza

said. 'I beg to no woman – so if you wish to send me back to Portugal, then do it.'

Paniatowski smiled. 'Nicely done,' she said.

'What do you mean?'

'*You* think that *I* think that if I sent you back to Portugal, you would end up in prison for your crimes under the dictatorship – but I don't think that at all. And would you like to know *why* I don't?'

'I don't care.'

'Oh, but you should care, because this is going to be very important to you,' Paniatowski said. 'You see, I put myself in your shoes and asked myself what I would have done if I had been a secret policeman who saw the end of the dictatorship coming. And the main thing I'd have done would have been to destroy any records that might connect me with my crimes. Did you do that, José?'

'You are talking like a mad person,' Cardoza said.

'Mounting a trial with only eyewitnesses would be a very tricky business, especially if – as I suspect – most of the potential witnesses never survived the prison experience. Besides, Portugal is still a divided country, and the democratic government would think twice before doing anything that might reopen old wounds. So, on the whole, I think you'd be safe enough.'

'So why do you want to send me back?' Cardoza wondered.

'Because I wouldn't really be sending you back at all – the moment your feet touched Portuguese soil, you'd be arrested and put on a plane to Brazil, because, unlike the UK, Portugal *does* have an extradition treaty with Brazil.'

'You couldn't do that,' Cardoza said, but he was starting to sound very worried.

'I could – and I will,' Paniatowski assured him. 'Your old friend Inspector Silva has already put all the arrangements in place – the only thing he's waiting for now is to be notified when you'll be arriving.'

'Evil bitch!' Cardoza spat.

'You wouldn't last long in a Brazilian prison – especially when the inmates learned you'd been a policeman,' Paniatowski said. 'So you have a choice. On the one hand, you could choose a long life sentence in Brazil, where you will come to regard death at the hand of your fellow prisoners as a merciful release. On the other hand, you can choose a much shorter life sentence in England, which I have no doubt you'd survive.'

'They could still send me back to Brazil, once I had finished my sentence in England,' Cardoza said.

'Yes, they could,' Paniatowski agreed. 'But during the time you're incarcerated here, the situation in both Brazil and Portugal may change to your advantage. It's a gamble, I won't lie to you about that – but it's a bloody sight better than the certainty of a Brazilian gaol.'

'All right, I killed Tom Crawley,' Cardoza said.

'Why?'

'He grew too greedy. He brought the poison in from Brazil, and then he tried to blackmail me about it.'

'And you simply couldn't have that, could you?'

'Nobody blackmails me.'

'Why did you kill Jordan Gough?'

'I did not kill him. I have an alibi for the time he died.'

'So you must have been working in partnership with Mrs Adams.'

'Mrs Adams knew nothing about it.'

'Then according to you, you didn't kill Jordan, Mrs Adams didn't kill him, and neither did Arthur.'

'That is correct.'

'Then who did kill him?'

Cardoza scowled. 'I cannot tell you how angry it makes me to have been caught by such a stupid policewoman as you – a woman who cannot even see the truth when it is staring her in the face.'

'Answer the question,' Paniatowski said.

'Let me ask you two questions instead,' Cardoza said. 'The first is – what do you think was in Jordan Gough's mind after his visit to Harley Street?'

'He went to Harley Street? In London?'

'Yes.'

'And what's the second question?'

'Since you now know that Arthur did not buy the poison in Brazil, why did Jordan send him there?'

And suddenly, Paniatowski thought, it was all starting to make sense.

The wall phone rang in Jordan Gough's elaborate kitchen.

'Answer it for me, will you, inspector?' Mrs Adams asked.

'I'm not sure I should,' Beresford said.

'Oh, go on,' Mrs Adams said, giving him a coquettish smile. 'I'm busy with the cooking.'

Beresford picked it up.

'Hello,' he said, awkwardly.

'Is that you, Colin?' asked the voice on the other end of the line.

'Boss?'

'Where are you?'

'I'm in the kitchen.'

'And is Mrs Adams with you?'

'Yes.'

'I want know precisely why she asked Jordan Gough to leave the dining room, the moment after she had served the steak. Got that?'

'Got it,' Beresford agreed. He hung up the phone. 'According to your statement, you told Gough you wanted a private word with him outside the dining room,' he said to Mrs Adams. 'What was that all about?'

Mrs Adams turned down the heat and then dipped a large spoon in the mixture. She blew on it, to cool it down slightly, and took a sip.

'Hmm,' she said.

She crossed the room and held out the spoon to Beresford. 'You try it, inspector.'

Beresford did as he'd been told.

'Delicious,' he admitted.

And then he thought, my God, she might just have poisoned me.

'It will taste even better when I've added it to the meat,' Mrs Adams said. 'It will be cooked in around three hours. If you stay around that long, you could share it with me.'

'I can't,' he said.

And he was thinking, Jesus, I really wish I could.

'You were telling me why you wanted to have a private word with Jordan,' he said, forcing his mind back on the job in hand.

'I didn't really want a private word with him,' Mrs Adams confessed.

'No?'

'No. I wasn't lying in my statement, but I wasn't quite telling the truth, either.'

'I think you'd better explain,' Beresford told her.

'Well, it wasn't me who wanted to talk to him – it was someone else.'

'You said there was no one else in the kitchen with you.'

'There wasn't. It was his lawyer who wanted to talk to him – on that kitchen phone.'

'The one I've just answered?'

'Yes. I have my own line, and Gough had his. Mine is connected to the kitchen and my living room.'

'I see.'

'Anyway, Mr Markham said it was urgent he speak to Jordan, but I wasn't to say who it was – which is exactly the same as he'd said when he made the first call, a few minutes earlier.'

Beresford felt the hairs on the back of his neck bristle.

'Did he speak to Jordan Gough the first time, too?' he asked.

'No.'

'Why not?'

'I'm not sure. He apologized for calling just as Jordan was starting to eat, and I said that didn't matter because, as it happened, dinner was going to be ten minutes late. You remember – I told you I had to start the pepper sauce again?'

'Yes, I do remember.'

'And once I'd said that, the line went dead, and he didn't ring back until exactly ten minutes later, when I was just about ready to serve.'

# TWENTY-TWO

Robbie Holland, the editor of the *Whitebridge Evening Telegraph*, was surprised by the unannounced visit of the detective sergeant – surprised and a little unnerved, because despite the fact that she was smiling at him, there was something scary about Kate Meadows.

'My boss, DCI Paniatowski, has been getting some very bad press from you,' Meadows said.

'I'm sorry it wasn't very favourable, but I had no choice in the matter,' Holland said, conscious of just how dry his mouth had suddenly become, 'I only print the truth as I see it.'

'As *you* see it, Mr Holland?' Meadows asked, still smiling. 'Or as *somebody else* sees it?'

'I . . . I am the editor,' Holland said.

'That's what it says on the door, anyway,' Meadows replied. 'The thing is, Robbie . . . You don't mind if I call you Robbie, do you?'

'No, that's fine, Kate,' Holland said.

'And you can call me Detective Sergeant Meadows,' the sergeant told him. 'The thing is, Robbie, the article was a tissue of lies from start to finish, and you could end up in big trouble.'

'Are you threatening me, DS Meadows?' Holland asked, noting the tremble in his voice.

'I'm making you aware of the situation,' Meadows said. 'Fortunately for you, help is at hand.'

'What do you mean?'

'We arrested Arthur Gough for his brother's murder, but now we know he didn't do it.'

'And you want me to run the story?'

'Yes, we do,' Meadows agreed. 'But we want much more than that. This really is your lucky day, Robbie, because we're prepared to give you an exclusive in which you get to name the real killer.'

'Has he been arrested?' Holland asked.

'No, he hasn't,' Meadows admitted. 'He will never be arrested.'

'I can't run a story accusing a man of murder if he hasn't been arrested for it,' Holland said panicking. 'He'll sue me.'

'No, he won't.'

'Even if he doesn't, Mr Markham will fire me for printing a story without the evidence to back it up.'

'You needn't worry your little brain about Spider Markham. He'll soon have enough troubles of his own to worry about. And we have got evidence against the killer – lots of it.'

'Then why, in God's name, won't you arrest him?' Holland asked, on the verge of hysterics.

'Robbie, Robbie, Robbie, you're going to have to trust me – because if you don't, I'll make your life a living hell,' Meadows said. 'You do believe I can do that, don't you?'

'Yes,' Holland said miserably. 'I believe you can do that. What is it that you want me to write?'

'Really, Robbie, fancy suggesting I should tell you what to write,' Meadows said in a rebuking voice. 'I couldn't possibly do that. I believe passionately in the freedom of the press.'

'But you just said . . .'

'What's this?' Meadows interrupted.

She bent down, and picked a piece of paper up off the floor. She scanned it with her eyes, and then she smiled again.

'You've been teasing me, haven't you?' she asked.

'I . . . I don't know what you mean.'

'Well, there were you, humming and hawing about writing the kind of story I wanted you to write,' she passed the sheet of paper across to him, 'and now I can see that you've already written it.'

Spider Markham leant back in his chair, and looked at the blonde woman opposite him.

'I never expected to see you in my office, DCI Paniatowski,' he said. 'I suppose I should be honoured.'

'But you're not,' Paniatowski said.

'But I'm not,' Markham agreed. 'You see, I know the reason you've come here.'

'Do you indeed?' Paniatowski asked. 'And what is that reason, exactly?'

'You've come to ask me to save your career,' Markham said. 'You want me to use the power of the *Evening Telegraph* to swing public opinion in your favour, so that even though you've made a terrible botch-up of things, your bosses won't dare to sack you.'

'And would you do that for me?'

'I might consider it if you were a little more contrite.'

'You mean that if I got down on my knees in front of you, and begged you to help me, there's a good chance you would.'

'I wouldn't say there's a *good* chance, but there's certainly *a* chance.'

Suddenly – unexpectedly – Paniatowski laughed. 'No, there isn't,' she said. 'I'm not just collateral damage here. My destruction is an integral part of the plan.'

'Whatever are you talking about?' Markham wondered.

'Jordan Gough was always an insanely vengeful man, but finding out he had a terminal brain tumour only made things worse.'

'Jordan had a brain tumour?' Markham asked, in mock astonishment. 'I didn't know that.'

'Of course you did,' Paniatowski said dismissively. 'I've done a little checking up since this morning, and it seems that you arranged for his treatment at a Harley Street clinic, so there's really no point in pretending anymore.'

'No,' Markham agreed, 'I don't suppose there is.'

'Why did he decide to go all the way to London, rather than to the hospital in Whitebridge, Mr Markham?'

'Because Harley Street was expensive – and Jordan was a great believer in the idea that the more expensive a thing was, the better it was.'

'So, he discovered that he was dying,' Paniatowski said. 'Most men in his situation would start thinking about their legacies – and he was no exception. Some of these men would donate the money to build a new wing on a hospital. Others would found a sanctuary for old donkeys. Jordan decided on one final act of revenge against his brother. And, as a small bonus, he saw a chance to ruin me – the only detective who ever arrested him.'

'I really think the strain of this has been too much for you,' Spider Markham said.

'Before you rang me at the Drum and Monkey, I wasn't exactly happy about investigating the supposed threats made against Jordan Gough, but I was at least reconciled to it,' Paniatowski said. 'Your call changed all that. You were so bloody objectionable that I determined then and there I was having nothing more to do with it. What I didn't ask myself then – and should have done – was *why* you were so bloody objectionable. But I know the answer now.'

'Do you? And why was I?'

'Because you wanted just the reaction you actually got. You see, if I'd taken the case more seriously, the plan wouldn't have worked half as well as it did.'

'You're babbling now,' Markham told her.

'All right, let's try another line of questioning,' Paniatowski suggested. 'Why did Arthur Gough have to go to Brazil, when Tom Crawley had already bought the poison? It certainly wasn't to make a deal with Brazil-nut growers.'

'I have absolutely no idea why he had to go to Brazil.'

'Then I'll tell you. He had to be seen to have had the possibility to buy the poison himself – because if he hadn't had that possibility, it would have been much harder to frame him for the murder.'

'So now someone else framed him for the murder,' Markham said. 'Is that how you cover up the fact the police were so incompetent that they arrested the wrong man?'

'Are you saying that no one did attempt to frame him?'

'Yes.'

'Then why did Gerald Dodd enter Arthur Gough's house illegally and hide some poison in the toilet tank?'

'I didn't know about that.'

'Of course you did. You've been in on the planning of the whole thing right from the start.'

'The planning of what?'

'Of Jordan Gough's suicide – a suicide which was designed to look like a murder.'

'So now you're saying that Jordan deliberately chose a horrendous death for himself?'

'He suffocated,' Paniatowski said. 'It can't have been much worse than drowning – and many people who commit suicide chose to drown themselves. Besides, his driving obsession was revenge – and, for all we know, the tumour may have intensified that – so it was not so much what happened to him that mattered, it was that Arthur should be punished for being their parents' favourite son.' She paused. 'Did Jordan ever tell you the story of Chippie Cousins, the woodwork teacher?'

'No.'

'I'm sure he did – I'm sure he told everybody – but I'll remind you anyway. Jordan could have beaten Chippie up, but that wasn't enough for him, because he wanted to do something the man would take with him to the grave – so he quite calculatedly and deliberately destroyed his life. It was the same in the case of Arthur. He could have had him killed – Cardoza would have done it willingly – but how much better it would be to ensure that Arthur spent the rest of his life in prison for a murder he hadn't committed.'

'Fascinating,' Markham said. 'And I hope you realize that I'm being sarcastic when I say that.'

'You didn't have to go along with it,' Paniatowski told him. 'He wasn't in real pain, and you could have persuaded him that what life was left to him was precious, and he could have used it both for learning to be at peace with himself and for doing good works – but you didn't do that. Did you make a lot of money from helping him with his scheme, Mr Markham?'

'I knew nothing about any of this,' Markham said.

'I'm going to charge you, you know,' Paniatowski said. 'Assisting in a suicide is a criminal offence, but conspiracy to pervert the course of justice is much worse, and in framing Arthur Gough, that's exactly what you did.'

'It's not true,' Markham said. 'I did no such thing. And even if it was true, you couldn't prove it.'

'We've got José Cardoza's confession, and he says you're in it up to your neck.'

Markham was visibly shaken. 'José's confessed!' he said. 'Why would he do that?'

'I made him an offer he couldn't refuse,' Paniatowski said.

'But so what if he's confessed?' Markham asked, recovering somewhat. 'It's his word against mine, and he's a known criminal.'

'And you're the sort of solicitor who gives the law a bad name,' Paniatowski said.

Markham smiled, showing his growing confidence. 'You may be right,' he said, 'but you'd never find a prosecutor willing to make such an unsubstantiated claim in court, so all any jury would see is a respectable lawyer and a foreign thug who was trying to bring him down. So you go ahead and try to make that charge stick – it will damage your reputation more than it damages mine.'

'That's probably true – so thank heavens for the phone call,' Paniatowski said.

'What phone call?'

'The one you made to Gough's house the night he died. You're not denying making it, are you?'

'No, why should I?'

'Can I ask why you rang the kitchen phone line, instead of the main one?'

'I'm not sure I know what you mean.'

'The house has two phone lines, one used mainly by Gough, and the other used mainly by Mrs Adams. Why did you ring Mrs Adams' line?'

'I must have got the two numbers confused.'

'So you had Mrs Adams' number?'

'Obviously I had it, or I couldn't have rung it.'

'Why did you have it? Did you often have occasion to ring her?'

'Well, there must have been one occasion at least, or I wouldn't have had her number, would I?'

'Fair enough,' Paniatowski agreed. 'But what I don't understand is why you made the same mistake twice.'

'What do you mean?'

'You say it was a mistake to ring Mrs Adams the first time, so why did you repeat the mistake by ringing her again, ten minutes later? After all, it wasn't her you wanted to speak to, was it – it was Jordan Gough?'

'I'm getting tired of this game,' Markham said.

'Here's how it was supposed to have worked,' Paniatowski explained. 'You ring up just at the time the food is due to be served, and say you want to speak to Jordan Gough. Mrs Adams passes the message along – except that she says *she* wants a private word, as she's been instructed to – and Jordan Gough goes out, leaving Arthur Gough alone with the pepper sauce. Then later, when she's being questioned by one of my detectives, Mrs Adams will say, yes, there were a couple of minutes when Arthur was alone in the room.'

'Any competent lawyer could blow holes in that theory without even thinking about it,' Markham said.

'Then go ahead,' Paniatowski invited.

'Why did there need to be a phone call at all? Why couldn't Jordan simply have left the room?'

'Because both Arthur and Mrs Adams would have wondered what he was doing, leaving the room just as the food arrived.'

'All right, why didn't Jordan simply ask Mrs Adams, before the meal began, to call him outside just after she had served up?'

'Because that's what she would have reported to the police, and they would have wondered why he would do that. But to get back to my story – things went wrong because the meal was delayed. Now the intelligent move would have been to abandon that particular idea then and there, but you couldn't, because Jordan Gough was still expecting to be called out of the room. So what did you do? You hung up, and rang back ten minutes later, when Mrs Adams had assured you the meal *would be* ready. So the next question the prosecutor is likely to ask is why you waited ten minutes if the call was so urgent that you had to interrupt Jordan Gough's meal. And there's really no answer to that.'

'It's all highly circumstantial,' Markham said.

'It's *somewhat* circumstantial, but combined with José Cardoza's statement, I think we've got enough to hang you,' Paniatowski said.

'Before we go any further, I'd like to congratulate you, Detective Chief Inspector,' George Baxter said. 'By exposing Jordan Gough's connection to drugs and prostitution, you've uncovered a whole stinking network which extends far beyond Whitebridge, and we expect police forces all over the country to be making multiple arrests soon.'

'Not to mention the fact that I've also made it possible for dozens of young women to be rescued from a life of white slavery,' Paniatowski said.

'That goes without saying,' Baxter replied.

'Really, sir?' Paniatowski asked. 'I don't think we can ever say it enough.'

Baxter nodded. 'You're right, of course. I should have mentioned the young women first.' He cleared his throat. 'However, we now move on to a much less pleasant matter.' He reached into his desk drawer and produced a copy of the *Whitebridge Evening Telegraph*. 'Have you read this, Chief Inspector?'

Paniatowski shook her head.

'No, sir, I haven't.'

Nor had she, though she had been told by Colin Beresford exactly what it said.

'Read it now,' Baxter said, passing the paper across the desk to her.

An Apology

This newspaper never hesitates to tell the truth, whatever the consequences. Equally, we do not flinch from admitting we have made a mistake, however big or small that mistake may be.

Today, we wish to apologize for a *huge* mistake. In our editorial two days ago, we accused the police of being negligent in the investigation of the murder of our late proprietor, Jordan Gough. We went further, and claimed that Detective Chief Inspector Monika Paniatowski could have prevented the murder.

We now believe not only that Mr Gough committed suicide, but that he framed his brother for his death and did all he could to make DCI Paniatowski seem incompetent.

We accept that Mr Arthur Gough and DCI Paniatowski were victims of a cruel manipulation. We offer Mr Gough our deepest sympathies, and DCI Paniatowski our heartfelt apologies.

'Well?' Baxter asked.

'I don't know what you expect me to say, unless it's "goody, goody",' Paniatowski told him.

'And you consider that flippant remark to be an appropriate response, do you?'

'What kind of response do you expect, sir? Shouldn't I be pleased that the article makes it very unlikely that I'll be dismissed?'

'It isn't the article that will save you – it's the fact that we now know Jordan Gough didn't die because of your negligence.'

'Maybe,' Paniatowski said, 'but my enemies – and I do have a few . . .'

'I know you do. You've been too successful *not* to have enemies.'

'. . . my enemies have got the scent of blood in their noses, and are not likely to let a small thing like the truth stand in their way, if they can possibly ignore it. But they can't ignore it now, can they?'

'That may be true, but it still does not justify leaking information to the newspaper,' Baxter said. 'I want you to find which member of your team was responsible, and give me his or her name.'

*Her* name, Paniatowski thought, she was willing to bet the farm on it being *her* name.

'I can't see any harm's been done,' she said. 'There's nothing in this article which will prejudice our case against either José Cardoza or Spider Markham in any way.'

'That's scarcely the point,' Baxter said. 'We cannot have officers on this force releasing information to journalists without the proper authorization, so I'm ordering you to conduct an inquiry, and find the guilty person.'

'Whoever did it – and I'm not admitting for one second that it was a member of my team – did it to save my bacon, and I'm not about to throw him or her to the wolves in return.'

'Maybe you haven't quite grasped what an order is,' Baxter said. 'It means that you have to do what I say you have to do. You simply have no choice in the matter.'

'Three days ago, you put your neck on the line for me, sir, and I'll always be grateful for that.'

'I only did what I had to do,' Baxter said, embarrassed.

'And I'm only doing what I have to do now,' Paniatowski said. 'You were prepared to defend me to the bitter bloody end, and I'll do the same for whoever leaked the information.'

'You'd really do that?' Baxter asked. 'Having just avoided dismissal by the skin of your teeth, you're prepared to appear before a disciplinary board – and risk dismissal again – rather than obey that order?'

'Yes, sir,' Paniatowski replied. 'And so would you, if you were in my shoes. You've already proved that.'

Baxter frowned. 'Well, since I really don't want to lose one of my best female detectives, it seems to me that I have no choice but to give way to you on this one,' he said.

One of his best female detectives? Paniatowski thought, surprised at how annoyed she suddenly was.

What was he talking about?

She was his *best* female detective.

The only other one who came anywhere near was Kate . . .

She saw it now! Baxter had known it was Meadows all along, and he could have asked any of a number of ranking officers to investigate the leak.

But he hadn't!

Instead, he had asked Paniatowski, knowing that she would refuse – knowing she would give him the excuse to look the other way.

'Thank you, sir,' she said.

'Thank you for what?' Baxter replied. He held up his hand to silence her. 'Don't bother to reply. You're dismissed, Chief Inspector.'

'Yes, sir,' Paniatowski said.

9TH MAY 1981

# EPILOGUE

Philip Paniatowski was digging a hole in the back garden with a trowel he had stolen from the potting shed. He wasn't supposed to dig holes, but that only made him want to do it more.

He was the clever one of the twins, and Thomas was the nice one. He knew that for a fact, because he had heard people say it.

'Look at them,' someone would say. 'Philip will be a great success one day. It wouldn't surprise me if he ended up very rich.'

'Yes,' someone else would agree, 'you're right about that. But Thomas is the one you would want your daughter to marry.'

They talked quite openly about it, even if he was there in the room, because he was only four, and couldn't possibly understand what they were saying. But he was a very clever four, and if he didn't understand all the words, he certainly got the general meaning.

The hole was getting quite deep now, and he had uncovered a worm. He took hold of the worm, studied it as it twisted and turned in his hand for a few seconds, and then put it on the ground. It immediately started to wriggle away to the left, but Philip put the trowel in its way, and it turned to the right. He blocked it again, revelling in his power.

There had been a lot of talk about something called poison in the last few days. He had asked Mummy what it meant, and Mummy had said that it was something he really didn't need to know about until he was a grown-up – which made him feel that it was something he really had to know about now.

Since Mummy wouldn't tell him, he had asked Reyes.

'It's what you give another person to eat or drink which will make them feel poorly,' she had told him.

Thomas didn't know what poison was! Thomas didn't know anything!

Philip liked being the clever twin, but he wanted to be the nice twin, too. It didn't seem fair that he wasn't.

He had grown bored of playing with the worm, so he lifted his trowel and cut it in half.

He wondered what he could use to poison Thomas.